WILL YOU STAY ANOTHER DAY?

SAMANTHA TONGE

B
Boldwood

First published in Great Britain in 2025 by Boldwood Books Ltd.

Copyright © Samantha Tonge, 2025

Cover Design by Lizzie Gardiner

Cover Images: Adobe Stock and Shutterstock

The moral right of Samantha Tonge to be identified as the author of this work has been asserted in accordance with the Copyright, Designs and Patents Act 1988.

All rights reserved. No part of this book may be reproduced in any form or by any electronic or mechanical means, including information storage and retrieval systems, without written permission from the author, except for the use of brief quotations in a book review. This book is a work of fiction and, except in the case of historical fact, any resemblance to actual persons, living or dead, is purely coincidental.

Every effort has been made to obtain the necessary permissions with reference to copyright material, both illustrative and quoted. We apologise for any omissions in this respect and will be pleased to make the appropriate acknowledgements in any future edition.

A CIP catalogue record for this book is available from the British Library.

Paperback ISBN 978-1-83533-009-8

Large Print ISBN 978-1-83533-010-4

Hardback ISBN 978-1-83533-008-1

Ebook ISBN 978-1-83533-011-1

Kindle ISBN 978-1-83533-012-8

Audio CD ISBN 978-1-83533-003-6

MP3 CD ISBN 978-1-83533-004-3

Digital audio download ISBN 978-1-83533-005-0

This book is printed on certified sustainable paper. Boldwood Books is dedicated to putting sustainability at the heart of our business. For more information please visit https://www.boldwoodbooks.com/about-us/sustainability/

Boldwood Books Ltd, 23 Bowerdean Street, London, SW6 3TN

www.boldwoodbooks.com

For everyone who longs for just another day

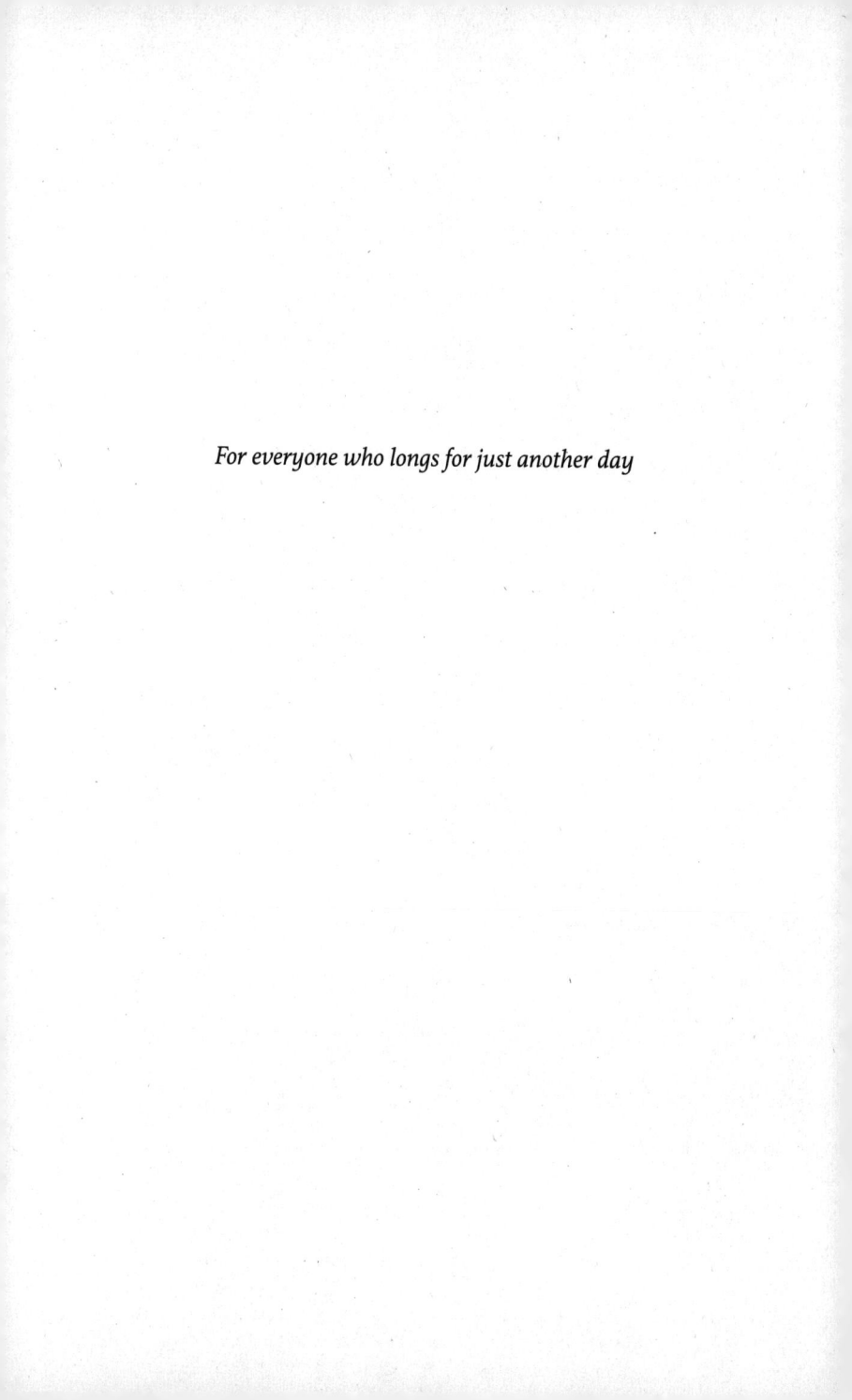

PROLOGUE
17 OCTOBER 2024

Lili and Em ambled into the local park, arms linked. They'd started the weekend early, on a Thursday evening, and taken a laptop to the pub near their cottage. After a couple of drinks, they'd finally booked the accommodation for the holiday they'd talked about for ages: four nights at the Pleasure Star Hotel on the Las Vegas strip in December 2025. The trip was to celebrate their thirtieth birthdays the following January. They both agreed that a full-on Vegas experience had to take place during the extra-glitzy festive season.

As she sat on the swing, Em stared down at her ripped psychedelic tie-dye trousers that lay on top of her Doc Martens. 'Do you think Vegas is ready for a punter not dressed in a tux or sparkles?'

Lili put down her laptop bag, collapsed onto the swing next to her and squinted through the night. 'It's not exactly our usual kind of holiday, but we deserve a luxury break with food we aren't likely to gag on.'

'Come on, Lili, you loved that corn fungus I got you to try

when we backpacked around Mexico. It must have been a bug that made you sick.'

'Ha! You told me it was truffle!' Lili swung forwards and backwards, propelled by her feet and indignation.

Em's laugh rang through the air.

Oh.

How lovely.

Lili's heart lifted.

She'd missed that sound, in recent months, when Em had drifted through each day like a deflated balloon. Lili glanced sideways as Em soared into sky, higher and higher, against the backdrop of frosty starlight. Vegas had been Lili's suggestion, a project she'd hoped would cheer up her housemate.

Her soulmate.

Maybe the worst times were over for Em. They must have been if she was prepared to go to that houseboat party tomorrow and prove to lowlife Sean that she was living her best life. Em didn't want Lili to go with her, insisting she needed to show Sean she was an empowered, strong, independent woman, who wasn't going to let a broken heart break her spirit.

'Remember how we used to jump off the swing whilst it was still moving when we were little?' asked Em.

'Only when our parents weren't around.'

'After three.' Em counted down and, whooping, the two of them plunged onto the ground. Good thing it was soft tarmac.

'Aaah! I think I've twisted my ankle,' said Lili, having landed right next to Em with a groan.

'Oh, God. I can't... breathe...' Em sat up and placed a hand on her chest. She jumped to her feet, pulled up Lili and they both grinned. 'I keep waiting for us to grow up.'

'Paying rent and the bills on time, holding down jobs, hardly ever getting drunk, cooking from scratch and mowing the lawn… I'd say the wait's over.' Lili picked up her laptop bag. 'Well, I mean, almost. Racing doesn't count. Last one back to the cottage makes the hot chocolates.'

'Lili, I don't think so. As you've just proved, we aren't children any more,' said Em haughtily before her eyes twinkled and she began to run.

'Oi! That's a false start!' hollered Lili.

It was good to see the old Em back.

Things would get better now.

Forget running after her friend; Lili skipped all the way.

1

Tomorrow was the anniversary of the worst day of Lili's life. Worse than Mum and Dad's divorce, the flood in the cottage and – she gave a wry smile – that Christmas she'd discovered Santa wasn't real and reindeer couldn't fly. She sat in her car and turned off the engine. The ancient tape deck ejected the 80s mixtape. Parked up outside Colin and Shirl's house, Lili shivered and peered through the October twilight, the Cornish crisp air sneaking through the gaps in the vents. Twelve long months had passed since their only child had died. They'd always treated Lili more like one of the family, but then she and Em had been like sisters, growing up in Manchester. Lili hadn't visited Colin and Shirl much this last year, unable to face their grief in case it triggered a return to the pain of those darkest days – the call about a houseboat accident, the investigations, a funeral that was decades too early.

When the news had first hit, Lili had cried enough to fill all the freezers in Cornwall with tears instead of ice cream. *What a travesty*, vanilla-cone fan Em would have declared. On impulse, this lunchtime, she'd rung Em's parents from work. Shirl had insisted Lili come around for pizza with garlic-sprinkled stuffed crusts tonight. Another favourite of Em's.

Her phone pinged and Lili took it out of her coat pocket. A text from the travel agency. Did she and Em want to reserve a taxi from the airport to the hotel they'd booked on the Strip? Lili shoved the phone in her bag and berated herself for not cancelling the December Vegas break. It wasn't a typical trip for either of them. Em loved authentic culture, Lili loved nature, but a luxury, festive trip to one of the most glamorous spots on the planet had unexpectedly appealed to both of them. After booking the hotel they'd beamed at each other with carefree mischief in their eyes, like they used to in school when the mean girls failed yet again to make them cry.

She went to get out of the car and knock on Colin and Shirl's front door, but paused as a pleasant flutter tickled her insides. Em did love a good Knock Knock joke. The two friends would frequently send them to each other. One of their favourites was:

Knock Knock.

Who's there?

Woo.

Woo who?

Woo hoo, I'm excited to see you too!

It wouldn't hurt to message her friend one last time. For the first few months after Em had passed she'd texted her often, found it comforting, even though she knew she wasn't around any more. Indeed, the texts had petered off in recent weeks. Lili's life needed to move forwards, that was what Mum said – and Dad. Them agreeing on anything was a rarity, significant, worth taking notice of. But there was no harm in one little final message, one final goodbye, before tomorrow arrived and life moved into another year in which Em didn't exist. Lili sat up straighter and shuffled to get comfortable. She took out her phone, swiped away the Vegas message and tapped into texts.

> Knock knock!

She added a turtle emoji afterwards. It was a private joke between them. She wouldn't hear back but that didn't matter. Leaving the joke open-ended made her feel Em would be chuckling about the message up in the heavens.

Lili got out and went up the drive, towards the terraced house. Em's parents only lived a few miles away from her cottage in Truro, the one she'd once shared with Em. Colin and Shirl had moved down to Cornwall, from Manchester, after the two friends, who'd travelled abroad in their early twenties, had settled in the southern county famous for its pasties and pirates.

She knocked on the door and it immediately opened.

'Lili, darling!' Shirl leant forwards and gave her a tight hug.

'Let the lass get in from the cold,' said Colin gruffly. He winked at Lili and took her coat whilst Shirl shut the door.

'Sorry I haven't been over for a while. Work's been hectic and... my trip to London took... How are you... Em's anniversary... I still...'

Shirl placed a hand on Lili's shoulder. 'It's okay, love. We never know what to say either. Em was such a big part of our everything.'

She'd been the missing quarter of their picture that, up until last October, showed the four of them enjoying sumptuous cream teas together and strolls on the beach. Colin and Shirl had both gained new facial lines and streaks of grey in their hair – the sparkle was gone from the couple, although they'd continued with their beloved Latin dancing. Their latest sexy, rhythmic moves had always caused Em to comically cringe. Whereas Lili had given up the Pilates class she and Em used to enjoy attending.

Colin and Lili headed into the lounge, cosy with well-thumbed books, boardgames, her puzzle books and his football magazines stored in shelves and on a nest of tables. He asked Lili about her sightseeing in the capital. Shirl brought in a tray of coffees and the three of them chatted about the charity shop that Lili managed, Colin's plans to retire next year and how Shirl would miss her patients too much to leave her job in a care home. There was a resident's hundredth birthday party on Sunday and she and Colin were helping out.

'Been up to Manchester lately?' asked Colin, and he bit into a custard cream. 'Have to say, Shirl misses the shops and I miss my United season ticket.'

'I'll be up in December, staying at Dad's for Christmas Day and then over to Mum's the next morning.'

'And how's the love life?' asked Shirl. 'Met that special someone yet?'

Em would have glared, full of indignation. To be fair, Shirl had lasted a whole twenty minutes.

'I have, but sorry, he asked me to sign an NDA.'

The three of them smiled and Shirl complimented Lili's hair. It was blonde and plaited at the sides, and Em used to call it her *Game of Thrones* look. She wore pumps and jeans and a baggy jumper, a far less distinctive style than her late friend's.

Late. Silly word for Em. Being on time was one of her things, drilled into her by her well-meaning ex-military grandfather.

Shirl got up the pizza shop app on her phone and they ordered food. Lili accepted a small glass of wine and a few sips in was laughing about a favourite story of when the four of them stumbled across nudists on a beach. Even though the drink was chilled, Lili felt toastie inside. Reminiscing. This was nice. Calm. Reassuring. For the first time in a long time Lili felt hopeful, as if her life had finally moored in steadier waters. Lili was glad she'd visited them today. Facing tomorrow would be easier.

With the pizza eaten and Lili facing an early start the next day, she waved goodbye, the three of them promising to keep in touch more often. As she drove home, there was a ping from her bag. Please, God, not the travel agency again. She pulled up on her drive, yawned and took out the phone. The screen flashed with a text.

> Who's there?

What the actual...? A reply to the Knock Knock joke?

Lili's hands started shaking. This wasn't happening. No. Absolutely not. And breathe... Fancy believing that Em had replied. Idiot. She inhaled and turned off the phone. It was just a glitch. She went inside. Lili brushed her teeth until her gums hurt, as if erasing the sight of that message. She got undressed, washed her face and slid between the covers. But as she reached to turn off the bedside lamp, curiosity got the better of her and she picked up the phone and turned it on. The Woo Hoo joke she'd remembered earlier brought to mind another favourite Knock Knock joke of theirs. Without giving herself time to change her mind, Lili typed back:

> Boo.

Neither of them would have ever replied with the expected

next line – in this instance, *Boo who?* Instead they'd be clever and go straight for the punchline, something like *Don't cry!*

That wasn't going to happen. As if someone could text from the dead.

But the screen flashed. Lili's eyes widened as she read the message.

> Now don't you cry!

2

Lili looked at the calendar on the wall, downstairs in Ware & Care, the charity shop she'd worked in for almost four years. The sun was about to set on 18 October, the date she'd felt prepared for in recent weeks, life feeling more anchored than it had in a long time, especially during that visit to Em's parents last night. But then everything changed when those texts arrived.

Lili and Em would have been getting excited about Halloween by now, the horror movies, the themed snacks and drinks. But this year Halloween was the anniversary of Em's funeral – the service at least.

What if it hadn't been *her* body taken for burial?

No! She wouldn't listen to the nonsensical thoughts that had whirred through her head all last night. Perhaps Em's number had been given to someone else. But Lili was sure someone had told her Em's mobile network operator took the numbers of people who'd passed out of service, out of respect.

The doorbell jingled and for the umpteenth time that day Lili's heart pounded. But she knew there was no way Em was back in Cornwall. A couple walked in. Despite the busyness a Saturday brought, she looked out of the window and scoured the pavement, kidding herself that she wasn't searching for her friend's shock of colourful hair and cocky walk. She hadn't tasted lunch, had burnt her tongue on coffee, nearly gave out too much change and almost tripped over a customer's guide dog. They'd have so much to catch up on! Like that final season of *The Umbrella Academy*, political elections, and those garlic-bread-flavoured chocolate bars the newsagents couldn't get rid of. Had Em's low mood passed? The doctor had offered Em anti-depressants during the months before her death. She'd been down after breaking up with that idiot, Sean, the first guy to ever mean more to her than simple fun. But Em had worried the tablets would dampen her natural spirit, unable to see that had already happened.

Lili gritted her teeth. Someone going straight to the punchline of the Knock Knock joke didn't prove a thing. She folded her arms, forcing herself not to jump up and down hollering with joy, an impulsive urge that sent adrenaline rushing through her veins, as if she were stood on a surfboard riding a steep wave.

But *what if*?

She wouldn't text back again until after work, after she'd had time to calm down and let common sense prevail.

Lili focused on tidying a pile of information leaflets by the till. Ware & Care had been set up seventeen years ago to fight UK poverty. It ran foodbanks across the South West, also handing out free clothes and homeware. The shop's buttercup yellow and white front made it feel warm and inviting, even on Cornwall's most rainy days. Back in Manchester, young Lili and Em had worked together in an Oxfam shop. Em left as soon as they'd completed enough hours for the volunteering section of the Duke of Edinburgh award. She'd then got a job at a crystal shop, in Afflecks indoor market, after sixth-form college – whereas Lili stayed on at Oxfam, switching to a full-time paid position there after A levels, until she and Em went travelling. She'd loved everything about the position. Helping customers was a big part of it.

Her fingers flexed. It wouldn't harm to reply to that text now. She'd waited long enough. However, the door jingled again and pensioner Glenda entered. She often popped by in the winter, after spending the afternoon in the village's library to keep warm.

'How are you today?' Lili asked as Glenda came over, bright red lipstick on and a matching light jacket, dyed blonde hair completing the glamorous look. It was only up close the bags under her eyes and frayed cuffs of the jacket became apparent.

'You know me, love, I never complain.'

They looked at each other and grinned.

'My hip's playing up and the new neighbour played rap until three this morning. He's a selfish bugger.' Thick foundation on her face exaggerated the lines as she frowned. 'But apart from that everything's tickety-boo. My nephew's taking me to an eightieth birthday bash this evening.'

'How is Simon coping now, after the divorce?'

'He's got a date through Bumble, whatever that is, determined not to be single for the festive season. Bloody silly name if you ask me. Drone bees don't have girlfriends; they only mate with the queen.' Her eye twinkled. 'Sure you don't want me to give you his number?'

Ignoring the question Glenda had asked before, Lili rolled her eyes in a friendly manner. She was far too busy for a committed relationship, happy to go on dates but staying single.

Em had agreed whilst they'd travelled, whilst they'd pursued their careers – until she'd met Sean, the liar.

'And how are you, dear?' Glenda asked gently, not saying the obvious. She'd gone to Em's funeral, being a customer of Crystoffees when she could afford coffee and cake out. Em used to work there.

I don't know. Fine! Scared! Elated! Confused!

'I'm okay,' she said and pointed to a rail, keen to move on. 'That full-length anorak has just come in. Looks brand new. I reckon it will be snapped up when the weather turns colder, especially as it's a festive plum colour. And there are a couple of new romances on the bookshelf.' Glenda's face lit up and she went to investigate.

Not all customers came in because money was tight. Some sought out a vintage or antique piece out of admiration or to sell on eBay for a profit. Dustbin bags of donations were like unopened treasure chests to Lili, with the ornate pottery, old embossed book covers, and the quirky fashion items Em loved to hear about. One person's junk was another person's jewel.

As she studied the window display, Lili's fingers ran over her phone in her pocket and she was just about to take it out when...

'I've set out the newly priced goods. What shall I do now?'

Lili turned to face dimples and a sun-tanned face. Meg was her only full-time worker, twenty-one and saving hard to fulfil her dream of opening an online vintage clothes shop. Today Meg wore a 40s-style tea dress with a cardigan and her hair tied up with a scarf. Lili stood in her usual uniform of smart jeans and a top. Glenda had left, wearing her new coat, and the shop was empty now.

'There's only ten minutes left.' Only ten minutes until she

could reply to that Knock Knock text. 'You might as well head off. Good job today. Are you out clubbing with Zoe tonight?'

'No. We broke up.' Meg sighed. 'Apparently I've got no filter. Just because I said her trousers looked tight. She didn't look comfortable and I said we should go shopping for a bigger size. It's best to be honest, right? But she flipped. I even bought her chocolates as an apology.'

Lili smiled as she waved Meg off. Em never had much of a filter either.

Having locked up, Lili crossed the small car park at the back of the building. Once in the driving seat, she took out her keys, but couldn't wait a minute longer. All day she'd been going over what to type, listening to her heart, which had done its best to silence her head, editing down all the news she had, all the questions. In the end it came down to six simple words, with an exclamation mark added to emphasise her happiness... or was it to soften anger, or disbelief?

> Where the fuck have you been?!

She paused before continuing to write.

> I've missed you.

Lili added a turtle emoji and pressed send. Mouth dry, she turned the key and gripped the steering wheel. The Saturday drive home from Mevagissey to Truro was never as bad as during the week, with the rush hour. Twenty minutes later, she turned into her drive and parked up. She peeked at her phone. No reply yet. Lili opened the front door and stepped inside the cottage, with its golden walls and mahogany ceiling beams, with the cosy lounge on the left and the farmhouse kitchen opposite. The place felt like home, even though it was rented and they'd not been allowed to redecorate. The property owner was a friendly sort. The cottage had used to belong to her grandfather and she'd drop in every six months to check up on things. One day Lili hoped to buy a place like this. She'd put money aside in recent years and then Em had left Lili her savings. She'd felt awkward and discussed it with Colin and Shirl, but they'd insisted it was what their daughter had wanted.

Good thing Lili hadn't spent any of the money, if Em was alive. She might have to give it back.

Lili exhaled, went into the lounge and dropped onto the chintz sofa, which wasn't to her taste when she'd first moved in. However, she'd grown to appreciate its cheeriness this last year. A pile of books sat on the low coffee table. Lili loved stories that reflected nature, and a series of novels about penguins were a current favourite. Em had read mostly on her phone, scrolling through Instagram and laughing at reels.

Her phone flashed and Lili picked it up.

> I've been travelling like you. Next stop Switzerland.

Oh my God! Oh my God! Em had put the green nauseated face emoji after the word travelling! It was part of the private joke they had, to do with the turtle one.

But wait... what...? *Travelling?*

Christ on a bike, or a ferry too, or hovercraft, plane, speedboat, coach!

Of course, that made sense, Em going off around the world, wanting to get away. She read the text again. *Like you.* What did that mean? Lili had recently forced herself to get away. She'd gone on a four-day trip to London, booked an Airbnb and caught a West End Show, shopped in Covent Garden and ridden the London Eye. She got up and went to the curtains, looking out, up and down the road. Was Em back in England and spying on her?

But how could Em even travel abroad now? Had her parents forgotten to cancel her passport? Em's mum, ever organised, never forgot a thing, not even in her grief. The funeral couldn't have run more smoothly. And Switzerland? Em had always said that country was conservative and boring and that she'd only ever go for the chocolate.

The two of them needed to speak.

Lili typed back, requesting a call, and gave a little jig. But hours later, as she sat in the lounge, foot tapping, pretending to read a book, there was still no reply.

Something didn't feel right.

And something stopped her from pressing dial.

Maybe someone else had ended up with Em's number, despite her phone company's policy. But no, that would be unethical. The company could get into trouble for that. And it wouldn't explain the green-faced emoji. Lili fetched her laptop from her bedroom and researched until late before picking up a notebook. Surprised with the possibilities she'd discovered to explain the texts, Lili scribbled. She sat back and re-read the list. Four concrete possibilities.

A car backfired outside and she jumped. What was she doing? This was all so stupid. With a tut she tore out the page, screwed it up and tossed it onto the coffee table before heading upstairs. Under the duvet, Lili determined not to think about Em. Instead she mentally ran through the ceremony she'd be holding tomorrow afternoon in her cottage. These ceremonies always took place on a Sunday and people only heard about them by word of mouth.

As she finally closed her eyes, downstairs a ray of moonlight snuck through the lounge curtains. It lit up the title and the list that Lili had written on the uncurled notebook page:

Is Em Really Alive?

1. *Yes. The texts are from her. Em ran away. Maybe she was in some kind of trouble or so depressed she needed time out.*
2. *Kind of – a medium is passing on messages from Em's spirit.*
3. *No, another person somehow has Em's phone and knew to skip the punchline of that joke and send the green-faced emoji. Have I met them before? Why would they pretend to be Em?*
4. *No. There are companies that send pre-programmed texts to loved ones of the deceased. The messages would have been written before her death and programmed to instigate a conversation with certain phone numbers. They can be triggered by location or a date. It might have been possible for Em to have programmed in responses to our favourite jokes. Have her parents received pre-programmed texts too?*

But if it is number four, had Em known she was going to die?

3

Lili got up early the next day, pulled on a T-shirt and jeans, grabbed a jumper and drove to Mevagissey. She bought a takeaway latte and croissant and walked up, through the village, to the coastal path, leaving the gift shops, the fishermen and dog walkers behind – a route she always took if life ever dealt out a low card. Today was unusual because she was treading that ground after being dealt the highest card possible: the chance that Em had aced it by making contact.

Eyes crinkling in the sun, Lili strode at a fast pace past Portmellon, shortening the walk that usually took an hour. Eventually she reached her special place, Gorran Haven beach. A curve of grey, pebbly sand with rocks either side, it looked out onto choppy steel-blue waters. Her jumper on now, she sat on a large rock, took the paper bag out of her small rucksack and tore off bites of croissant. It wasn't long before a speckled baby seagull strutted up to her, an adult one hovering nearby. Lili tossed over flakes of pastry, then sat sipping her coffee, lukewarm now but still comforting. She reached into her jeans pocket and pulled out the list of possible explanations for the texts. Reading the words, she sighed, screwed the list up again and threw it to one side, like she had last night. The wind caught the paper and it rolled across the sand. Not one to drop litter, Lili balanced her coffee on a rock and charged after the list as it headed towards the sea. She just caught it before a wave would have sucked it into the ocean, and carried it away forever. Jaw set, she stomped back to her drink and stuffed the notebook page back into her pocket.

The horizon attracted her gaze – the fishing boat in the distance, the sun reflecting off waves that shimmied against the wind. The invigorating salty scent of the bay, the ripple of air against her skin, the splash of water sounding in her ears all helped her forget the stressful things that seemed to matter so much, back in the village, back in the cottage, like the tumble dryer playing up or Netflix buffering. Lili's eyes narrowed and she focused harder on the horizon. There it was! Fifty metres out, in the sea, a large grey head popped up. She liked to think it was the same seal every time that dropped by to say hello as it always appeared in the same patch of water near a sea stack. Neptune, she called her – or him. Cornwall excelled when it came to phone detoxes, due to the lack of signal in so many appealing places; Lili couldn't receive texts, couldn't go on Google. Instead she stared at the sea. She followed Neptune.

Breathe in, breathe out. She pulled out the list again.

As if it were a computer program that could sort rambling, excited thoughts into a rational order, the bay's atmosphere gave her clarity.

She stared at the sea again. She followed Neptune.

Two clear choices presented themselves: Lili could forget those phone messages, consider them a quirk of fate, and leave her past with Em well behind now. Or she could embrace the jaw-dropping, unexpected possibility of holding a hand out to the past and Em slipping her fingers into it.

One hour later she stood up and stretched. She smoothed out the list, folded it up carefully and slipped it into her purse. Lili never had been one to turn down a challenge, and she knew what she had to do: she'd set herself a deadline; put on a detective hat. One way or another, by Halloween, Lili would go through the list and find out if Em really was back.

It was still early but Colin and Shirl would be getting ready for that hundredth birthday party, so Lili would speak to them tomorrow, after work. That gave her time to plan how to tell them that their dearly loved daughter might not be dead after all.

4

Lili sat down in Colin and Shirl's lounge.

'Thanks for letting me call around again, at such short notice.'

Shirl still had her work tunic on. Colin brought in a tray of coffees.

'Everything okay, lass?' he asked and offered her a slice of marble cake. Too nervous to eat, Lili declined.

'Yes... I mean, it could be brilliant... and if not, nothing lost. When I say nothing lost, I mean, obviously...' She exhaled. Staring at the ceiling until the early hours last night hadn't helped her put together the right sentence.

'Start at the beginning,' said Shirl softly. She and Colin sat on the sofa. Lili was in an armchair opposite.

'I was wondering...' Lili took another sip of coffee, even though she wasn't thirsty. 'Can you remember what happened to Em's phone? I was scrolling through my contacts the other day and realised her number is still in there.'

'Got lost,' said Shirl in a flat tone. 'I obsessed about it in the beginning.'

'It would have been great to flick through her photos.' Colin exhaled. 'But at least we've got the WhatsApp messages going years back that we shared with her.'

'We found a spreadsheet of her passwords on the laptop, for her social platforms... but it didn't seem right going through her private life so we only used them to close the accounts.'

'There's a possibility it could have exploded in the fire.' Colin bit into his slice of cake.

'You should have mentioned it,' said Lili. 'I'll send you some of my photos if you want.'

'Thanks, petal,' said Shirl, her face brightening. 'Only if it doesn't stir up memories you don't want.' She picked up a crumb from her empty plate and put it in her mouth.

Colin caught her and tutted. The two of them smiled. 'Em used to do that,' he said.

'I remember,' said Lili. 'It used to drive you mad, Colin.' It would never not feel weird to call her childhood bestie's parents by their first names instead of Mr and Mrs Evans.

'We grounded her once – well, a few times, as a teenager, for worse things, like getting home later than promised, you may recall,' he said. 'She got her own back by chewing with her mouth wide open at every meal until the curfew ended, eyes like daggers, knowing how important table manners were to me. She always wore her feelings on her face.'

'That was one of the worst things at the end... when we identified her body,' said Shirl.

Oh thank God, Lili wasn't going to have to push for answers about the identification. She held her breath.

Colin nodded. 'She died of drowning, as you know, Lili – but parts of her body were swollen and... and the buildup of gasses... Are you sure you want to hear this?'

Lili nodded. She needed to.

'The gasses distorted her face.'

'We were advised not to look at it,' said Shirl. 'So we never got to see her face one last time.'

'That must have been incredibly hard... You could still easily identify her, though? Sorry... you don't have to answer that.' *But please do.*

'It's okay,' said Shirl. 'One year on and most family and friends are still too scared to mention her name around us. That call from the police... I'll never forget it. No idea how we got to the hospital. We didn't recognise the pile of her drenched clothes a nurse gave us and most of her body was under a sheet. But she had that tattoo of a dolphin on her wrist.'

'And that large freckle on her other arm.'

'I just knew, by the look of her,' said Shirl. 'We both did. That's all we needed to identify her and we didn't want any tests done on her body. She'd suffered enough.'

Em wouldn't have cared what she looked like after any drowning... only in terms of it upsetting her parents. She took pride her in outfits, her hair dye and accessories, but not in a vain way. Even though she was going to be stuck with it for ten years, Em couldn't stop laughing at her dreadful passport photo that had made her look as if she'd been hauled into a police line-up.

All the evidence pointed to the body being Em's and yet... Dolphin tattoos were really common, as were freckles and...

No, no, no. Keep your head, Lili. And neither of Em's parents had mentioned getting strange texts.

But why did it niggle that Colin and Shirl hadn't seen their daughter's face? That the dental records or DNA hadn't been verified? After the accident, the houseboat party company had been investigated. Its safety standards were well below par and there was no record of exactly how many guests had been on board that night. The body could have been anyone.

'I was just thinking about Em's passport photo – how she looked like a convict.'

'I'm her mother but yes, that wasn't a look even I could love,' said Shirl, and her eyes twinkled for a second.

'Did you get to keep it?'

Colin shook his head. 'No. We thought about it a few months ago, when we went to Spain. Her passport wasn't in with her stuff. We really should contact the passport office.'

'It's not like me to miss something like that,' said Shirl. Her voice hitched and a small, unexpected sob escaped. 'I should have cancelled it but it's so very final, ending someone's citizenship.'

So the phone wasn't found. Nor the passport. And Em's face wasn't actually identified.

Lili put down her mug and leant forwards. 'I'm sorry to ask this...' Her voice wavered. 'I don't want to cause either of you any pain but... have you ever considered that Em might not be dead?' she blurted out.

They both frowned.

'You see, just before I came into yours, on Friday, I... I sent Em a text. A silly one. To do with a joke and...' She explained about the replies she'd got back and why the number couldn't have been passed on to someone else; told them only Em knew to jump straight to the punchline in any case, and to send the green nauseated face emoji. 'So I did some research, trying to work out what's going on.' She shoved the creased list into Shirl's hands, who then showed it to her husband. 'These are the four possibilities. Have either of you received any odd texts this year? That could have been pre-programmed or...'

Colin and Shirl stared at the list. Then gave it back to Lili. Shirl slipped her hand into his. He squeezed her fingers. The two gazed at each other, sad smiles crossing their faces momentarily, and then they nodded. Lili's mum and dad used to exchange looks like that sometimes, back in the day, when they got on, as if married couples shared a secret language.

'Lass, you know we love you like one of our own,' said Colin. 'We respect your opinion. We know how much you miss Em.'

'What Colin's trying to say is... we haven't received any texts, love. We don't believe in psychics.'

'Right. So that means—'

'Em isn't alive, love,' continued Shirl firmly. She placed a hand on her heart. 'I'd know. I wish so very much that there was a chance she'd walk back into our lives, but as soon as I saw my girl in that part of the hospital they call Rainbow's End... Don't torture yourself like this.'

Colin's face turned red. 'This is just someone who's found Em's phone and is playing a prank. You let me know who it is if you find out and I'll...'

Shirl patted his arm.

'But why would anyone do that?' Lili asked. 'I never told anyone about Em and me jumping straight to punchlines or about the emoji. They were our things. If Em had told a friend, why would they play such a cruel joke? It doesn't add up.'

'Leave it, love,' said Shirl.

'When we got the news about Em, those first few hours, before we saw the body, we doubted what the police had told us,' said Colin. 'Even on the way to the hospital we ran through a thousand reasons as to why Em could have gone missing. It was a dark, dark place to be in and I never want to go back there again.'

Shirl let out a juddering sigh.

'Then when we came out, denial hit harder,' he continued. 'We told each other that was *not* our daughter. But our eyes didn't lie.'

'You're only going to tie yourself in knots, petal. Delete those messages. Throw away the list. Oh, I wish it wasn't true, sweetheart, but believe us, our Em isn't coming back.'

'Not everything in life has an explanation,' said Colin, the bags under his eyes looking even heavier than usual. 'I realised that when Em died, and it makes things a little easier. Technology gets bugs and faults. That's all those texts are. Or someone with a warped sense of humour, so don't feed their nastiness by trying to find out their identity. Don't go to that hopeless place and try to locate the phone. We've closed all of Em's accounts. It's only got the photos on and you reckon you've probably got copies of a lot of them. Shirl's right. Give it up.'

'I did request a call but got no reply.'

'There's your answer,' said Shirl in a gentle tone. 'If it was Em, she'd have dialled back straight away, probably have called in the first place...'

Would she? What if she was scared of a backlash for putting her loved ones through the last twelve months?

'...whereas if it's a prankster and not some kind of technical fault, they're probably too much of a coward to actually speak to you.'

Lili gave them each a big hug. Apologised if she'd upset them. They both said not to be silly and that they'd arrange another pizza night again soon. When the front door closed, Lili took the list out of her pocket. She walked over to the public bin, on the pavement where she'd parked her car, and was about to throw it in when a leaflet caught her eye. It lay on top of a squashed Coke bottle, almost as if someone had put it there just for her. She picked it up and the words jumped out.

> Wellness and Craft fair, Jubilee Hall, Mevagissey. Psychic readings.

5

Lili yawned, exhausted even though it was only Wednesday. Thank goodness it was almost time to close. She'd decided not to text Em's number again until she'd completed her investigations and found out exactly who – or what – she was dealing with. Lili had a plan in place that would kick off as soon as she cashed up and could get to that wellness and craft fair that ran from two until seven. At lunchtime, needing fresh air, she'd popped into the She Sells café, right on the harbour front – such a pretty setting, with pastel houses dotted across the surrounding hillside. The other café she frequented, Crystoffees, wasn't quite as big. Its name was a fusion of the words 'crystal' and 'coffee' because half of its floor space was given over to the crystal-selling side that Em had once managed, always carrying a lump of citrine in her pocket on work days, saying it gave her energy, not that Em needed extra.

At least not until the months before her death. Sean, her long-term boyfriend – well, long for her at six months – had been hiding a secret. His parting gift, on their last night together, had been to give her whiplash from a car accident.

He'd been driving and inadvertently let slip his betrayal after Em questioned him about why he hadn't returned her call the evening before. He'd mounted the pavement and crashed into a lamppost. Despite having physiotherapy, it left her with backache for months. For the first time in her life, dynamo Em couldn't rush around, go clubbing, swim in the sea, or do a little dance every time something pleased her, from a half-price cocktail to getting her wages.

Ohhhh.

Lili's breath caught as a memory came back from when Em's back was bad. She was on painkillers and dwelling on Sean's lies. The two of them had been sitting in the back garden, chuckling at a seagull stomping on the lawn to draw out worms. There'd been a right hullabaloo at the front of the house. A canoe had fallen off the top of a passing car.

'Remember the canoe man, John Darwin, who went missing and faked his death, Lili? He was all over the news when we were little.'

'We made up stories about the fantastical lands *we* would disappear to.'

'Wouldn't it be great to disappear for a while?' she'd muttered. 'No social media. No responsibilities. No stupid ex-boyfriends or useless physio appointments.'

A burst of joy made Lili glow from head to toe. She'd not taken Em seriously at the time, but what if that had been the beginning of her friend making a plan? What if Colin and Shirl were wrong?

Tommo came downstairs from the stockroom of the shop, his loud footsteps bringing her back to the present, those footsteps also quicker than normal. He looked like a fisherman with his wispy white hair and beard, the baggy corduroy trousers and his trademark colourful braces. Countless villagers seemed to have cleared out their lofts last weekend. Black dustbin bags had been left in the car park out the back, full of musty-smelling books, clothes, ornaments and toys. Retired Tommo had only just finished sorting through them. He volunteered frequently since losing his husband. He'd never forgotten a period in his life when he'd been homeless and had had to couch-surf. He was in today, and he'd heaved the bags upstairs on his back, one by one, like a diligent Santa. Only difference was he rode a motorbike and not a sleigh and would never have delivered presents in time due to his frequent cigarette breaks.

Eagerly, Tommo held out a worn-looking green book with a duck on the front. He gave a raspy cough, not due to smoking, he'd insist, but supposed pollution from the nearby harbour. 'A Beatrix Potter first edition! I'd bet my last stick of rock that this is worth something.'

Lili examined the inside. 'Wow, you could be right!' They pored over the dates inside and Lili looked it up on her phone. 'Let's get it properly priced.' Rare finds, by the staff, never landed on the shelf, but were sold off by Ware & Care to raise as much money as possible.

'Joe would have wanted to see it, being such an avid reader,' said Tommo. He sighed and rubbed his hip. 'I still haven't thrown away all his books, even though it's been two years. He threatened to haunt me if I ever gave away his Lee Child collection and tried to make me promise to read them when he'd gone, during his last chemo session.'

'Have you?'

'What do you think?' he said gruffly, and she laughed. 'More of a movie man, myself. As a compromise I've watched the Jack Reacher films and Joe's not made the lights flicker or blown cold air down my neck yet.'

She went to speak but changed her mind.

'What?'

'Oh, nothing...' She pointed at the clock. 'We'd better get going. I want to visit the fair in Jubilee Hall. It's running for another hour or so.'

Tommo gave her a fierce look. 'Spit it out. I may be getting on but you can't pull any wool over my eyes – not with these glasses on.' He adjusted his spectacles, the frame ocean blue like his eyes.

She leant against the till counter. 'How did you... accept, you know, what happened to Joe?'

His face flushed. 'It's one year since Em, isn't it?'

It was so much worse hearing it out loud.

'It... it's been a struggle.' Tommo's voice sounded full for a few seconds. 'But I guess I got to say goodbye... I reckon that's the main reason. We said the things we needed to before it was too late, a silver lining of the bastard cancer. Whereas you didn't get that chance, gal.'

Lili's eyes prickled.

'But it will get easier. Around Joe's first anniversary, the summer before last, jeez, the loss felt as raw as a newly skinned mackerel.' The tanned skin around his eyes crinkled, his usual humour returning. 'Doesn't help that us soppy British sods are as keen to talk about death as much as a diet or how much booze they knock back each week.'

'How *is* the cholesterol?' asked Lili sweetly.

'I thought we agreed not to mention the c word.' A serious look crossed his face. 'Always happy to talk – if you need to. Even though your Em would have called us a couple of wusses.'

Lili's breathing hitched. *Her* Em.

She locked up and headed upwards, towards Church Street. The hall was a functional building about ten minutes away, available for hire within the local community. She pulled open the blue door. Deep breath. It smelt like a school gymnasium. She scoured the room. There in the corner sat a man behind a table. A simple purple cloth covered it. A pile of business cards lay next to a water bottle. Across the front was a sign saying Psychic Reading. She walked past a candle stall, the air around it welcomingly fragrant, then past a local author who looked at her hopefully. A table stacked with homemade Christmas cards was next. Em and her both believed the festive season could never come too early. The two of them ate mince pies when they came into the shops in September and watched Christmas movies as soon as they landed on Hallmark.

She approached the table. The psychic was around her age and dressed smartly, with ruffled boy-next-door short hair, a work shirt and bow tie – definitely not her type, although she'd said that once before, after first moving into the cottage. A city type lived next door – suit, briefcase, smart mac. Turned out he was funny, confident and keen on Lili. They dated for several months but then it became... comfortable, and she couldn't be doing with that. Comfortable made for resentments and taking a partner for granted; comfortable made it easy to lie. Her mum and dad had proved that and Lili had sworn, at a young age, amidst the sobs that racked her chest in bed night after night as they argued, that she'd *never* fall into the same trap as her parents.

The single life was safer.

'I'm not here for a reading!' she blurted out. Spiritual readings were a load of gobbledygook. Lili had watched a programme about them once. How fraudulent fortune tellers, mediums, seers, whatever, studied clients for giveaway reactions, analysed body language, used broad statements and asked leading questions. Em had been less cynical and Lili was doing her best to keep an open mind and work her way through her list.

The man's face broke into a smile. 'Please sit down,' he said with a warm London accent. 'My name's Greg.'

'Oh... um, I'm Lili.' She perched on the chair.

He tilted his head. 'Why are you here, Lili?'

'Aren't you supposed to already know?' she countered, unable to stop herself. 'Sorry, I don't mean to be rude... I've never done anything like this before.'

He gave an infectious laugh. 'Believe me, people have said much worse.'

Her shoulders eased. 'It's my best friend. Em. It was the anniversary of her death on Saturday, and...' Oh God. This sounded stupid, but she explained about the texts and how she was investigating them. 'I'm trying to eliminate all possibilities. I went on the internet and have drawn up a list of—'

'Ah, the internet. The great all-knowing that has the answer to everything.'

'Now and then it does. You learn to spot the BS, right?'

'Oh, I wasn't criticising you, we all do it. I tried to lose weight last year. Read some advice about detoxing with lemon water every morning. My dentist was horrified. The acid corrodes enamel.'

Lili relaxed. 'So... I read a case of a woman getting texts from her dead boyfriend. Eventually a psychic texted and said the boyfriend's spirit was passing the words on to her and she was merely acting as a conductor; said she needed paying for any further time. Is this likely do you think? His death had been in the papers as he was a B-list celebrity. Do you think it was more likely the girlfriend was being scammed? No offence to your profession...'

'Every profession has charlatans.' He took a minute. 'Technically, someone acting as conductor in that way is possible, but I don't think it would happen out of the blue like that. For a start, us psychics do indeed have to eat. I think they'd have contacted you first, as themselves, before you got these texts, and charged you a fee upfront. I mean, it's not like they get paid by the dead.'

A smile flickered across her face. 'Fair enough.'

'More importantly, they'd have found out first if you wanted to hear from your loved one. Not everyone does. It's too upsetting. Nah. It doesn't add up. I'm sorry, Lili, but I'd be very surprised if these texts were from Em's spirit.'

She took out her purse. 'Thanks for your time. How much do I owe you?' She looked around for a notice with a price.

He stood up. 'Nothing.'

She got to her feet. 'But...'

'I've not earned any money by contacting a spirit, with the help of a photo of the deceased one usually. This hasn't been that kind of consultation. All we've done is chat, and I'd be a rich man if I charged people for every time I did that. Mum always said I had more to say than a bird during the dawn chorus.'

'Why do you need the photo?' asked Lili. 'Don't you just ask the room "who's there?" Or have I watched too many movies?'

'The face is everything about a person. It holds their true identity. Expressions give a clue as to how their energy flows, as do the eyes, which many believe are portals to the soul. I can pick up a lot from a shot – as long as it isn't a robotic passport one.' He smiled, shook her hand and Lili left. In a blur.

Oh. My. God.

Perhaps her views on people like Greg were wrong.

He'd dropped the word 'passport' into the conversation, a clue perhaps that Em *was* travelling. More importantly, he'd talked about the importance of a person's face. His actual words were 'it holds their true identity'. That must have been his way of saying that Colin and Shirl's apparent identification of the body was irrelevant, his way of encouraging Lili not to give up.

This was the strongest proof she had yet – the psychic *knew*, he did, that Em wasn't dead.

6

Lili locked up the shop and turned to face Tommo and Meg. The three of them started walking, Lili studying passersby, looking for that familiar face. On the last Friday of every month, she took staff members out for a drink in Mevagissey. It had been a tentative idea but Em had insisted she go for it.

'Don't be a dick. Of course you must do it. Most of the managers I've worked with think criticism is the way to inspire staff, instead of free cocktails. It's not rocket science.'

An assistant manager, Andrew, worked half of his time in Mevagissey, the other half at a Ware & Care store in Truro. Hers was only a small shop but Lili had a reliable team of volunteers, mainly retirees or unemployed youngsters. But like tonight, sometimes the Friday night drink out ended up just being Meg, Tommo and Lili who'd built a solid friendship despite the differences of three generations. Tommo didn't work on a Friday but was always up for a free drink, he said, but Lili knew it was for the company. Both Meg and Tommo lived in Mevagissey but now and again would come over to hers in

Truro to look around Lemon Street Market and have dinner at her cottage.

'It's hard filling the time since Joe died,' Tommo once said. 'I'm busy with the garden, I read, I keep Ware & Care running a few times a week...' He'd attempted a smile. 'But I never realised how much time Joe and I spent simply... being. We didn't need clubs. We didn't need a whirlwind social life. We had each other and that was enough.'

It had been like that for Lili with Em. Any spare time after work they just chilled by cooking – well, Lili did. Cup-a-soup queen Em would wash up. They'd watch Netflix and argue over their celebrity crushes – Glen Powell for Lili, Tom Hardy for Em.

'I was almost going to stick to mocktails tonight. Nearly got an ear infection after going cold water swimming with my neighbour's son.' Tommo dragged on his cigarette as they walked along the back streets to a favourite bar that had a collection of fishing rods across the ceiling.

Lili trailed behind. Every now and then she took out her phone.

'Good for the heart,' said Meg, chewing gum. 'My gran swears by it. She and her mates go most weeks throughout the year.'

'Join them, do you?' he asked.

'Not on your life!' She gave an impish grin.

Lili got drinks whilst Meg and Tommo talked quietly together. They stopped when Lili returned carrying a tray. She sat down and handed out the drinks. 'There was a new special – a Dark 'N' Stormy daiquiri.'

Meg drank and closed her eyes. 'That rum is amaziiiing.'

They chatted about Meg's twenty-first birthday last week, Tommo asking her to spill the tea about a night out with her friends, looking very proud of his use of modern slang. They moved on to Christmas, or at least Meg and Tommo did, him protesting at how his younger colleague had already begun her festive shopping and it wasn't even Halloween. A shop regular, a teacher called Callum, came up and they spoke about how they hadn't seen him for a while. Lili zoned out, thinking about Greg the psychic and everything he'd said a couple of days ago. She zoned back in when Meg pulled a comical face and mentioned the special ceremonies at Lili's place.

'I overheard two elderly customers talking. They'd heard about your Sunday afternoons but didn't know the detail. One said her friend had seen three men coming out of your cottage the other week. I almost burst out laughing when I heard the words "sex parties".'

Tommo bellowed with laughter. Lili almost choked on her drink. Let people think what they wanted. What went on was private to the people who took part and not for broadcasting.

Lili knocked back the last mouthful of her cocktail and exhaled. 'I needed that.'

'Busy day?' asked Tommo.

She shrugged.

He shot Meg a glance and she cleared her throat. 'I... we... need to say something.'

'You actually hated that drink?'

'Of course not! And you know me – no filter according to my ex. I'd have said something after the first sip. No, it's just... well... the last month or two—'

'Are you okay, gal?' cut in Tommo, and he ran a thumb behind one of his bright red braces decorated with seashells. 'Me and young Meg have been worried. You haven't been your usual self this last year, but just when you seemed happier, things have taken a downturn.'

'You don't smile as much, haven't bothered with make-up – not that you need it,' Meg added hastily.

'I'm fine.'

'You didn't chase that shoplifter this morning like you normally would have, you called the police instead,' said Tommo.

'And you didn't sing when Taylor Swift came on the radio yesterday. It was as if you weren't listening.'

'Honestly, everything's all right!'

'Calling BS,' said Meg.

'Since when did you get so cheeky?' protested Lili. 'I remember that sixth former who first turned up and wouldn't say boo to a goose.'

Tommo turned to Lili. 'What's it all about?' He tilted his head. 'Em?'

'Got to be honest, I used to have a bit of a crush on her...' Meg gave a sheepish look. 'She was so cool. I loved that sleeveless, floor-length coat she wore, made of silk. That's true style. Not caring about the weather or occasion, just wearing what you love. And she complimented me on my nose piercing the first time we met; said my parents must be great to have let me get it done when I was sixteen.' A flicker of something painful crossed her young features. Lili and Tommo shot her understanding looks. Meg had confided in her two colleagues about how her parents had her when they were teenagers themselves and couldn't cope. Out of the blue they'd upped and left, selfishly expecting Meg's mum's parents to take on the responsibility of a baby.

Meg had effectively lost her mum and dad. Tommo had lost his husband. Lili met their earnest gazes. Okay. She could trust them.

'This first-year anniversary of Em's death has hit me harder than I expected, and to cap it all I've started getting these weird text messages...' Cheeks blushing, Lili got up. 'Look, you don't want to hear all of this... Come on... I'll get another round in.'

Tommo reached up and gently pulled her back down. 'What messages?'

'Oh, it's nothing. Now, I don't know about you two, but I want to try a Shipwreck Woozy. I'll have the virgin one as I'm driving, but apparently the alcoholic version contains...'

Tommo raised his eyebrows and folded his arms, staring at Lili. Meg did the same.

Lili sighed. It took her back to the looks she'd get from her parents when she was little and had been naughty. When she was older, they became the looks that they gave each other. 'You'll think me crazy if I explain. I'll lose all that respect you two show me, as your boss... Oh wait...'

The three of them smiled, then Lili reluctantly explained about the Knock Knock joke, the emoji... her list... her chat with Em's parents and how adamant they'd been that their daughter was dead, but then she'd seen the psychic...

When she stopped, Tommo got to his feet. 'Bloody hell, gal, I need that Woozy. And I'll be having words with Joe later as to why *he* hasn't texted *me*.'

Meg was about to speak when her phone rang. The call with her gran ended as Tommo came back, smelling of smoke. He dished out the drinks and collapsed into a chair.

'Christ, you must have been as shocked as a fisherman hooking a shark, Lili. If Joe messaged me, I'd... Damn, I'd be surprised above all else because he hated mobile phones.' His voice wavered. 'He was a silly old sod when it came to technology. I'd do anything to be able to show him again, just once, how to copy and paste a link or use a gif.'

Tommo would put on a brash, happy-sailor front, but Lili sensed that something sadder lurked underneath, trapped.

'Em always seemed so extra, in all the best ways – no one's ever laughed so loudly at my jokes as she did,' said Meg. 'Texting like this is exactly what she'd do, I reckon. What have you found out about those companies, on your list, that send pre-programmed texts?'

'I tracked down a handful online. It took forever – but there isn't much detail about how it works. You have to sign up to find out and I'm not doing that. Some charge several hundred pounds.'

Meg took out her phone and tapped for a few moments. She skimmed the page, then handed her phone over to Lili.

'Here's one. A company called Happy Ever Endings. Ring them. They might pick up, you never know. A lot of online businesses run 24/7.' She shook her phone. 'Go on. I want to hear what they say.'

'They won't just tell me. They're out to make money.'

Tommo shrugged. 'They may have good intentions as well.'

What the hell. She had nothing to lose. Lili pressed the call button and it rang out. She was about to hang up – it was a Friday evening after all – when someone picked up. Lili got to her feet and made her way outside, into the quiet, Mevagissey lit up as if it had not one but a hundred little lighthouses like the one on the end of the wall of the outer harbour.

'Hello? I'm wondering if you can help me.' Lili explained her situation to the woman who picked up.

'I'm very sorry about your friend. It sounds as if you've researched what a service like ours does – how pre-planned messages can be activated by all sorts of things. Like location – someone could programme a message to be triggered every time a loved one visited their grave. Or on a particular date, say a birthday. So I agree that... Em, was it? She could have programmed a message to be triggered by the words Knock Knock; she could have stored your favourite jokes and programmed in the appropriate answers – and appropriate emojis.'

Lili held her breath.

'But a text from a deceased loved one wouldn't simply come through. A link would have been sent that would have led you to a secure platform where the message could be viewed and then downloaded and saved if you wanted. I think all companies like ours would follow that procedure. I'm very sorry, but I don't think the texts you've received were pre-programmed by your friend.'

Lili made her way back inside and handed Meg her phone back. She told her and Tommo what the woman had said.

'Ah. Yes. That makes sense,' said Meg.

Tommo placed a hand on Lili's. 'How do you feel?'

'Okay. Now I can rule out number four on my list. That leaves two options – either...' Her face lit up. 'It's a living and breathing Em texting me...'

'What, despite everything her parents said?' Meg asked.

Lili coloured up. 'Yes – because of the unfound phone... the passport... what the psychic said about faces... that emoji...'

Tommo rolled his lips together. Meg simply nodded.

'Or,' continued Lili swiftly, and she shrugged, 'it's someone else. And boy, that joker better be scared of ever meeting me if that's the answer. But I've just got this feeling...' Eyes shining, she went to buy crisps.

When she got back, Tommo was fiddling with a beer mat.

'As you say, spit it out,' Lili said to him, tearing open one of the crinkly bags.

'We just hope you aren't going to be disappointed if it's not

Em,' he said. 'The heart wants what the heart wants, but sometimes that means it leads us astray like... like a pod of whales that accidentally beach themselves, convinced they're swimming in the right direction.'

'You definitely pressed her name in your contacts list, when you messaged? The texts definitely came from her old number?' asked Meg.

'I did check. Of course I did. And remember, *you* reckoned this is exactly the sort of thing Em would do.'

Meg's face softened. 'Yes, but now it's all sunk in... I don't think it's likely. Her parents saw the body. They saw the body, Lili. They'd *know*. Oh, I so very much want it to be her. But like Tommo, I... I also don't want to see my brilliant boss get hurt.'

Lili's eyes pricked. 'I've got to get a definite answer. One way or another.'

Meg and Tommo looked at each other.

'Then we're here for you, gal, if you keep looking into this,' he said. 'Just... be careful. You don't know what – or who – you are going to discover.'

7

Early the next morning, Lili stood in the kitchen, yawned and sipped her first coffee of the day. The morning light caught the stained-glass bird suncatcher that hung from the window. She gazed out onto her back garden. Another day of unusually warm autumnal weather was waking up. Their home was small, on the outskirts of an estate near Truro, but picture-postcard pretty, with the garden's apple trees at the far end, a curved wooden bench, and colourful borders that framed the lawn. Em had teased Lili for installing a bird bath and feeding table, saying she'd become *so suburban*. However, Lili would often catch her friend sitting out on the patio before work, tossing generously sized crumbs of toast to sparrows.

As the sun rose, so did an uncomfortable feeling in her chest. Were Tommo and Meg right? Was she a fool to chase this dream of having Em back in her life?

It wouldn't be the first time she'd been foolish. She'd thought Em's ex, Sean, was decent too. He was a dentist and Em had suffered pain with a tooth for months but couldn't get registered anywhere for treatment; the waiting lists were far too long. Sean had opened a new practice, close to them in Truro, and had sorted out her months of toothache in a matter of minutes. They started dating. He persuaded her to deregister though, so that he wouldn't get into trouble, and sent Em gifts. Neither Em, nor Lili, could see that the charm was a distraction from his other woman. And when it ended, oh so badly, not only was Em left broken-hearted, with whiplash, but also the tooth problem came back and the same old issue of not being able to get treatment. Em was taking painkillers for the tooth and for the whiplash. Was it any wonder that drinking on the houseboat risked her falling in? If the body found belonged to Em.

Sean's lies did untold damage.

However, when under his spell, even Lili began to soften towards the idea of having a long-term relationship of her own, especially after yet another friend from Manchester got married. But then if she partnered up, had kids, built a home out of love and not just bricks, was that risking it tumbling down and hurting a child as much as young Lili had suffered? Despite their own torrid, painful history, Mum and Dad were always asking Lili if she'd met anyone special. Lili didn't get it, and what happened to Em had made Lili promise herself that she'd give even less thought to the idea of meeting Mr Right. She already had the right job, the right friends, the right health, the right passion, the right house, the right location. That was more than enough.

And the right garden. A smile crossed her lips as a squirrel tightrope-walked the fence like a jittery circus performer. Lili's parents' bitter divorce had taught Lili, from a young age, that pinning your future dreams onto another human being was dangerous. Even though Colin and Shirl were happy, Em had always agreed that romance wasn't the be all and end all. Her feelings for Sean had taken both of them by surprise. Lili's mum had been okay; she'd kept positive once her marriage was over, but her dad stayed depressed for months. It took him a couple of years to rebuild a life for himself and ever since, he'd lurched from relationship to relationship, making the same mistakes, looking for something he thought was missing, when all the time it was within him. Unlike Tommo, who had his biker friends, his volunteering, a sense of self-worth, self-reliance... She'd only seen him wobble at Christmas, having known him for the last two Decembers. Poor Tommo. She kept his festive secret to herself.

Lili put down her coffee and her face lit up in a way it rarely had these last months. There was the robin who'd been calling by this year, first last winter, then more so over the summer and now, as autumn arrived, every day. She'd named her Bobbin, a real bird for sure. She'd spent many mornings in the summer getting up early and training the bird to come onto her hand. At first Lili would just sit quietly in the garden. She'd thrown food down on the ground, near her chair. Over a few weeks she dropped the food nearer and nearer, until one day she put it in her hand and stretched out her arm. Oh the joy when two little feet landed in her palm, a V-shaped head bobbing up and down! That was one of the ways she'd decided Bobbin was female – the males' heads were more U-shaped apparently. Also she'd seen Bobbin standing next to another robin that was slightly bigger with brighter colours – no doubt a male.

She went outside, onto the patio, and shivered. She stretched out her arm with a handful of seed mix.

'Hello, Bobbin,' she murmured as the bird landed on her hand and pecked away, every now and then stopping to look at her. 'You get it, don't you?' she said. 'Why I'm investigating Em's death?'

Lili didn't know why but the bird had offered enormous comfort during the last year. She'd told Bobbin about her texts to Em and often sent them whilst in the garden. Bobbin was wild – it didn't have to stay put, but often after eating its fill, the bird would hang around. Sometimes Lili put down a dustbin lid of water and Bobbin would bathe. This year she would buy Christmas cards with robins on.

'Or do you agree with Tommo and Meg that it might be better to leave it be and pretend no one ever replied to my Knock Knock text?' she asked.

The robin stopped eating, looked Lili dead in the eye and then did the strangest thing: shook its little head. She couldn't get that image out of her head as she drove to work, as she restocked shelves, supervised staff, tried to eat lunch.

Finally, the day done, she stood outside the shop, under the twilight sky so clear near the coast. Bobbin was right. Lili wasn't being a fool. She'd get home and ring Em, pronto! Except Glenda, who'd left the shop about ten minutes ago, was still hanging around outside, tightening her scarf, pulling on gloves. Then she took out her brolly as rain began to spit down. Lili always knew how Glenda's life was going by her choice of story. On good days, she picked out Jackie Collins bonkbusters, or a Jilly Cooper countryside romp. Feisty, funny, the characters and plots in those books reflected her mood. Yet when life was proving more of a struggle than usual, she'd avoid contemporary scenarios and lose herself in the past. Today's choice had been a Regency-era story. Lili pulled a tube of Munchies out of her coat pocket and offered one to Glenda.

'Don't mind if I do,' she said and shivered, taking one. The weather was cooler now and more like the norm for October. It had even rained at the weekend. 'I'm already looking forward to visiting the library on Monday and am beginning to dread Sundays when it's closed.'

'Hold on,' said Lili, and she popped back into the shop. She returned with a long, full-body hot water bottle in a sealed bag. 'Have this. Company policy – we don't accept hot water bottles. Even if, like this one, they're brand new. Rules are rules.'

'I can't possibly accept that,' said Glenda, but her eyes lit up. 'Although it certainly would be good between the sheets with that length.'

They looked at each other and burst out laughing.

'Is it true what I've heard about your Sunday afternoons? That you're a dominatrix? Wouldn't this long bottle come in handy?'

'Glenda!' Lili started laughing.

'Only teasing, but I am intrigued. Could it be Tupperware parties, séances, or a new militant political party?'

Lili pushed the water bottle into Glenda's hands. 'If you could ever benefit from attending, I'm sure fate will lead you to my cottage.'

Glenda gave her a hug and walked off.

Lili locked up and stared at the Closed sign with a sigh. Saturday 25 October – only six days to Halloween. Normally, she and Em would have already carved pumpkins. Lili had bought one a few days ago but it still sat on the unit without a toothy smile. Perhaps she'd try her hand at baking pumpkin pie instead.

Right. Off home to ring Em's number, to find out the truth once and for all. With a fast pace she started to walk, but wait... Was that Callum, the regular customer they'd not seen for ages? She caught his eye and went over.

'Callum... how are you? How's the little one? Jack running you ragged as always? You've been missed in the shop. Tommo's got no one to talk football with.' She pulled a face. 'He tries with me, convinced anyone who grew up in Manchester must live and breathe the Premier League.'

'Cheers, Lili, I've missed those chats too.' His cheeks flushed.

'I... I hope I'm not being nosy, but is everything all right? We've become used to seeing your face in the shop, what with all the clothes and toys you buy for Jack.'

Callum looked sheepish and hesitated. 'It's... going to sound stupid.'

Lili thought about the texts, and Tommo and Meg's faces when she spoke about them. Colin and Shirl's as well. 'Stupid might just be my speciality at the moment. Do share. It will make me feel better.'

Callum smiled. 'My place is only small, a tiny two-bedroom flat – all I could afford after the divorce from my wife Alice. We share custody but I still need space for when Jack's with me and... it's cluttered. All my stuff is piled up in my room and now spilling into the lounge. He's forever growing, forever changing, but I've avoided coming into the shop because, to be honest, I don't know where I'll put anything new.'

'Is there nothing amongst all the clutter that you can get rid of?'

'I should but... it's hard. You get attached...'

She tilted her head. Perhaps it would do him good to come to one of her special Sunday afternoon events. The rain began to pelt down. Now wasn't the time to mention it.

'Well, if you change your mind, we've had an influx of toys. I know Jack loves board games and one's come in to do with building dinosaurs. Maybe a visit will inspire you to declutter a bit.'

Callum gave a non-committal shrug, smiled again, and they

said goodbye as a group of early Saturday night drinkers jostled past. Head down, coat collar up, she went to pass Crystoffees where Em used to work, breathing in the smell of joss sticks as the door opened.

'Hey! Lili!'

It was as if fate was trying to intervene, to stop her continuing her investigations. She looked up. It was Paul, Em's old manager.

'Hold up,' he said. 'I've got a spare pasty that needs eating up tonight.' He disappeared and came back with a bulging paper bag. 'Right, better go and close up. I'm off to the cinema tonight.'

'Thanks so much, Paul.' But he'd already gone.

Back at the cottage, Lili hung up her coat, put on her slippers and poured out a glass of cold water. A clear head was needed. She settled on the sofa and took out her phone.

Autumn pot pourri filled the room with the aroma of pumpkin spice. Smooth Radio played gently in the background. She'd never lived alone until this year, moving straight from a life with her parents to one with Em, so she'd worked hard at filling the emptiness of the cottage with fragrances and sounds. Lili had taken up crocheting, bought jigsaws and invested in a tin of coloured pencils and big drawing pad. None of the hobbies had lasted. None of them had got rid of the void Em had left. Not even the occasional date. Meg encouraged her to go through dating app profiles on their lunchbreak, but the idea of a romantic distraction didn't work. It was so not what Lili was about. One positive from her parents' divorce was that each of them, in their own way, afterwards, showed their daughter the foundations of inner confidence.

'If you ever have to compromise yourself to fit into a relationship then it's not good, even if that partner is a good person,' said Mum.

'Pretending I was something I wasn't slowly killed me,' said Dad. 'I should have spoken up earlier, stood up for who I was. It wasn't your mum's fault.'

Both those comments stuck with a young Lili and made her realise that the most important thing in life was honesty, through and through.

Right. No more procrastinating. Lili ran a finger over the phone's screen and was about to go into Contacts when the corner cabinet caught her eye. She and Em had laid out souvenirs from their trips. They each collected something different. For Em it was boxes of matches. She smoked back then, until her dad had a lung cancer scare and she wanted to support him stopping his forty-a-day habit. Lili herself also stopped vaping, even though she enjoyed the faces Em would pull every time she tried a new flavour that her friend would deem sickly sweet. Lili's souvenirs were small ornaments to hang on the Christmas tree once a year, like the pair of clogs from Holland, and castanets from La Manga.

Where might Em have gone travelling this last year?

How dare she go without her!

Lili pressed dial, blocking out the possibility a total stranger might pick up. Or would it be a stranger? Could it be someone she knew, playing a twisted joke? What if dicko Sean... She'd bumped into him once, after the break-up. He'd smiled and said hello in that smooth tone, as if nothing had happened. Lili told him in no uncertain terms what a selfish, two-faced jerk he was. His whole demeanour changed in an instant and Sean had snarled back that Lili had always been jealous of Em dating him; he'd scoffed at how she'd never had a boyfriend, little realising that had been her choice. Could he have been playing a joke? No, no, no, she wouldn't entertain that notion. Surely even Sean couldn't be that spiteful?

The phone rang out. And rang. Her stomach twisted and... Oh. The call clicked into an automated voicemail. Not Em's usual recorded message. Lili went to speak but ended the call instead. She hadn't waited one year to simply speak to a digital voice. As the radiators gurgled with hot water, Lili shivered and wrote a text.

> Hey Bestie, let's meet up. I can't wait to see you again. It's time us interlopers show Cornwall how to live it up again xx

She put a turtle emoji. They'd called themselves interlopers when they'd first moved down from the north. Truth was though, the rugged coastline and down-to-earth Cornish banter quickly felt like the perfect fit. An idea came into her head and she carried on typing.

> It's Halloween on Friday, how about then? We could dress up!

Determined not to obsessively keep checking her phone, Lili went for a long bath. She ate the pasty. Only then did she pull out the charger and look at the screen.

A message was waiting!

> Sure, mate! Sounds good. Thursday gives me time to get back from Europe! Halloween? It's got to be The Rough Tor in Bodmin then. See you at eight.

No emoji this time, but no matter! Whoop! Friday it was!

Lili stared at the words on the screen. My God. What was she doing? Was this really happening? This felt right, and Em did occasionally call her mate, although she wasn't familiar with Bodmin.

> See you then! xx

A sob escaped her lips. These messages shone a torch into what had felt like such a gloomy future. Lili knew that whatever the outcome, she was going to this meeting. If there was the slightest possibility that this was Em, it was worth it.

8

LILI AND EM AGED TWELVE

On the first Monday of the summer term, they sat at the bottom of the playing field. Lili let a ladybird run over her hand.

'Hannah and her friends are such bitches,' said Em.

'I thought they'd get bored of the nasty comments by now.'

'Kamal said they're idiots and it's only because they're jealous that we can play football and got to meet Katy Perry last Christmas.'

'That's cos he fancies you,' Em said, and they both giggled. 'Those VIP tickets were pretty amazing though. Your parents were so cool getting them for us.'

Lili rolled her eyes. 'Yeah, yeah. A guilt present – for them getting a divorce.'

'I blame Dad for my problems. I mean, who the hell calls their daughter Myrtle?'

'It *was* after his favourite aunt who couldn't have a kid of her own though, right? Anyway, my mum's not much better, naming me Lydia after some random doctor who delivered me. I know it was a difficult birth but...' The ladybird flew away. 'No wonder Hannah and her friends say we've got old lady names.'

'Gotta admire Hannah's English skills, really, nicknaming us Myrtle Turtle and Lydia Bacteria within the first week of high school. Kinda catchy.'

'And now she's calling us lezzers.'

Em raised an eyebrow.

'Kamal told me that as well. Hannah's saying that us wanting to meet Katy Perry cos we liked her song "I Kissed A Girl" means we must secretly be into each other. Why do you think I held your hand crossing the playground today?'

Em grinned. 'Lydia Taylor! That's why those losers jeered. I wondered why Kamal was laughing. You really don't give a shit, do you?'

'No. For a start, why is being called a lesbian insulting? Mum's best friend at work, Jill, is gay, and a far better person than Hannah will ever be. I only care about the opinions of kind people – like my nan. I can talk to her about anything. She said answering back to people like Hannah, or showing you are upset, feeds them; that they're insecure, they get desperate and think the only way to feel better is to put others down. Our old classmates from primary school still like us, and Laura in my maths set has invited us both to her party next week. We play football with the boys and I reckon most of the teachers think Hannah is a brown-nosing idiot... you and I are doing okay.'

'As always, you are right, my friend,' said Em. She leant forwards and kissed her on the lips.

Lili pushed her away, laughing, and wiped her mouth on her sleeve. 'Too far.'

Em laughed too and got up. 'Come on. Kamal is waving. Time to thrash him and his mates at footie again. Hope I'm on the same team as Zach, he's sooo hot. Race you there!'

She went to run but Lili stood up and caught her hand.

'You and me won't change, will we? Whatever happens? We'll always be there for each other?'

'Course. You know that.' A mischievous look crossed Em's face. 'In science the other day we were doing marine animals and Mr Morley said turtles can carry salmonella bacteria on their shells, which is really dangerous to humans. So as long as we always stick together, we'll always be able to keep the dickhead humans in their place.'

'Forever and ever,' said Lili in a satisfied tone. 'Till we're old ladies, when our names will finally suit us.'

'Yep. Together forever. Apart from the next two minutes when I run so far ahead you'll never catch up!'

9

The Rough Tor pub suited its name. Halloween decorations didn't hide peeling wallpaper and a chunk of missing plaster. The tables were scratched and the carpet was stained. However, the bar and glasses shone like beacons of light guiding the way. Immediately, Lili could tell why Em had chosen this place. It confirmed all of Lili's hopes that she'd faked her death and run away from such a difficult time in her life. Laughing punters had got into the Halloween spirit, wearing an array of witches' hats, skeleton jumpers and zombie make-up. Lili had booked a room, not knowing if Em would come straight from the airport. It meant Lili could stay up as late as she wanted, catching up with her friend's news. She'd decked it out in the way she and Em always prepared their lounge for the spookiest night of the year, with suitably themed snacks and a bottle of caramel apple Martini. Only a double room had been available, which was fine. Travelling the world, Em and Lili had often crashed out together, Em shrieking about how Lili would dribble on the pillow during her sleep, Lili waking in the morning to find her friend had stolen most of the duvet.

Happy memories the last year had lacked. A spurt of emotion flared in Lili's chest, unpleasant, angry, a sense of having been betrayed even. Had Em ever stopped to think how much her actions would devastate those who loved her? How could she make her parents, make Lili, go through a funeral? Had things really been that bad?

And breathe... The main thing was that Em would soon be back. There'd be plenty of time to hear her explanations.

Lili smoothed down her pumpkin-themed jumper and headed to the bar. She perched on a stool and ordered a glass of wine. Em would have grinned and called her a posh idiot. Bottles of beer were more her style. Lili pulled out her phone. Three minutes to eight. Two messages. One from Tommo, one from Meg, both wishing her luck, despite their reservations.

Lili hadn't thought anyone had noticed her struggle this last year. She'd put on a smile for staff and customers, gone home up to Manchester with Easter eggs in the spring, hosted northern friends from the Oxfam shop who'd visited Cornwall in the summer, danced at a beach party, eaten pasties and ice creams with gusto, got to know a visiting American, a nice, no-strings holiday romance if you could call two weeks of hangovers that. Life was tough for most people these days; Lili wasn't going to drag others down. That had been the great thing about living with Em. They'd show each other everything, the good, the bad and the fugly, as they joked. They'd get the bad stuff out of their systems. That way it never festered.

Bobbin the robin had been Lili's only true listening ear since Em.

Five minutes past eight. Someone sat down beside her. She looked up to meet the gaze of a man in a Dracula cape with black shoulder-length hair and a shadow of stubble. He was nothing like pale Em, who consistently dyed vivid colours into her boring mousey hair. Well, she called it that. To Lili it was a lovely shade of brown.

The man was around Lili's age and kind of cute. Okay, he was hot! She couldn't take her eyes off him. He was up there with Glen Powell, she admitted to herself, but real, here, with an earthiness coupled with a friendly smile. Em would have given Lili a pointed look and then gone over to chat him up.

Em.

Her being five minutes late turned into ten, turned into twenty. Soon it was a quarter to nine and Lili was on her second glass of wine. The man next to her hadn't moved either and kept glancing at the clock above the bar. With a heavy feeling, she watched the funny impromptu dancing going on by the jukebox as themed song after song played, 'Monster Mash' being the current favourite.

Punctual Em would have been early if anything.

At that moment the door opened and both she and the man next to her jumped as someone came through the door. A woman, around Em's height, with bright purple hair, crowned with black evil queen horns – that was so like Em to stand out!

Oh my God, it was really her! The nightmare was over!

Lili waved, heart thumping, heart singing!

The woman took off her mask. She gave Lili a friendly smile before... she turned away.

Lili gulped, hand still in the air.

Time stood still. Reality slapped her on the cheek. She downed the remainder of the wine and wiped her mouth with the back of her wrist.

'You okay?' asked the man next to her, now looking as miserable as she felt. 'You've been stood up too?' She couldn't answer. He held out his hand. 'Dylan. Dylan Davis. Pleased to meet you.'

'Lili Taylor.' She slipped her hand into his. It felt warm and somehow comforting. She pulled hers away, having left it there for several seconds.

'Sorry. Just a bit distracted. I've been waiting for Em, my friend. We... we haven't seen each other for ages, but I finally heard from her.'

Dylan gestured at her glass. 'Fancy another?'

Lili paused. 'Why not?'

The barman topped up her glass and passed the man another beer.

'How long is it since the two of you have been in touch?' asked Dylan.

'It's been a year since...' Lili exhaled. 'Since her funeral.'

Dylan put down his beer.

Lili gave a small smile. 'It's complicated and my colleagues think I'm crazy but... I sent her phone number a Knock Knock joke, you see. It was our thing to go straight to the punchline if we knew the answer. The reply came back. *She* did! It must have been her!' God, it was good to talk to someone objective. Perhaps the wine had loosened her tongue, but who cared? She'd never see this guy again.

'Wait, what? A Knock Knock joke?' Dylan's skin turned a shade as pale as the chalky skin of the man dressed as a ghost behind him, no mean feat as Dylan's had a sun-kissed depth to it.

'Then Em told me she'd been travelling, and I realised... What if she faked her own death? You hear about that sort of thing, don't you?' continued Lili. 'But she hasn't turned up and I'm left wondering... hoping still that...' Lili talked about their cottage in Truro and how she'd not had the heart to move anything into Em's old room. She gave an apologetic look.

'Sorry. Rambling.' She gulped her wine. 'Who are you waiting for?'

Dylan brushed a hand through his hair, pulling it back, making his features more prominent – the strong eyebrows, the sharp jawline and eyes as black as a witch's cauldron. What would he be like to kiss?

For God's sake. Get a grip, Lili. He's not the person you wanted to see tonight. He's not your best friend ever.

'My brother. Harry. You see... he's a huge fan of pranks. He's been travelling too, and I thought...' An expression she couldn't read crossed his features. 'He sent me a Knock Knock joke. It's a while since we've been in contact too.'

'Oh, that's a coincidence!'

Dylan bit his lip.

Her chest tightened. Unless...

Oh.

Fuck.

Unless it wasn't.

'But you went straight for the punchline.' Her voice wavered.

'Harry and I always try to outwit each other. I'm so sorry. It was an easy Knock Knock joke, I guess, with really only one answer.'

'Why did you say *you* were travelling? Or were you?' She studied him intensely.

'To catch him out. That's why I said I was travelling *like you* – to let Harry know that I'd realised the random text was from *him*. It's exactly the sort of thing he'd do. I was hoping he was back. Even if he does drive me mad. I mean *really* mad. Harry set a fake account up on Tinder and fooled me into a prank blind date with him once. He's signed me up to weird newsletters, hidden alarms in my bedroom and covered my laptop screen with a fake cracked one. That's why I didn't let on that I had no idea who the text was from. I wasn't going to give him the satisfaction. And the word "interloper" also convinced me it was him.'

'Why?' A lump had formed in her throat. Em wasn't coming. That meant... Of course it did...

Em. Wasn't. Alive.

'We come from Tavistock, born and bred in Devon. Bodmin is in Cornwall...'

Oh, yes, the old rivalry between those two counties, like the scone debate over whether you spread on jam or cream first.

Lili put a hand over her heart, acid rising in her chest as if she'd actually eaten something horrible.

'Why did *you* use the word?' he asked. 'Oh, hang on, your accent... You're a northerner, right?'

'Em and I grew up in Manchester but moved down here after travelling together in our early twenties,' she said, straining to keep her voice steady. 'Why did you suggest meeting at The Rough Tor?'

'For old time's sake – Harry and I had a crazy Halloween night here years ago. We were teens. A mate from our football club invited us. His parents used to run this place. We got stone drunk on booze we nicked from the bar and then went trick or treating at midnight and woke a load of locals up.' He gave a wry smile. 'The police had a firm word with us and our mate was grounded for a month. Harry and I still live together now, and even though life's been a lot more peaceful with him being away... it's too peaceful. Though I'd never tell him that. But this isn't about me and my brother.' He cleared his throat. 'What made you text your friend after all this time?'

'I...' She gulped and couldn't continue. 'Sorry. I just need a moment.'

His face flushed. 'Don't you apologise. This mess is down to me. I feel like a complete shit.'

Lili raced to the toilets. She stood in a cubicle for what seemed like an age, locked the door and bit on her fist. A tear rolled down her cheek. She punched the door. Did it again.

'You okay in there?' asked a voice.

Lili tore off a piece of toilet roll, wiped her eyes, flushed the chain and left the cubicle, apologising to the queue waiting for being so long. She returned to her seat.

'Sorry about that,' she said.

'Honestly, don't worry.'

'I texted because it was the first anniversary of her death. How come you've got her phone?'

He looked puzzled and handed his over.

'Oh. Yours is a different model to Em's.'

'I've got two phones. I decided to get this one for personal use and to use my other one for business only. That way I'm not bothered by work stuff out of hours. I emailed my new number to everyone, including Harry.'

'Who's your provider?' she asked. Why didn't Lili listen to Tommo and Meg? It was all falling into place. His provider was the same as Em's. 'Right. They must reuse old numbers once contracts aren't renewed. I was told they didn't.' She curled her fists in her lap.

'They only take it out of service for the first six months after someone dies... I read that in the contract when I signed.'

'Oh. Right. Six months? Most of this year I've been texting her, talking about my problems, how I miss her... Did you read some of those texts as well? They were private! You should have messaged back before.'

'Lili... slow down... remember, I thought your messages were from Harry. I wouldn't have believed that if I'd been getting loads of texts all this time. That wasn't his way. His jokes were always spontaneous. And I only got this phone a few weeks ago.'

'No, of course, sorry, I'm not thinking straight.'

She couldn't look him in the eye. She'd texted Em about a date she'd made herself go on, just to get out, about a doctor's appointment, about personal memories they shared.

Dylan clicked into the message from Lili and passed the phone to her.

'Scroll back. Put your mind at rest.'

'No... I believe you.'

He held his palms in the air. 'I insist.'

Her finger flicked up the screen. He was right. Dylan also showed her the receipt for when he bought the phone. He wasn't lying.

Those messages to Em had gone nowhere, into the ether, into the ashes of a phone that had probably melted in the fire. Suddenly the buoyant happiness, the excited bustle of the pub weighed her down. Ridiculously unhealthy snacks would help but she couldn't face going up to her room alone.

'I... I booked a room, for me and Em. Pointless now. We used to love Halloween.'

Lili would never normally go into a private space with a man she hardly knew, but tonight wasn't a normal evening. And she'd got to know Dylan. A bit. He wasn't a liar, at least – and after what happened to Em, with Sean, that was the most important thing.

'Fancy some caramel apple Martini and all-you-can-eat in Halloween-themed crisps and sweet treats?'

10

The room was basic with a small desk and chair and beige throw over the double bed. However, in the bathroom there was an array of free toiletries, including a mini shampoo, scented soap and a packet of condoms. Lili had brought paper cups and poured out two martinis. She passed Dylan a bag of Monster Munch crisps and offered him gummy vampire fangs.

'Classy,' he said and took a handful. She smiled back and they leant against the headboard as they sat on the bed, their legs outstretched in front of them on top of the duvet. 'You and Em spent every Halloween like this?'

'For as long as I can remember. We were at school together, travelled the world, then moved down from Manchester to Cornwall eventually.' Their life together summed up in one sentence. How was that even possible? She told Dylan about the countries they'd visited and some of the stories about the beautiful sights and friendly couch-surfing hosts. Also the time they accidentally ate dog in Vietnam and ran out of the restaurant without paying. And once they got stranded on a mountain in India, having gone hiking too near nightfall. Years later, the two of them used to look back, never sure whether to laugh or recoil in horror at their high jinks.

He pointed to a pile of leaves on top of a chest of drawers, acorns and conkers lying on top.

'Oh those... I always have a bowlful of autumn treasures in the house. They are so cosy, the colours so warming and perfect for Halloween. Love seed pods too. In the spring and summer I bring in flowers, weeds being a favourite – dandelions, daisies, buttercups. People just mow over them but I think they're as beautiful as anything you'd get in a florist's.' She gave a sheepish look. 'I always was a cheap date.'

Dylan burst out laughing. 'What line of work are you in? And what did Em do?'

'I run a charity shop in Mevagissey. Em helped manage a café that sells crystals, up the road from me.' It was hard, going back to talking about Em in the past tense. 'Tell me about Harry?' she asked swiftly, hyper aware of Dylan's proximity, the soft sound of his breathing, the way his throat caught just before he spoke.

'Two years younger than me. Both of us born in Devon and stayed there ever since. Dad ran a house clearance business and met Mum on holiday in Italy. She married him and eventually got British citizenship. They retired five years ago and Dad passed Express House Clearances onto me and my brother. The last couple of years they've spent as many months as they're allowed on the Amalfi Coast, where we have relatives, and have decided to start the process to see if they can move there permanently.'

'Wow. And house clearance? That must be interesting. I love going through new stock that comes into Ware & Care.'

Dylan shrugged. 'Not really. I'm there to do a job. I never cease to be amazed by the useless junk people hold on to. I try to be sensitive after a bereavement, but my job's to help them get rid, so we're in and out as quickly as possible.'

A practical attitude. So unlike Lili's. He'd be baffled if he knew about her occasional Sunday afternoon freedom ceremonies, as she called them, that helped people move on. Lili wouldn't talk about them with Dylan. Often people didn't understand. It was best to keep them, and exactly what went on, secret.

'You're half Italian?'

'Yep. Voted one of the sexiest nationalities in the world, don't you know?' He took another fang sweet, lodged it in his mouth and bared his teeth at her, pulling a gruesome face. 'Easy to believe, right?'

'More like one of the most misguided nationalities,' she replied smoothly.

He grinned and chewed the sweet. 'Mum's favourite flower is a lily.'

'My name's actually Lydia. Em's was Myrtle.' She took another sip of martini. 'We got bullied by a group of girls at school who called us Lydia Bacteria and Myrtle Turtle.'

'Ouch.'

'When I say bullied... we didn't much care. Their unkind comments about our supposed old lady names said more about them than us.'

'That's why you put a turtle emoji on your message?'

He'd noticed; he'd remembered such a small thing. She glanced down at their legs. They were almost touching.

'Yes. And Em used the green nauseated face emoji to represent bacteria when she messaged me. It looks like someone feeling sick with an infection. We started using the emojis after we left school and were travelling, and the habit stuck. So I thought...'

Dylan rubbed the back of his neck. 'Ah. Of course. But I put that in the text after the word "travelling" because I get very travel sick. Harry knew that and it was meant as a clue that I was onto him.'

'Oh. Right.'

'I kind of get it – having a name that stands out, that is, not the bullying. Harry and me... I don't tell everyone this...'

Lili raised an eyebrow, forgetting Em for a second.

'His middle name is Luigi, mine is Mario.'

'No!' Her spirits lifted for the first time all night. She laughed, bumping against him. He bumped her back. 'Honestly, what *are* parents thinking?' She shook her head.

'Mine swear they never saw the connection. Funnily enough though, the other kids were jealous when they found out – thank you, IT teacher, for announcing it in my class. Harry's mates soon found out as well. Everyone loved those games so much. They'd sing the theme tunes whenever we went by. We used to walk with our knees and fists up every time they did it.'

'Me and Em would hold hands cos those girls started saying we were lesbians. That used to shut them up.'

Lili became overwhelmed by the memory of them both in school uniform, planning out their futures, talking about how they'd end up in the same care home, causing havoc. She put her drink down on the bedside table, slid off the bed, walked over to the window and looked out across the town.

What had made her think Em would want to meet up in Bodmin? She'd always considered it grey and ugly, despite what tourist reviews said and the nice walk they'd had up Bodmin Moor's highest hill, Brown Willy (they couldn't stop laughing). And a guy Em had really liked came from there – the relationship before Sean-the-cheat. The boyfriend from Bodmin had been called Gus. Em had been really taken with him – whereas he was taken with her backpacking stories, took a year off work to travel and she never heard from him again.

Now Lili really was never going to hear from Em again.

A hand touched her shoulder. She turned around and looked up. Dylan had joined her.

'Em fell off a houseboat and drowned. Her funeral was exactly one year ago today,' she mumbled. 'Halloween appropriate – the scariest day of my life.'

'I'm so sorry,' he said.

'Don't be, Dylan. You've been disappointed tonight too. Come on, I need to hit a bigger sugar high – let's open the gobstopper eyeballs.'

'Would you rather I leave?' he asked.

No. Her eyes scanned his body, the height, the breadth, the confident movements, and like had happened, now and then, this last year, the pull to lose herself with a man tugged at her heart, so that just for a moment she could pretend that Em wasn't gone. Em had got the words "carpe diem" tattooed on the base of her spine. She used to say there was a lot of truth in clichés.

In any case there was something about Dylan; not just the angular features, the wavy midnight hair, the black pearl eyes and Atlas shoulders. Christ, those descriptions. Em would have laughed, but the physical attraction had set her body and mind on fire. She imagined him in a Roman gladiator's gear, with a loincloth, sandals and helmet, holding his armour and speaking in Italian.

But the attraction was more than that, to do with an air about him completely opposite to that of an armed fighter – gentle, caring, interested.

Whatever. She'd never see him again but... but that didn't

mean they couldn't make the most of an evening when they'd both been let down.

Lili moved forwards and slipped an arm around his waist. 'No, don't go. Please... stay.'

Dylan cleared his throat. 'Right, you mean... That's, um... You're a great girl, Lili... but you're upset, I wouldn't want to...'

'I'm a woman, Dylan, I know what I want. And right here, right now, that's you – if you want that too,' said Lili, feeling more brazen than she was used to. She stood on tiptoe and slipped her arms around his neck, pulling him down gently so that she could kiss him.

11

Dylan reached forwards and took the bobble out of Lili's hair. Blonde locks fell around her face.

'I've been wanting to do that since I first met you,' he said.

Lili took his hand. 'Come on, Mario,' she whispered and led him back to the bed.

Dylan swept an arm under her legs. He easily carried her over and lay her on the mattress. He stood in front of her, holding her gaze, and undid his shirt buttons, slowly, methodically. Nice. Dylan took his top off and threw it on the floor. He moved nearer, his black shoulder-length hair falling forwards. Pulse racing, Lili made room for him on the bed. His hand went down to her jeans. He undid the button and pulled down the zip.

'Okay?' he asked, still looking right into her eyes.

Oh. Considerate. Lili nodded and pulled off her jumper. He'd tugged off her jeans and now the two of them were under the covers. Impatiently, she slipped out of her T-shirt and Dylan wriggled out of his trousers. Lying sideways, their lips met, heat building in between her legs. Oh God.

Will You Stay Another Day?

She'd never been kissed like this, with such a light touch, yet he couldn't hide his eagerness as he explored her mouth. It unnerved her. Lili felt a… a lack of control.

This was new.

She kissed him back and her fingers slipped around the waist of his boxers. Taking the hint, he removed them. His index finger slipped down the top of her bikini briefs.

'You sure about this, Lydia?' he murmured, those eyes still piercing, yet touched with something else more compelling – concern; respect.

In response she removed her underwear, pushed herself up and straddled him. Lili took his hands, pinning Dylan down on the sheets, and when they got as close as they could, and an all-consuming urgency drove them both, a moan, small at first, built within her. Oh God. Oh God. Her head filled with a vortex of lights, of colours. An intense, addictive, dirtily euphoric sensation overran her emotions, followed by… oh… oh… a sense of relief that swept across her whole body, deeper and deeper until it was almost too much to bear.

Lili panted, hearing her heart beat. What had just happened?

When it was over, when he pulled her into his arms, when he kissed her head and told her she was so beautiful, before nodding off, Lili turned away and held a hand over her mouth, concerned she'd let out another a cry of ecstasy, unable to remember the last time she'd felt so very happy.

* * *

Baffled as she recalled the way he'd held her as she'd fallen asleep and how, during the night, she'd woken up to feel him covering her bare shoulders with the covers, Lili crept out of bed when dawn broke – baffled because she wished she could stay longer. What was that about? Last night her mind hadn't wandered to an upcoming holiday or problem at work, as it had with other men she'd slept with over the years.

Her whole attention, in the moment, had been on Dylan.

She pulled on her clothes, apart from a sock that must have got lost in the sheets. Hair tousled on the pillow, Dylan slept soundly, arms reaching out to the side now as if looking for her. An urge almost drove her to lie down next to him again, and breathe in his sexy bergamot scent. She reached into her bag and pulled out a clean tissue and pen.

Lili would normally make it clear, in advance of first sleeping together with one of the men she'd dated in the past, that she wasn't looking for a serious relationship. That saved any awkwardness or anyone getting hurt, and it made it easier to stop seeing someone after a few weeks, a few months at the most.

She should have done that last night but had got carried away, in the moment, after only a few hours with Dylan, what with Em not turning up. Lili had wanted an escape from reality and hadn't been able to resist his laughing mouth, those serious eyes, and that gentle nature combined with a Roman gladiator vibe.

Lili stared at the tissue.

Hi Mario. Wahoo! It's-a-me, Lili! Thanks for a fun evening. Bye Bye! x

No. Stupid, stupid, basing a message on a video game! And what was with the kiss? She hardly knew him – although Dylan had known just what she liked, as if they'd been together her whole life. She stuffed the tissue into her pocket and took out another.

Hi Dylan. Thanks for an enjoyable time. Look after yourself. Lili.

Gah! That sounded as if they'd spent the night playing Scrabble. Why did she care? It was a goodbye note, after... the best sex she'd ever had.

Lili gritted her teeth. *Come on, get on with it.*

Good to meet you, Dylan. Take care.

She left the tissue on the pillow next to his and put one of the autumn leaves she'd brought next to it, a beautiful orange field maple one. Then she packed up everything, crept out of the room and closed the door behind her.

12

Lili sat in the back garden, a throw around her shoulders. The sun shone and warmed her cheeks, even though the air was crisp with a chill that had set in the last couple of days and now embraced the first of November. She sipped her coffee and a smile spread across her lips at the memory of Dylan with those gummy vampire fangs in his mouth, last night.

Bobbin appeared on the garden table next to her and tilted its little head.

'I've been waiting for you,' said Lili, and she put down her coffee. Bobbin hopped a few steps nearer, no doubt recognising the special Tupperware bowl that was full of its favourites. Now and then Lili made up the bird food herself. She'd never been able to face feeding her garden friend mealworms, instead offering a mix of chopped peanuts, raisins, suet and a little cheese. Lili poured some into her hand and stretched out her arm. Bobbin hopped over and two small feet landed in her palm. Lili's heart lifted as Bobbin began to sing. The bird had only done that once before, so close to her. A robin's song was utterly joyous, a melodic, rapid tune built up of cheerful whistles and perfect high notes. It soothed the crushing realisation that had set in, that Em was gone for good. There would be no reunion. Lili focused on the bird's beautiful red feathers and how they matched autumn leaves on the ground. Small details that cheered the soul.

'You're so clever,' she said as Bobbin pecked at a raisin. 'Whenever I sing, I sound as if I've been eating toothpicks... Dylan had really nice teeth.'

The bird stopped dead and stared into her face. Lili couldn't help laughing.

'I know... One night only with Mr Cool. Sounds like a West End show, doesn't it? And between us... my God, it was right up there with any blockbuster. He was totally my type. I'll tell you all the important deets I'd have shared with Em, because you're as good as she was at keeping secrets.'

Bobbin waited patiently.

'When I think about last night, even now, hours later, a zing runs through my entire body. Everything was so easy – the talk, the laughs, his moves, mine. That's why I absolutely can't see him again...' Bobbin accidentally pecked her hand. Or was the robin trying to tell her something? Em's voice came into Lili's head. *For God's sake, stop being so uptight! Go for it! Sweet and sexy – that's a killer combination!*

No. Lili didn't need a man in her life, especially at the moment.

'He works in house clearance,' she continued. 'And his attitude to clearing clutter couldn't be more different to mine. But then Japan changed me; it's why I set up my freedom ceremonies.'

Bobbin leant forwards.

'Okay. I'll tell you. But don't laugh like most people do when I explain. You see, Em and I loved Japan – the gentle manner of its people, the ornate traditional buildings contrasting super-modern ones, the cuteness overload in shops regarding clothes, plushies, food; oh, and the cherry blossom! Everything! We rented a little house for a few days in Kyoto and the woman who owned it told us how a nearby temple... well, it held funerals for inanimate objects.'

Bobbin squawked and Lili chuckled. 'I know, right? It sounds bonkers.'

At first this idea had struck Lili and Em as utterly ridiculous. But the landlady had explained about Shintoism, a belief that *everything* has a spirit, even things made of metal or plastic.

'I researched and discovered ceremonies held in Japan for dolls and gaming machines about to be discarded, can you believe? When we moved to Cornwall and I carried on working in a charity shop, the idea of such funerals began to make sense. Although the ceremonies in Japan are about gratitude and appreciation, whereas I had an idea that resonated deeper with me, that would address an issue I'd seen through my work and—'

Was that a stare of disbelief from Bobbin? Lili almost chuckled again. No. Surely not. 'I know, it's hard to get your head around. Let's just say, sometimes it's not as easy as we think to throw away old objects. One day, a customer broke down. I took him out the back, made tea and listened to why he felt so conflicted about donating the vase he was clutching.' Lili's eyes crinkled. 'It was Em who finally pushed me into turning my ambition into a reality. She told me to stop messing around and follow my heart; to plan out my Sunday afternoons, to create my own style of funerals, and help people move on from their past.'

Lili sighed. *I miss that straight-talking. Miss Em so much.* Her phone bleeped and carefully she moved her arm to the table.

Bobbin hopped off and she emptied the contents of her hand into a pile next to the bird. It dived into the cheese – cheddar always went down well.

'Bye bye, Bobbin, see you later.' Lili pulled the throw tighter as she made her way through the cottage. She dropped onto the sofa and looked at the message.

A punch to the stomach. Em's old number had sent a message.

And breathe. No. It wasn't *Em's* number any more. Lili clicked into Dylan's text to see a photo of her sock, followed by a vampire emoji. She burst out laughing.

Laughter was a precious commodity. Em had always laughed a lot, at least until the split with Sean. She lifted people, like a shot of coffee, sweet and syrupy but with an edge. Cheeky banter was her currency and she spent it often. In between her friend's death and the funeral, Lili had taken time off work and laid in bed staring at the ceiling, missing the sound of Em's giggle, the cheeky one-liners, the witty comebacks. Lili had texted her mum and dad saying to only come down to Cornwall for the service; that she was coping okay. But Meg and Tommo called round one day and saw the aftermath of Em's death. They didn't fuss; didn't ask too many questions, just tidied up and made mugs of tea. But from that point on, they took it in turns to drop off food. She'd even been grateful for Tommo's blow-your-socks-off curry. And over time she'd picked up the reins of her life again, a life that had begun to trot along nicely again, with working hard, with no meaningful romantic commitments. They said grief changed you, but Em wouldn't have wanted that.

She looked at the photo again.

There was something about Dylan, something that told her if they slept together again, she'd fall hard for him, and by doing so, she'd risk losing someone special again, risk getting hurt.

She couldn't go through that a second time.

> Keep the sock. I'm nothing if not generous! Thanks again. All the best.

Lili took a deep breath and deleted Em's number from her contact list.

13

Monday. End of day. Just another ordinary day. Lili yawned and went up to the stockroom. She hadn't slept well last night, two days on from Halloween, lying awake, taking it in, the cold hard fact that Em really wouldn't hit thirty after all. Yet she still couldn't quite bring herself to cancel the hotel in Vegas. She hadn't told Tommo and Meg about her Halloween meeting in Bodmin with Dylan, and now it was over she was glad she hadn't. Lili had been so wrong about Em coming back from the dead.

She looked around. Good old Tommo had done a brilliant job as always, leaving everything tidy before going downstairs to put out stock. A new arrival, a mirror with a frame like sunflower petals, caught her eye, already priced up, along with a tall pile of Terry Pratchett novels. Plus a T-Rex soft toy; little Jack would like that. His dad, Callum, still hadn't been back.

Footsteps sounded and Meg appeared. 'I'm off,' she said in a reluctant tone.

'Everything okay?' asked Lili.

'Sure.'

'Dating woes?'

Meg sighed. 'No. For once.' She managed a self-deprecating smile. 'Gran ones. She messaged today; said could I be quieter getting in if I'm out late again as last night I woke her up and today she was getting up super-early for a swim.' Meg gave an even deeper sigh. 'I can't wait to move out, but she doesn't know anything about it yet. She'll be devastated.'

'She might surprise you.'

'I don't think so. Gran's talked about dipping into her savings to build an extension so that I can have my own workroom, with a sewing machine and racks for the clothes I make or old ones I upcycle. She's in it for the long run and I get it, I'm basically her whole family without my parents around. And she's mine. But it's time for me to branch out on my own. It's not like I'll go far. I was going to share a place with a mate, but that fell through. Renting's so expensive. I'm saving as hard as I can, but then I've got this year-long online business studies course to pay for that I've recently begun and... I don't want to upset her. I've hardly seen my parents over the years. Last I heard they were squatting in Edinburgh. We couldn't even contact them for Granddad's funeral. I owe Gran so much.' Being brought up by an older generation was probably why she got on so well with Lili and Tommo.

Lili nodded. 'But you also owe it to yourself to live the life you'd never have had if your gran hadn't been so amazing. When you know, you know, right? About moving out? Try to talk to your gran, sooner rather than later. She's going to find out anyway.'

Meg shrugged and went downstairs.

After the divorce, neither Mum nor Dad's place had felt like home as Lili was shuttled between them, but eventually the new norm felt easy. And she didn't miss the arguments. The new situation also made it easy for Lili to strike out on her own, being away from England for weeks on end with her travel. Yet her big move to Cornwall had shocked them both, and in their own way they'd each sounded her out, made sure it was the right decision. In fact, they'd actually agreed to pool resources and gift Lili enough money to cover her half of the deposit on the cottage. Dad had hired a van and driven her and Em down. And as if she were a teen again, Mum had taken Lili clothes shopping before she left, and out for lunch.

Footsteps sounded again and Meg hurried in once more, followed by Tommo.

'Where have you been hiding *him*?' Meg hissed.

'What? Oh, that big porcelain robin with a Santa hat on? Striking, isn't it?' said Lili. 'It's a bit early for Christmas stock but I couldn't help putting it out. It'll sell quickly, I reckon and—'

'Gal, we aren't talking about a robin,' said Tommo. 'We're talking about… Woah, if I were forty years younger…'

'Or if I were into guys…' Meg interrupted.

Lili frowned. 'What are you two talking about?'

'I think you mean *who*,' replied Meg. 'I'd just flipped the open sign around when a man turned up, asking to come in.'

'Black wavy hair and like a fishing boat master, who could ride the wildest seas with his eyes closed, the sun on his face, salt in his lungs. Looks like he knows what to do with a tiller between his hands.'

'All right, Tommo, calm down,' said Meg. 'But yeah, a striking guy and pretty tall.'

'Kind eyes,' said Tommo. 'They remind me of Joe's. That was the first thing that attracted me to Joe, in fact – even though he was standing next to his new red Suzuki.'

No. It couldn't be.

Tommo pretended to warm his hands against Lili's cheeks, rubbing them together in the air. 'I could have done with this fire on my beach walk at the weekend.'

Lili glared and the two others laughed.

'It might be Dylan. He's just an... acquaintance.'

Meg gave her a long hard look. 'You slept with him!'

'Meg! We're still at work. Show some respect,' said Tommo, and he leant forwards. 'Let's go to the pub instead, and then all bets are off.'

'Where did you meet him? How long ago?' Meg demanded.

'Don't hold back,' said Tommo. 'I've lost my husband, Meg's girlfriend is still haunting her...'

'It's ghosting,' Meg whispered.

'We need to live vicariously through our boss.' Tommo gave a mischievous, irresistible grin that, Lili begrudgingly concluded, must have been the thing that had attracted Joe.

'Okay, okay. Later.' Lili hurried downstairs. Meg and Tommo followed and busied themselves with tidying the shelves, even though it was gone clocking off time now, and in any case, everything was already perfectly symmetrical and alphabetical. Tommo prided himself on making sure Ware & Care in Mevagissey was the tidiest charity shop in Cornwall.

Gosh.

There he was.

Apart from him, and her two colleagues, the shop was empty. With Dylan around, she had a feeling it would have seemed that way, even if there had been other customers.

This was... really annoying. Her plan had been to cut all ties.

'Dylan, how are you? This is a surprise.'

He leant forwards and kissed her cheek. Was that a snigger

from behind the clothes rail? He pulled a sock out of his pocket, like a magician revealing the answer to a puzzle.

'Pairs shouldn't be separated, be those from the animal kingdom or wardrobe,' he said and pointed to a pair of salt and pepper shakers in the shape of avocados. 'Or even from a charity shop.'

'Like Mario and Luigi,' she suggested.

He paused. 'Yes, even Mario and Luigi. I was passing, a bit of business.' He looked around the shop. 'Nice place.'

'I'm about to lock up,' she said and turned to her friends who'd given up any pretence of working now. 'Dylan, please meet my colleagues, Tommo and Meg.'

'Great to meet you, pal,' said Tommo, and he punched him on the arm before adjusting his glasses. 'Wow. Feel those muscles. You'd have no problem steering a trawler.' He gave a nervous laugh and swayed from side to side.

Meg pointed to Dylan's wrist. 'Love the friendship bracelet,' she stuttered and stared at him, as if he were on the page of one of her celebrity magazines. Meg didn't get lost for words. Not ever.

Lili had seen the bracelet last Friday but not given it much attention. Now she could see the beads on the front spelled out the word 'twat'.

'My brother gave it to me,' he said. 'Don't think he believed I'd actually wear it.'

Tommo punched Dylan's arm again and snorted.

'Excuse me, Dylan, I won't be a minute. Tommo, Meg, I've forgotten something about a new pricing policy and mustn't forget to tell you. Could I have a minute?' She jerked her head and the three of them went upstairs and stood in the stockroom.

'What *is* wrong with you two?' she hissed.

The pair of them looked sheepish.

'Don't often get a rockstar in Mevagissey,' said Tommo. 'Certainly not a Cornish one.'

'Well, he is half Italian.'

Oh Jesus. Lili shouldn't have let that slip. Due to the wonderstruck looks on their faces, she ordered them to stay put and she went downstairs again.

'Sorry about that. I would say to stop in the staffroom for a coffee, but I've got something on after work.' *It's for the best.*

Dylan held up his hand. 'Can't stay in any event. I've got a video call arranged with Harry tonight – he'll be telling me about amazing sunsets and exotic food, I'll be sharing the latest figures from the business's books.'

That was good. Absolutely. Exactly what she'd wanted.

'But seeing as we spent Halloween together, do you fancy joining me for another important calendar date? A Bonfire Night display this Friday? My brother's obviously not planning to come back any time soon. So I'd appreciate the company. Lots of my mates are married now or have family stuff going on for fireworks night.'

Dylan just said it how it was – she liked that. However, she bit her lip. 'I don't think... You see...' As if she was breaking up with him before they'd even dated, she continued. 'I'm not... looking for a relationship or anything long-term.'

'Who said anything about that? See – I just friend-zoned *you*.'

'I think I did that first,' she said.

'Whatever you say.'

Lili laughed before she could stop herself. Damn this man! Friends. Okay. This was good. They both wanted the same thing. One last meet-up wouldn't hurt.

'I'll text you the details,' he said and opened the door. 'Oh. The sock.' He put it over his hand. '*Arrivederci, amica,*' he said, making the sock talk, like a puppet. He gave it to her and headed off.

She pulled the sock over her fingers, for some reason wanting to feel where his hand had been. Something rustled inside and she pulled out a beautiful mustard-coloured silver birch leaf.

14

Lili sat in the garden, finished her sandwich and stretched out her arm, having saved a few scraps of cheese. Friday 7 November – the day of her fireworks date with Dylan. Not that it was a date. Far from it. All week she'd thought about him, even though she'd told herself not to. The brain was a contrary thing, prone to demand avoidance. It was easier to think of her dwelling on Dylan as a malfunction of an organ.

Bobbin flew over.

'*Buon appetito,*' she said. Lili absolutely had not been thinking back to a trip to Rome and imagining her and Dylan walking hand in hand past the Colosseum. Because that would be like a teenage crush and Lili was almost thirty with a far bigger handle on her emotions.

'It's true, right?' she said to Bobbin. 'I'm strong, steadfast, my head won't be turned by a guy, even if he does look great in a Dracula cape.'

Bobbin stopped eating and hopped from foot to foot. She could have sworn the bird was laughing.

Lili waited until Bobbin finished eating and then got up.

The firework display was at Craymouth, a northern Cornish town near the Devon border, around an hour's drive for both of them. She'd had the day off, which had timed well and made the night out less of a rush. Craymouth was a market town with ancient buildings, wonderful independent shops and big public flowerpots, bursting with rainbows of blooms in the summer. Lili had visited with Em a few times as it hosted musical festivals. Dylan hadn't said much in his text, just that its Bonfire Night display was a must-see. The event started at seven. They'd agreed to meet at five.

A few hours later she got out of her car at one of Craymouth's beach car parks. The wind blew strongly enough to chase away the clouds and leave the darkening sky clear of blemishes. Lili should have worn a hat. At least she'd wrapped up with a thick scarf. Over the ocean, the sun was setting, a semi-circle of gold resting on the water, illuminating crests of waves; it highlighted a flock of passing gulls and the striking jagged outline of rocks nearer the shoreline. Its glow reminded Lili of her friendship with Em and how a special person in your life made everything brighter, raising the volume on laughter, intensifying the taste of a meal out, bringing the little, wonderful things into focus.

'Lili?'

She looked to her right. Dylan was walking away from a blue saloon car. He wore a beanie hat and snug duffle coat, tight jeans and walking boots. Not that she cared about his appearance; no, not at all, nor the fact that Tommo and Meg were right about the air of fishing boat master – someone who was in charge, capable, decisive, and unafraid of facing the elements at their worst. His face broke into a grin and he pointed at her car.

'Sorry, Lili – nice as it is to see you, I'm compelled to introduce myself to that vision next to you, before we chat. Although I might need a magnifying glass to get a good look.'

Lili was not unaccustomed to such a reaction. Dylan bent over to look through the window. Em had left Lili her car as well as her savings – a classic Mini, tiny compared to its modern equivalent. Em herself had inherited it from an elderly aunt. Colin and Shirl had thought their daughter should sell it, but it had been love at first sight for Em, who promptly named it Colonel Mustard due to its colour. Its engine sounded as loud as an aeroplane's when you drove fast, and Lili spent most of her journeys expecting it to break down. Yet it had been reliable so far, was cheap to run and easy to park. Both she and Em supported recycling, and taking on this car suited the ethos of Lili's job. Dylan ran a hand over the bonnet. Every journey in that car also brought back memories of driving with Em. The time they'd almost come off the road because a bunch of lads in the MPV in front had pulled down their trousers and wiggled their bare backsides. Em had flipped them the finger, even though she and Lili were laughing. Then there was the time Em rushed Lili to A&E whilst she was having a heart attack. Okay, it was acute indigestion, but Em liked to dramatise when telling people how she'd make an ace ambulance driver. Colonel Mustard had a tape cassette player, and they'd put in Shirl's old 80s mixtapes. God, they'd had fun, singing along to Wham and Spandau Ballet on long journeys. Lili had a car of her own but it had been more expensive to run and the seat had never been comfortable. So she'd sold it when Em passed and taken on the classic car instead.

'Anyway, back to you.' Dylan bent down and... Oh. He kissed her on the cheek again, like he had in the shop.

Friends did that. They did. It meant nothing.

'Fancy fish and chips on the beach before we head to the

fireworks?' he said and pointed ahead to a van. 'The display is near the pier, about a half mile walk to the right.'

They both had cod with a dollop of tartare sauce and Dylan insisted on paying since Lili had provided the snacks on Halloween. The slope down to the beach wasn't smooth and at one point Dylan reached out his arm. Lili could manage on her own but an urge to slip her hand into his overwhelmed her. Dylan's firm hold guided her down and she inhaled as the sea air blew even more strongly against her face, through her hair, like an air purifier, removing the dust, the dirt... the sad thoughts.

'How do you know Craymouth?' she asked as they sat against dunes, facing the tide, barely visible now through the twilight.

'Harry and I used to come to music festivals here.'

'Same! Me and Em. Well, they were more for her really. We'd make a deal to arrive early. I got to browse the shops, which she found boring, then in return I would stand on my feet for three hours, dehydrating and getting tinnitus.'

'Ha! Relatable. A swim in the sea was my bargaining point. Harry endured it, to laugh at my dancing later on. He was a natural. But no one wants to see my cheesy moves.'

I wouldn't say that, she thought as an image came into her head of him sweeping her up into his arms last week, laying her on the bed.

God. Could she be any more mushy? If she was texting this to Em, her friend would have sent back laughing face and vomit emojis.

The fish and chips gone, Dylan put their polystyrene trays into a nearby bin and they walked towards the sea. Bitter salt air, crashing waves, unsteady sand underneath her feet, chilly air... Lili linked her arm with his. Which was okay. They were only mates.

But what if she wanted more?

There. She'd said it – at least in her head.

Willing it to give her an answer, Lili fixed on the ocean. There was no end to the horizon; the water stretched onwards forever. Life was not like that. You had one short chance to find happiness. Was she really going to deprive herself of love until the end of her days? Wasn't she brave enough to risk it when the prize could be so very exciting?

A large wave crashed onto the sands as if the ocean was telling Lili to wake up to the fact she'd not felt like this about a guy since a schoolgirl crush on her biology teacher. Lili looked up at the sky, searching for the first star of the night. Starlight took thousands of years to reach earth and as stars lived billions of years; the light people saw now probably mostly came from ones that were still alive. But like humans, eventually they aged. Did Lili want her light to go out before she'd experienced love and passion – the things that had always been missing with dates previously?

She shifted her head down from the sky to Dylan and his strong features, the carefree hair sticking out from underneath his hat, a man content to just stand and watch, without feeling the need to talk, even though they hardly knew each other. That was self-confidence. Yet a frown was etched into his forehead.

Perhaps he had a question for the ocean as well. Dylan looked at her and went to speak but stopped.

'What?' she asked.

'Nothing. It's nothing.'

They walked up towards the pier and onto the promenade where crowds were waiting. On the way she smiled to herself and discreetly tucked the amber hawthorn leaf she'd brought with her into his pocket. He'd probably soon get bored of this joke between them. The aroma of hot chocolate and mini donuts gave a demanding call and they surrendered to it, their lips soon covered with sugar. Dylan took photos to send to his brother later. Apparently Harry's favourite childhood food was fairground donuts. A DJ played the latest hits as they strolled past a stall sizzling with sausages, but despite the heat from it, Lili shivered. Dylan immediately pulled off his beanie and pulled it over her head. Laughing, she protested but he insisted. Seven o'clock arrived and the show kicked off with bursts of psychedelic sparks. The crowd jumped at bangers and clapped as fragments of light rained down. Afterwards Dylan and Lili went back on the beach, to return to the car park.

'Great night,' she said, linking arms again, daring to pull him in closer than before. 'Thanks for asking me. That fountain firework at the end was stunning.'

He pointed to a bench and they sat down. 'Not too cold?' he asked.

Yes, and she knew how he could warm her up.

'Because there's something I'd like to discuss,' he said.

No need. I feel it too. She looked out at the ocean and ran a finger over the beanie. Okay. Grief had changed her. Maybe in an adventurous way. Despite loving the single life, despite the misery that played out as her parents' marriage disintegrated, maybe now was the time to go for a relationship that had meaning. She turned to face him, tilted her head upwards, and she leant forwards, directing her mouth towards his.

15

Dylan sneezed and she jumped back. 'Excuse me,' he said and smiled. 'Harry has this condition where he sneezes when the sun comes out. Believe it or not it's called ACHOO syndrome. Perhaps I'm sensitive to the moon.'

'Well, you did wear that Dracula cape. Don't tell me you avoid sunlight. I mean, I haven't actually seen you during the day.'

'You'll have to find out.'

So he wanted to meet again.

'As I was saying...' He pulled a pair of gloves out of his pockets and put them on. 'I had an ulterior motive in inviting you here today. I haven't been able to stop thinking about it since we met.'

Was it possible to beam on the inside?

'It's great that we are only mates,' he said.

Wait. What?

'Because I've got a professional proposition, and you know what they say about not mixing business and pleasure.'

She didn't blink.

'When we clear someone's house, we sort the items into four categories. Ones valuable enough to be sold, those to throw out, any we need to take to the recycling plant and items we can donate to a charity shop. A collection of bags of items to donate has built up at our warehouse. I tend to take them further afield where the house move is down to a local bereavement. People often worry about walking down the street and, say, seeing a stranger in a loved one's clothes.'

Lili forced herself to focus.

'And it's occurred to me that you'd be a great outlet to team up with. It would make my life a lot easier too, having a direct contact like that. How about I bring some bags over?'

'Right... of course... I mean... will Ware & Care be charged?'

'No way! You're helping me out. Does any day suit, to drop them off?'

'If we're closed, there's a large bin out the back where people can leave donations. You just push the bags through a large swing lid,' she stuttered, still digesting his motive for inviting her out. 'You get to it via the street behind the shop. Great, sounds really great,' she said. Lili stood up. He'd done nothing wrong. Lili was the idiot. 'Sorry, Dylan... you may have a reaction to the moon, I think I have one to the wind. I'm freezing and am going to head off.'

He stood up, eyebrows furrowed together. 'Oh... right... unless... why don't we go to a pub and—'

'No. Honestly. I think I need an early night. No... don't you hurry, enjoy the moment.' Lili yanked off the hat and dropped it in his lap, before half-running back to Colonel Mustard.

As she drove home, she thought about the Cluedo board game that had given Em the idea for her car's name. The two of them had driven to a board game café once and not spoken on the way home. Lili managed a smile. They took it in turns being the sorest loser. Lili had missed all the clues tonight. The chaste kiss on the cheek for starters.

No matter. Life was fine, life was good, she didn't need anyone else.

However, a niggly voice in her head, sounding like ocean waves, whispered that maybe Em's death had to mean something; maybe life shouldn't just continue as it always had done.

Lili had come close to getting hurt with Dylan. Em had got hurt by Sean, Mum and Dad had got hurt by each other... Lessons learnt. Lili should have known better. Thank goodness Dylan only saw her as a business associate.

That voice again whispered in her ear, said what a crock of shit, that being with Dylan could have been amazingly different.

Lili pulled up into the drive and entered the cottage, cleaned her teeth and was unable to stop herself going into Em's bedroom. Colin and Shirl had stripped it bare, as if the possessions were the only memories they had left, apart from the Caravan Place poster on the wall, an electro swing band that always got Em dancing. Lili sat on the bed and bounced up and down, like they had when they'd first moved in, unable to believe their new home effectively doubled as a sunny, scenic holiday rental. This last year Lili had considered using the room as a crafting space. She and Em had bought secondhand furniture for the cottage and Lili had taken a course to learn how to restore it. She found it cathartic to strip wood and sand, to paint, stain or varnish, to hunt out interesting textiles. The shed at the bottom of the garden was big enough to work in and a little oasis during the warmer summer months. What went into it battered and inconspicuous came out transformed into an item of beauty, as if the shed secretly contained a hidden source of alchemy. Yes, the shed suited that best. And this room wasn't empty in any case; memories of Em filled it.

Lili closed the door behind her, crawled into her own bed and, she didn't know why, sobbed under the duvet in a way she hadn't since the week her friend died.

Finally she fell into a fitful sleep...

* * *

Lili and Em are in Colonel Mustard, singing loudly to Human League's 'Don't You Want Me Baby', eating their favourite chocolate, Rolos. Lili passes one to Em every time they take a breath from singing. The sun shines. The traffic isn't bad for a Sunday morning. They play 'cheese on wheels' and shout every time a yellow car passes by. On the back seat is a big bag containing their towels. They've also packed a picnic for the beach and are going to brave the water, even though the sea still felt cold in June.

They wave at passersby who suddenly look familiar... Em's parents, Glenda from the charity shop, that hot Crystoffees customer Em told Lili about, who had a Mohican and pierced eyebrow. Em parks up. Lili gets out a tissue and wipes chocolate off Em's chin, even though her friend protests like a toddler.

'How do I look after last night?' asks Em and wipes her chin with the back of her hand.

'Going to bed after dancing until the dawn chorus has taken no effect,' replies Lili. 'You look as bright as those birds sounded.'

Em grins. 'Liar. Right, beat you into the sea!'

'But we need to pay for parking and—'

Em tosses the car keys to Lili, climbs out, gets their bags from the back and runs off. She calls over her shoulder that she'll split the parking cost later and will lay out their towels and test the water. Smiling, Lili shakes her head, gets the parking ticket and puts on her sunglasses. She heads onto the sand and finds the spot where Em left their towels.

But where is her friend?

Lili squints through the bright sunlight at the sea, turning her head from left to right. Nothing... not a single swimmer. Other people are walking, playing beach games or sunbathing. But then... yes, a head bobs up and down, out in the ocean, someone with green hair. Em! But... Lili's eyes narrow. Em's arms are flailing in the air. Lili kicks off her sandals and runs as fast as she can towards the waves, over the sand and dried seaweed.

'Lili, Lili!' Frantically, Em waves. 'Help me!' She disappears under the surface.

In the cold water, as she strides against the tide, Lili shouts at others to find a lifeguard, but it's as if no one can hear.

No! This isn't happening.

Em's head appears once again. Lili is closer but can't quite reach her. 'Em! Em! I'm here! I'll get help!'

Wordlessly, Em gazes at her friend, and then just like that, she's gone.

* * *

With a start, sweating and shaking, Lili wakes up.

16

Lili sat in the staffroom, eating her tuna sandwich, still unsettled by last night's bad dream about Em in the sea. She sipped her cup of tea. It had been a while since she'd had one of those nightmares. She'd always tell Bobbin about them whenever they happened. The bird would cock its head and listen patiently – nothing to do with the feed in Lili's hand, she'd insist with a wry smile. Although Bobbin would never eat whilst she recounted a dream, which always started off with Lili and Em having fun, based on a real memory – like last night's, with the two of them driving to the beach, eating Rolos, something they'd done often. But then events would take an unexpected turn and end with water and drowning.

Neither Meg nor Tommo were in today. A team of retired women held the fort, enthusiastic, highly organised and thankfully unafraid of the computerised till that often had a mind of its own. She finished her lunch and went upstairs into the stockroom. As she briefly passed through the shop, Lili waved at Glenda, whose visits were now daily since yet another friend had died. Always a smile. Always a slash of lipstick. Getting out and connecting with people was her method of coping. Lili's was to carry on as normal. It had worked. It had. That was why last night's sobbing had shocked her – and yet been necessary, as if the tears had emptied a wounded part of Lili that now had space to... to perhaps be filled with something more positive.

She peered at two bags that Tommo had carried up yesterday but hadn't had time to sift through. The usual flicker of excitement danced in her stomach as if Santa had delivered the donations. Every object in the shop had, originally, been bought for a reason; had been worth the money that owner spent. What would she discover today? Whatever it was, she would never call it junk, like house-clearer Dylan did.

Not him again, with eyes and hair that belonged to a sensual night, with hands, with lips, that matched that too... Push the thought of him away, Lili. It won't do you any good.

She pulled open the first bag at the top and stuck in her hand. Lili pulled out a bundle of Babygros, small shoes, and after that, a pile of baby's first books. Ah, someone's child was growing up. Expensive years lay ahead for this parent, now on the never-ending hamster wheel of accommodating an ageing child and changing needs. Potties to My Little Pony toys to pocket money. A few baby jumpers lay at the bottom. Oh. How beautiful. Clearly hand-knitted, one lemon yellow, the other white, both unisex. They'd be snapped up. Underneath those, the very last item was... She lifted it out. Wow. What a stunning snow dome. Inside the glass was a white rocking horse. Intricate lines of gold artwork danced around the porcelain base. On one side was a small silver key. A musical box! Gently, Lili wound it up. It played 'You Are My Sunshine'. Neither the glass nor porcelain were scratched.

Carefully, she put it on a shelf where other objects waited to be priced. Lili opened the other bag, bulging and ripped on one side. She dug both arms in and pulled out a big pile of clothes – trousers, jumpers, some of them too worn to sell. All smart casual, old-school style, a jacket in decent condition and a collection of cravats that confirmed Lili's view these had belonged to an elderly gentleman. Next out was a pile of dog-eared LPs, jazz music mainly – Cole, Brubeck, Armstrong. Lili reached in again and took out a carved smoker's pipe. She'd seen several of these over the years, often made from beechwood. However, this one was unusual. Its dark orange bowl was carved into the shape of a bull's head, and the stem had been fashioned into a lovely butterscotch colour. No doubt it was made from amber. Last out was a pile of puzzle books, some half-filled. They were no good. Lili went to throw the bag away but it still pulled down at the bottom. She reached in and took out a small plastic case containing...

A pair of dentures!

Not the first time, nor would it be the last, and a sad confirmation that this gentleman had no doubt passed. Ware & Care had a list of items it wouldn't accept – medical, like this, gas or electrical appliances, toys without the safety CE mark, nothing made from banned products such as ivory; the list went on, including sex toys. Meg and Tommo hadn't been able to stop laughing when she'd once brought down a vibrator. A glint in her eyes, Glenda had been there and offered to buy it.

Lili tidied the bags away and went down to the shop. Frost had nipped the air this morning and she hoped Glenda was doing okay. No doubt she was using her new hot water bottle.

The door jingled and opened.

'Callum? And hello there, Jack, how are you?' Lili and the little boy high-fived.

'Dad told me there's a dinosaur board game in here.' Jack put up his two hands and gave a roar.

Callum patted him on the head.

'Great to see you in here,' she said whilst Jack headed over to the toy section. 'You collect LPs, don't you? We've just had some new jazz ones come in. They'll be on the shelf next week. Brubeck. You've bought him before?'

Callum's face brightened.

'And one by a Chet Baker.' She shrugged. 'Never heard of him myself.'

'Seriously?' he said. 'I'll try to get in during a lunch hour next week.' He sighed. 'No. No, I mustn't. I just haven't got the room. Jack's needs should fill any space.'

'Dad! Come and look at this!'

'In a minute, Jack,' said Callum. 'Thanks, Lili. I... I appreciate you looking out for me and my son. Marge, my neighbour, she said she's catching the bus over to your place, in Truro, tomorrow afternoon for some special event. She said how very much talking to you had helped. I thought you should know, that's all.' He headed over to Jack, who'd dropped the box's contents onto the floor and was picking up the pieces.

What happened at Lili's on a Sunday could help Callum too. But it wasn't her place to say more, not at the moment anyway.

17

Lili got up early and made herself pancakes and syrup. She hadn't gone to such effort at home for breakfast since Em died. Then she walked down to the newsagents to buy a Sunday paper and came back to the cottage and read it in the back garden with a large cup of coffee. She put a bowl of feed out for Bobbin and the robin kept her company, eating on the table. She'd covered her knees and legs with a blanket as frost still lay around, reminding Lili that Christmas was around the corner. When her toes became numb, she went inside and baked fresh scones for the afternoon. On the way home yesterday, she'd bought clotted cream and always had strawberry jam in the fridge.

After lunch, with only half an hour to go until two o'clock, she quickly vacuumed, pushed back the sofa to give her three guests more space and lit incense sticks. She covered the coffee table, in the middle of the room, with a white cloth and a small vase of flowers. Lili also set down a box of tissues and an instant camera. She turned on a Spotify playlist of relaxing, instrumental Japanese music. She left the scones in the kitchen. They would restore everyone later.

The doorbell rang and Lili hurried into the hallway. She opened the door. 'Hello, Marge. Come on in.'

A woman entered with pure white hair, in a cloud of rich, heady perfume, wearing large, black-rimmed glasses and an embroidered multi-coloured coat. Marge often frequented Crystoffees. She had been one of Em's favourite customers, a well-spoken lady who sounded as if she originally came from a posh part of London. She carried a plastic bag. Lili gave her a hug, hung up Marge's coat and showed her into the lounge. The doorbell rang again. It was Tarone from across the road, still in his postman's outfit that fitted tightly around his generous waist. His face was covered in perspiration. His extra shift in light of the looming festive season had just finished and he had a rucksack on his back. He wore shorts throughout winter and had done for every day of his twenty-year career. Lili was handing out glasses of water when the third guest arrived, in practical jeans and flat shoes and hair scraped back into a tight ponytail – Jill, who cleaned the charity shop every night, a single mum. A small leather bag was slung across her shoulder. Nervously, the three of them sat on the sofa and Lili joined them, settling in a small wooden, upholstered armchair. She and Em had bought it from a flea market and its curved legs shone thanks to Lili's re-varnishing.

Tarone rubbed his forehead, brushing chin-length dreadlocks away from his face. 'Before we start, can you explain about the ceremony again? What exactly am I supposed to do? I've mulled over everything you told me, Lili, and I've prepared myself, but I'm worried I'll get it wrong.'

The three of them clutched their bags tightly. In recent weeks, one by one, they'd asked about her Sunday afternoons.

Marge's hairdresser had told her about Lili's special events, Tarone had heard from his neighbour and Jill found out from one of her children. What was about to happen was private, personal, not to earn money, nor status, nor kudos. It was about attraction, not promotion, and since moving to Cornwall, since Em encouraged her to follow her gut with her mission, Lili's Sundays had attracted many people in need. She always prepared her guests thoroughly. Tarone wouldn't need her to go through it again – but she sensed he was simply procrastinating; he was anxious.

'You can't do it wrong, Tarone. It's down to you.' Lili smiled. 'I've told you about my travels and how I learnt... how I grew to believe that inanimate objects are not much different to us humans. Certainly not in terms of the building blocks of life. They just lack the processes necessary to be called living – how to eat, reproduce, respire, how to move and adapt.'

Tarone nodded. 'I did my own research after speaking to you. It's like... at the end of the day everything on earth is just a mass of protons, neutrons and electrons. We're all the same.'

'Exactly.' Lili took a sip of water. 'That's why, in Japan, some of these objects are given funerals. They've played an important part in people's lives. Over the years I've known several people who, for example, have felt sad saying goodbye to an old car, even though they're excited for a new one. The car holds so many memories, good times, bad times. It becomes part of a person's personal history and therefore they've attached emotions to it.'

'Those emotions we feel around certain objects, it's why we find it hard to let go of particular objects,' said Marge.

'Yes. Now and then, someone returns to the shop after dropping off an object. They take it back if we haven't sold it. Others, you can just see, are massively relieved when they hand over their belongings. Sometimes holding on to this stuff can hold us back, in the past. When an object means that much, it's about giving it some sort of send-off, rather than just dumping it in a bin.'

'It's an opportunity to find closure,' said Jill.

'Yes. All sorts of people have taken part now in these ceremonies, with all sorts of objects. The job of this afternoon is to set you free from whatever is holding you back. That's why I call it a freedom ceremony.'

Tarone's frown lines had eased.

The serious expression on Lili's face lifted. 'Then there are freshly baked scones for afterwards.'

Tarone fiddled with one of his dreadlocks. His cheeks flushed. 'At first I wasn't sure about approaching you but my neighbour, Pete, insisted that what happened here dramatically helped his daughter after a break-up with her boyfriend. I feel a bit stupid about it all though, to be honest, saying goodbye to something made of metal.'

'There's no pressure,' Lili said. 'You can change your mind. Perhaps someone else would like to go first?'

Jill squirmed in her seat.

Marge adjusted her glasses. 'Delighted to do it. Ever since my hairdresser first mentioned this, I've been itching to take part.'

Lili gave a thumbs up.

'Do I stand?' she asked.

'Whatever you are comfortable with.'

Marge pushed herself up, walked over to the window and turned around, in front of the others. She reached into her plastic bag and pulled out... a bird feeder, rusty and scratched. Her chin trembled ever so slightly.

'I lived with my sister until she died nearly two years ago.

Neither of us got married. She was older, and more outgoing – or so I always assumed. I realised, when she passed, that I'd been living in her shadow...' Her voice broke, just a little. 'Hence the big glasses, the colourful clothes now. I'm making up for lost time. One is never too old for change. That's my motto these days.' She swallowed, held the feeder in the air and looked at it straight on. 'I'm against discarding items unnecessarily, which is why I've not got rid before. But every time I look out to admire my garden, I don't see the lush plants or vibrant lawn, all I see is this – and my sister. And sometimes I... I hated her.'

Marge's voice faltered again, and Lili nodded encouragingly.

'I didn't comprehend clearly at the time, but she was a bully. I don't use that word lightly. Over the last couple of years, as that realisation has sunk in, I've had no issue with getting rid of her personal items. She put me off a young man I was engaged to years ago; said she'd witnessed him kissing someone else. Now I wonder if that was true. He denied it, became upset, and one of the reasons I was so fond of Alfie was that he had no side to him. But one should be able to trust their relatives, surely?' Marge's voice broke again. 'She made me do so many things around the house – cleaning, cooking. She said her career as an administrator for a marine insurance company was far more important than mine as a teaching assistant. As the years passed it was simply easier to keep the peace. I did most of the housework. And that was acceptable. I enjoyed baking, and scrubbing was cathartic.' She looked at the feeder. 'But the one thing I detested doing was topping this up with seed. Freda made me do it, however inclement the weather. She'd moan if it became dirty and send me outside in snow or ice. She didn't care as long as the birds were content.'

Marge's face softened and she swung the feeder gently from

side to side. 'You're a small thing but you represent so much – how I surrendered to her whim; couldn't stand up for myself; got stuck in a rut of doing everything she asked, to avoid confrontation. Well, that's not me any more. And... I'm no bird lover! There, I've said it!'

The other three smiled, even Lili, who was glad that Bobbin couldn't hear.

'They do their business everywhere, especially pigeons, and make a dreadful racket first thing in the morning.' She held the feeder in both hands and addressed it directly. 'It's not your fault. You did your job. And thank you. But I need to move on. The house, inside, now feels like a safe place, free from her memory, happy, kind, cosy. Now I need to be able to look out onto my garden and feel peace and see the joy in my flowers and shrubs.'

Marge looked up. Lili got to her feet and went over. She stretched out her hand and Marge passed her the feeder.

'Would you like a photo to keep?' Lili asked gently.

'No. Thank you. I would not.' She reached out and touched the feeder. 'You've been extremely fit for purpose...' She hesitated. 'Thank you, dear chap, for your service over the years. Many birds have survived the winter because of the food you've provided. I have no bad feelings towards you.' Her fingers stroked the wire casing for the briefest of moments.

Lili patted Marge's arm and then placed the feeder on the windowsill, a temporary home until her guests had left. Then she would dispose of it.

'Well done,' muttered Tarone as Marge sat down. 'That was... nicely done.'

Jill gave Marge a sideways hug. Then she looked at Tarone. He took a deep breath and stood up. He went over to where

Marge had been and took the toaster out of his rucksack. He held it in front of him and exhaled.

'I saw the doc a few weeks ago. My cholesterol's higher than the Brown Willy hill and diabetes is in the post – no pun intended. This has been a long time coming. You see...' He held the toaster more closely and ran a finger over a dent in it. 'When I was little, Mum used to call me Porky and she was always commenting on other people's size. I grew up thinking everyone would judge me. It's not her fault my health has got to this point. I could have reacted differently. Instead I've had a messed-up relationship with food. I've chosen to deal with my problems, over the years, by stuffing my face with cakes and takeaways. And you, my trusty toaster' – he ran a hand over the dial at the side – 'you've been my favourite mate. Nothing beats a slice of toast with bubbles of butter, as my granddad used to call it; with honey or jam, with peanut butter. I went through a whole loaf once, in one sitting. And toast is cheap. Whenever I'm on a downer, you've been a reliable friend and I've gone to you time after time. Out of everything in my kitchen – the cupboards full of tasty grub, the microwave – it's you that represents a lifestyle I need to leave behind. The doc said stuff about cooking from scratch and putting in the time to get into better shape. I won't replace you – at least not for a long time.' His voice wavered. 'Cheers, mate. Cheers for always being there – during that fallout with my boss and the time I was mugged. A cuppa and a slice of toast always made the day seem better, quick and tasty, instant satisfaction. You and me...' He grasped the toaster more tightly. 'We've been through a lot together.'

Tentatively, he looked up at Lili, Marge and Jill, whose faces showed nothing but compassion. Lili went over. 'How about a photo?'

Tarone nodded.

Lili set the toaster on the coffee table, next to the flowers, and took a shot. The instant camera printed out the photo and she passed it to Tarone before he sat down again. Lili placed the toaster on the windowsill next to the bird feeder, before sitting back down in the armchair. Jill got to her feet and stood where Tarone had been. She reached into her shoulder bag and pulled out a small box. She opened it. Inside lay a metal ring with a gaudy flower in the middle.

Jill looked up nervously. 'I was married for eighteen years, then one day, seven years ago, Tony up and left. Worst time of my life.' Her eyes filled. 'Still gets me now,' she said and wiped her cheeks. 'Not because I miss him but because of the pain and how stupid I felt. And then there was the effect it had on my girls... I sold my actual diamond engagement ring, and the wedding band, putting the proceeds towards taking me and my daughters on a much-needed holiday. I also swore I'd never marry again; wouldn't risk it. But...' She stood a little taller. 'I met someone eighteen months ago. A wonderful man. We took things slowly at first. He understood why I had trust issues and was so patient – and nervous when he proposed to me a couple of weeks ago.'

'Oh, congratulations!' said Lili.

'What lovely news.' Marge smiled broadly.

'Good for you,' said Tarone.

'Thank you... thank you so much... but I haven't told anyone yet, you see... I haven't given him a reply.' She looked down at the ring. 'I've hung on to this because it holds so many memories. When Tony left I... I didn't want to feel as if I was losing everything. He proposed on holiday in Santorini and the restaurant gave us free champagne. It was a spontaneous thing and he hadn't got a proper ring, so he bought this one in a cheap gift shop the next day, to tide me over, as a joke. We had lots of laughs back then. I insisted wearing it when we got back, until he'd saved enough to get me the little diamond ring he wanted to. The girls would borrow this ring playing dress-up when little. So many happy memories are attached to it... but now holding on to this ring makes me feel as if, somehow, I'm still pining for Tony. And I'm so not. He's out of my life and the children and I love my new man.' She took a moment. 'My eldest told me about these freedom ceremonies; one of her friend's aunts took part. It was news to me and I work in your shop! So... I decided to be brave. It's time.' Jill lifted up the box, gazing inside. 'You represent one of the most exciting periods of my life – young and carefree, full of romance and ambition. At the time you were perfect. Thank you so much. You were on my finger for several months, back when I was growing my cleaning business, back when we got our first house and made lots of plans for the future. But it's time now that I moved on completely from my first marriage. I have the good memories in my head and that's enough.'

Jill didn't want a photo. Unexpectedly, when she sat down on the sofa again, she burst into tears.

'Silly, because I'm so happy these days,' Jill said. 'In fact... these feel like good tears. I can't wait to get married again.'

The others comforted her as Lili went into the kitchen to boil the kettle. This often happened. Giving up an object you'd invested yourself in, for whatever reason, was often a cause for the remnants of past hurt to come to the fore one last time.

Jill would be okay.

The four of them sat around the table in the dining room. It was opposite the lounge, linked to the kitchen at the front, with wide French patio doors. Clouds had gathered in the sky, but this only added to the cosiness of the cottage, with a tall lamp on and the smell of incense wafting though from where Lili had held the ceremony.

Lili, Jill and Marge reached for the scones. Whilst the other two women spread on thick clods of clotted cream and dollops of jam, Lili glanced at Tarone. He caught her looking.

'A new start,' he said and gave a wry smile. 'I can't give away my beloved toaster and then carry on eating like I did before. What would be the point? It has to mean something.'

The others stopped eating and Jill clapped. Lili and Marge joined in.

'That's inspiring, Tarone,' said Lili, thinking about how she'd realised things had to change in her own life after the last year.

'It is early days, mind,' he said.

'I've every confidence in you,' said Marge. 'You did a courageous thing today.'

'Like you all did,' said Lili, and she went to the fridge. She came back and put a low-fat yogurt in front of him. 'Strawberry flavour at least.' She passed him a spoon.

'Thank you for today, Lili,' said Marge as Tarone tucked in. 'I've had trouble getting rid of the feeder... feeling guilty yet angry too; a sense that I needed to express how life had been. Now I've done that and I... I feel heard. I feel empowered.'

'I feel as if a weight has been lifted off my shoulders,' said Jill. 'I'm going to invite my new man around tonight and say yes!'

The atmosphere became more jolly as they talked about Christmas approaching and Tarone dreading the uptick in the amount of post he'd have to carry. They all raved about the pasty shop in Truro that did seasonal flavours – turkey and stuffing, mince pie filling and custard. They had another cup of tea and Lili packed up scones for Marge and Jill to take home.

As the sun set, Lili waved them off. Tarone's neighbour, Pete, worked at the local tip and she'd give him the bird feeder and toaster. He'd kindly offered to dispose of any old, unwanted objects discreetly for her. If someone ever let go of a valuable item that could still be used, Lili would get it valued and the profit from its sale would go to Ware & Care. Or if they let go of a reusable belonging that wasn't expensive, like Jill's ring, she'd send it to another branch of the charity shop to go on display, not wanting to risk someone spotting it in Mevagissey – a bit like Dylan taking his house clearance charity bags out of area.

Dylan.

Lili went into the lounge and tidied up. Then she stood in the middle of the room and gave a determined nod. In the spirit of Tarone already making changes, instead of sitting down in front of Netflix and rewatching series she used to enjoy with Em, maybe it was time Lili mixed things up a bit. She got dressed, grabbed a thick coat and torch and climbed into the car. She drove to Portmellon, the night-time drive reminding her of trips with Em, returning home after weekends away, and the shouts of glee if they spotted a Starbucks on their way.

Despite the coastal wind, despite the night, she strode the forty-five minutes to Gorran Haven beach, a beam of torchlight leading the way. Sweaty and shivering, Lili sat on the rocks and took out a water bottle. A break in the clouds let through moonlight and she glanced out at the water. Lili sat up straight. Really? There was Neptune! His unmistakable head bobbed up and down in the water, near the sea stack! Warmth rushed through her limbs. Selkies were mythical creatures that transformed from seals into humans if they ventured onto land. Lili needed to transform, from a person stuck in a pity party into the woman Em used to be proud to call her friend.

Out of habit, she checked her phone. A tingle ran down her

spine. Dylan had texted earlier. She'd told herself he wouldn't get in touch, having explained to him about the outhouse and how he could just drop off any donations.

She stared at the sea. She followed Neptune.

Then Lili read the text once more. It asked if he could drive over next week and drop off the bags.

She stared at the sea. She followed Neptune again.

Eventually, Lili put the phone away. She'd reply when she got home and had a signal and tell him no, he couldn't. She didn't want Dylan coming over to Mevagissey again, to leave a mark on any part of her life. It was best to keep distance and respect those lines laid down by a relationship not being romantic. She would drive over to his place of work in Tavistock and, if he didn't mind, sift through some bags and just take the bits that would sell. In any case, her shop was happily overflowing with donations at the moment, people having a clear-out before Christmas gifts arrived. This was the truth – and a surefire way to keep control, to limit their time together, was for her to be the one visiting.

Lili got to her feet, looked up at the moon and stretched upwards, hands high in the air, eyes closed, crashing waves providing a heavy rock soundtrack. She had a sudden urge to scream. The howls of the wind duetted with her voice as she ran, out of breath, salty air on her lips, as fast as she could back to the car park, the torchlight helping her narrowly avoid tripping over. She stopped by the car and bent over, panting, utterly spent, throat hurting. Lili didn't know what had escaped her body, out of her mouth, into the briny air to be blown out to sea, but its release had left her feeling truly alive for the first time in months. She got into the driving seat, blew her nose and revved up Colonel Mustard.

18

The following Friday evening, Lili, Meg and Tommo sat in the staffroom, nursing cups of coffee and the lush donuts that Andrew had brought over from the Truro branch. The regional manager had called by the bigger store to announce that the company was celebrating a growth in profits, and she'd handed over a large tray of the treats. It had taken a while to start recovering from the pandemic. More profits meant more help to those in need; good news all around. It didn't surprise Lili. She'd seen a change in customer behaviour over the last couple of years, the fading fear of possible germs on second-hand goods, the increasing footfall due to the cost of living and energy crises. Lili had just cashed up. Heavy rain beat against the window and none of them were in a rush to get home.

'Meg and I have been talking, Lili,' said Tommo, and he stretched. 'How about we help you put up the Christmas decorations in here tonight. Neither of us has got anything on. It's about time now, in the middle of November.'

'Living life on the edge,' muttered Meg and then blushed.

'No offence, guys, but I bet you two were doing something far more interesting with your Friday nights at my age.'

'November, at twenty-one? Let's think.' Lili concentrated. 'I was in Sweden on the Scandinavian leg of one of our trips – so much untouched nature and brilliant public services, but boy was it expensive.'

'As for me, I was employed in hospitality on a cruise ship, still not knowing what I wanted to do with my life; in the kitchens, washing-up mainly. Hardly glamorous, but I did fall in love with a Frank Sinatra tribute singer though. Mike. Great guy.' Tommo's voice softened. 'He used to sing "The Way You Look Tonight" to me. It was my first proper romance, away from the whispers and sneers that existed back in 70s Britain.'

'See.' Meg shrugged. 'You two had a life. I've no girlfriend. No car. Not got my own place yet. I'm looking at another flat this coming weekend.' She glanced at Lili. 'I took your advice and told Gran about moving out. You were right. I had to. But it went really badly. Oh, she didn't say much and that made it worse; in fact, she put on a brave face and said much as she'd love me to stay, it filled her with pride to see me forging my own life – especially after everything with my mum and dad. But that night I heard her sobbing in bed.'

'That's really tough, gal, sorry to hear that, but you've got to follow your heart,' said Tommo. 'I learnt that a long time ago. You can't live your life to please someone else, to please other people's expectations. Like you said, you won't be moving far.'

'I know. And she's got lots of friends and a busy life. Yet it leaves me feeling ungrateful. But I do, I have to weigh up everything. I feel I should be so much further on with my own goals, you know? Personally, professionally...' Meg sighed and bit into the donut. The others shot her sympathetic glances. 'Gah, ignore me,' she muttered and wiped her mouth. 'I'm still stinging from my ex Zoe saying I needed to grow up and get a proper job, to forget my online vintage clothes shop dream.'

'Sour grapes if you ask me,' said Lili. 'At the wise old age of twenty-nine, I can inform you that the most important thing in life is to have a passion. It gives your life meaning and purpose. Mine is the charity shop and dealing with unwanted objects. You're lucky to have found your calling, I reckon, Meg. Not everyone does. And look at you, working hard to carve out a future, with the business course, the research you do, too, learning about vintage fashion. Anyone can see you live and breathe it.' She waved a hand in the air, referring to Meg's outfit, the high-waisted pleated trousers and floral embroidered cardigan.

'It took me till my late twenties to fully realise that my passion lay in life outside of work and all I wanted was a job to pay the bills and give me a comfortable retirement. Banking administration ticked the box,' said Tommo. 'My heart was in going on tours and attending events with my motorcycling. Christ, I missed the roads when on ships, and that helped me work out what was important. At least you know what excites you at twenty-one. You're doing pretty damn well, if you ask me.'

Meg's face brightened and she drained her coffee cup. 'Okay, then. Let's get this place decorated. I'm in! As long as I get dibs on choosing the playlist. None of those sentimental Christmas ballads for me. But first...' With a flourish she checked the time on her phone. 'Yes, it's now officially out of hours, so, before we start...' She faced Lili. 'What's the latest on signor Dylan? You hardly said anything in the pub, after he visited, and Tommo and I haven't been given a crumb of news since.'

Tommo rubbed his hands. 'We want the low down. It's not been forthcoming despite me humming "That's Amore".'

'And I brought in those biscotti to have with our coffee on Wednesday,' said Meg. 'But subtlety isn't working so... have you seen him again?'

'You two really need to get a life,' said Lili.

They sat expectantly.

'All right! We went to a firework display together last Friday.'

'You never told us!' said Meg.

Lili had done her best to forget that evening.

'Not much to tell. He simply wanted to discuss us kind of doing business together. Long story short, I'm seeing him on Sunday because he works in house clearance and has some bags for me to look through, for the shop and—'

'Express House Clearances,' said Meg confidently.

'How do you know that?'

'You can't have expected me not to look him up on Facebook.'

Lili gave an exasperated tut.

'Not that I found anything juicy on his business page, and everything on his personal one is set to private. Although the profile picture on that is of him with his arms around a guy with the same colour hair cut short, and he wasn't as tall as Dylan.'

'That'll be his younger brother Harry. He's away travelling at the moment.'

'What are you going to wear?' asked Meg, grinning.

'Don't forget your toothbrush!'

'Tommo! This is highly inappropriate!' Lili gave a small smile. 'And... irrelevant. It's never going to happen...' Telling them the truth would get them off her back, and she reckoned they'd understand. 'I'm focusing on me at the moment... wondering if I need to make changes in my life, now that my situation is… different.' She gulped and tears sprung to her eyes. What was going on lately? 'Perhaps change has been a long time coming, since Em. A romance would just muddy the waters. And anyway, he's not interested.' She braced herself for their disappointment.

'Me and my big gob.' Meg covered her mouth. 'Sorry, Lili. Shouldn't have pushed.'

Tommo held his mug with both hands. 'I get it, gal. Apologies too. I should have known better, after losing Joe. Life couldn't continue as it had been but it took me a while to realise that. Helping out here was part of my plan to forge a new life.' His mouth drooped at the corners, his Cornish craic gone for a moment.

Lili got up, walked around the table, stood in between them and gave both of her friends a side hug. 'Right. I'll pull out the Christmas decorations. Who wants to do the tree? Meg, you were great at spraying the front window last year.'

Two hours later, they left the shop as Jill arrived, rain spitting now, the air smelling of gingerbread from a passing vape. Tommo stood with his motorcycle helmet under his arm. The three of them glanced back and admired their work. It was one of the last shops in Mevagissey to embrace the approaching Christmas season. Meg had sprayed a reindeer on the window. In the corner of the shop Tommo had methodically dressed the tree with colour-coordinated baubles, all equidistant to each other. Lili had hung shiny foil decorations from the ceiling. They'd already erected a stand displaying Christmas cards several days ago.

Tommo left, whistling 'The Way You Look Tonight'. Lili's heart squeezed as she thought about that festive secret of his that she'd discovered. His pride might be hurt if she mentioned that she knew about it. Meg walked off in the direction of the chippy, too hungry to wait for the cottage pie her gran had made earlier in the week and frozen. Lili waved goodbye to Jill through the window and then took a different route to the car park, the long way around, heading down to the harbour first. She stopped as the sea water came into view and breathed in the slightly fishy smell that she'd found so off-putting when they'd first moved here. Now she appreciated it – a pleasant change to Manchester's smoky fumes. It was the second largest fishing port in Cornwall but was in constant need of funds to repair and protect it in the face of climate change and severe weather. An array of moored boats bobbed up and down, as if a secret disco was taking place under the ocean. Lili turned the corner and went to sit down on one of the benches facing the water. A man sat there, collar up.

'Callum?'

His lips upturned 'Hi, Lili. Late night at the shop?'

'We've been decorating, ready for the festive season. How about you? Fancied some fresh air?'

'Just taking some time out. Boy, my pupils were restless today. Always gets like that during the weeks running up to Christmas.' He inhaled. 'I grew up by the sea and sitting here, feeding the gulls, eating ice cream, it reminds me of the good times with my school mates. They really were some of the happiest days of my life. It's comforting in a way, if I've had a hard day, to come down here to the harbour and have a chuckle about old frivolous memories. Us throwing chips down for the gulls, and hoping to spot the girls that we fancied, pretending to push each other into the water, and arguing about who supported the best football team. Sounds a bit mad, I know.'

'Not at all. It's funny the things that make memories stick. Like my friend Em's car, that's mine now.'

'The mustard Mini? You've driven past my place. I live in a

ground-floor flat and sometimes we're outside in the garden. That car is difficult to miss.'

'There are lots of memories in that Mini, even though it's small, as I drive along familiar routes.'

'Good memories mean a lot, don't they? When the present is tough. I'm still reeling from my divorce. Worried about Jack. Worried about money. Thinking about happier times keeps me moored to sanity!' His cheeks flushed. 'Guess that's why I've held on to so much old stuff.' He rubbed his hands together. 'Anyway, listen to me blathering on.'

'Is Jack at a friend's tonight?'

'Yes, he's got a sleepover – unsuitable name for it because he won't get any sleep at all!'

Callum and Lili said goodbye. She walked along the pavements sparkling with frost and headed back to Colonel Mustard, got in and ran a hand over the passenger seat. How she missed sitting there, in charge of changing the mixtapes and passing Em her Starbucks when it was safe to take a sip.

Lili started the engine and switched on the mixtape that she hadn't removed since last year. 'Pink Cadillac' by Bruce Springsteen came on. Lili hummed to it, tapping the steering wheel in time with her hand, nodding her head. Whenever this came on, Em would insist Colonel Mustard was as sexy as any fancy motorcar.

She was about to drive off when a text flashed up on her phone.

> Looking forward to seeing you Sunday. Why not come over earlier, say one, for a roast dinner? It's no fun eating alone. The address is the same as the business one I gave you. Mine's the house on the immediate right of the warehouse. C u then! Dylan

A meal? At his? A more intimate setting? Lili could do that. Sure. No big deal. It's not like anything was going to happen. She'd explain that her visit was a one-off, that the shop had a continuous stream of donations and didn't need extra.

Their business arrangement and what was effectively a friendship would then be well and truly over.

19

Lili hadn't driven to Devon often since moving to Cornwall. Her new home had everything she needed – coastal walks, her very own seal, cream teas just how she liked them, and a robin for meaningful conversation. However, she had been walking in Dartmoor and found the landscape breathtaking. She'd also visited a heritage site, of which there were many. Today was the first time she'd been to Tavistock and what a beautiful market town it was with unique shops and classical architecture – a wrong turn had taken her through the centre. She also saw the River Tavy. Dylan's place was on the outskirts. She drove past a suburban estate and then turned onto a main road. A couple of miles along, Lili turned right, passing semi-detached homes that faced woodland. At the end was an industrial area with two big vans parked outside and a large warehouse with a visible office.

The address she'd been given was the last semi. She parked up on the road outside and got out, greeted by a rejuvenating breeze. Lili carried a bag. Making a crumble didn't mean a thing. Bringing a dessert was simply polite. The house stood out from its companions along the road, with their neat borders, mowed lawns, with the hanging baskets and garden ornaments. Dylan's lawn was full of moss, the borders straggly and overgrown. In a large ceramic flower pot, a half-dead plant had wilted. As she walked up the drive, the front door flew open and Dylan shouted hello, wearing an apron that said 'Eat if you dare'.

'Another present from Harry?' she asked and entered the hallway, head down, to avoid him kissing her cheek. She passed the bag to him and wrapped her arms around her body, pretending to be cold, not wanting to risk being swept into a hug. Walking past a row of sports shoes, she followed him into the kitchen. The smell of roasting chicken welcomed her in and her shoulders relaxed. *Lili, stop being so uptight,* she told herself.

Dylan placed the bag on a magnolia worktop and ran a hand over the apron. 'How did you guess? This one's from abroad. Harry kicked off his travels by going to a mate's wedding in the US. Apparently, Texas, I think it was, is the capital of barbecues.' The kitchen was large, with a small pine dining table matching the cupboards. A wide window looked out onto a back garden that was as untended as the front one. He picked up the bag and peered inside at the crumble, wrapped in clingfilm, squirts of purple juice across its surface. His face broke into a smile.

'A favourite of mine! Cheers, Lili. Let me guess... apple and blackberry?'

'Correct.'

Water bubbled on the hob and he went to the fridge and took out a bag of vegetables he'd clearly prepared earlier. Dylan waved it in the air.

'Sprouts okay?'

'I love it when they come back into the shops every Christmas. Can I help?'

'Get us drinks, if you like. There's a bottle of fizzy elderflower in the fridge. I assumed you wouldn't be drinking.'

Dylan had set the table and turned the roast potatoes. She took off her coat, opened the bottle and minutes later they were clinking glasses.

'Great size kitchen,' she said and looked around. 'Your place is much bigger than my cottage.'

'Yeah, it's not bad. Grew up here. Harry and I have tried to put our own mark on it. We got rid of the chintz wallpaper in the lounge and a mate replaced the old avocado bathroom. I'd love a new kitchen. Pine's not really my thing. But we insisted on paying Mum and Dad the going rate of rent so that they could take on the mortgage of a small bungalow for their retirement – that was all before they decided to settle in Italy. Their money is tied up in the business, you see. It means there's nothing left over for further changes here. I suggested they sell this place, Harry and I would rent elsewhere, but they wouldn't hear of it as it's so close to the site for us.'

'I can't wait to get out of renting. I want to invest my earnings. I've saved up, so hopefully in a year or two… whereas your rent, in a way, it's being re-invested into your parents' estate – and your future, I suppose?'

'Yep. Harry and I will inherit at some point – hopefully not for a long time though.'

* * *

Over lunch he told her about his parents' trips to the Amalfi Coast, specifically Vietri sul Mare, a fishing village where his mother came from, with cliffside restaurants, unobtrusive avenues and traditional ceramics. Growing up there had made his mum's move to Devon easy, as she was used to the coastal life and loved scones as much as the pear and ricotta cake popular in her hometown.

'Sounds wonderful. Want to hear about the sights where my parents live in Manchester? The house is five minutes from a motorway and not far from a row of tower blocks.' A smile flickered across her mouth. 'Although the truth is, it was a brilliant place to grow up, with a lovely park nearby and amazing cafés. I miss the museums, the city vibe, the eclectic nature of everything in the centre, from the shops, to buskers, to passersby. The one thing that makes Cornwall feel like home is that the locals are as friendly as Mancunians.'

'Us Devonians ain't so bad,' he said and sat down again.

She jerked her head towards the window. 'Big garden. Dad always used to joke that his and Mum's was the size of a postage stamp.'

Dylan gazed outside. 'The garden is Harry's terrain. Last week, on Instagram, he shared photos of a botanical park he'd visited. Not much interested in plants myself.'

'I'd love to see them.'

'They aren't there any more. Harry put them in his story so they disappeared after twenty-four hours.' Dylan shook his head. 'I can't keep up to be honest. His itinerary is ever-changing.'

'When's he back from travelling?'

'God knows. I thought he'd be back by now. He keeps delaying his return. Having too much fun. But then my brother always has been more adventurous than me.'

'You don't mind? Isn't the business difficult to run without him?'

'I have to admit, it annoyed me at first but I make do. And recently I hired a great manager, Jags. The business has gradually expanded in recent years. It was time anyway. The nature of the work has changed over time, too, so we've been used to adapting and taking on new staff. Most stuff used to be taken to a landfill. Now there are regulations governing the environmental impact and customers make more demands in terms of ensuring what we take away is recycled where possible.'

'Which is a good thing.'

'Agreed.' Dylan took the chicken out of the oven.

Conversation faded whilst they ate the roast and Lili secretly basked in his compliments about the crumble. He wouldn't let her help wash up, so she nipped upstairs to use the bathroom. A few minutes looking at the bags in the warehouse and she'd be gone. Except part of her didn't want to leave. Visiting Dylan had felt... comfortable, companionable. It was a feeling that had been missing from her life these last months – little moments of happiness. There had been many of them with Em, and Lili wished she could recall every single one. She'd always believed making new memories with her friend would never stop.

She was about to go back downstairs when a framed poster caught her attention, visible past the door, on the wall in a nearby bedroom. It was of a concert headlined by Caravan Palace – the same as Em's poster! Underneath, on a desk, was a stack of books, on top of a chest of drawers, all of them musicians' biographies... Ozzie Osbourne, Kylie, Elton John, Jay Z, Bob Dylan, Melanie C.

Dylan cleared his throat behind her. 'I thought you'd got lost,' he said, 'but the house isn't that big.'

She jumped and turned around. 'Sorry... didn't mean to

pry... I just saw that poster. Em loved Caravan Palace. Have you seen them live?'

'Oh, this isn't my room. Harry's the musical boffin.' He hesitated and led her in. On the wall was a guitar. 'He was in a band at school and still meets his mates to jam now and again.' Dylan pointed to the poster. 'He loves their Parisian vibe.'

The room was so neat – vacuumed, not a crease in the bed cover. A leather jacket hung from a peg on the wall.

'Great coat.'

'His pride and joy. The stallholder said it once belonged to Adam Levine. I'm not convinced but Harry believes it and that's all that matters.' He shook his head. 'Music means everything to him. Any genre. Big or small artists. Big or small venues. He always talks about going to Vegas, one day, to catch a singer who might have a residency there. The ultimate experience, he reckons. And he does love a scratch card – probably thinks he'll win big in the casinos.'

'Em wanted to visit there too! In fact we booked a trip for our approaching thirtieth birthdays. Well, the hotel, at least.'

'What a shame you didn't get to go,' he said and closed the door to Harry's room behind them as they left. They went downstairs.

'I still need to cancel it.'

Dylan raised an eyebrow.

She exhaled. 'I know. I just haven't been able to face it. Em had been so excited. Me too if I'm honest. I'm more of a walk-through-the-woods-holiday kinda person, but... she was feeling down in the months before she died. I wanted to cheer her up and we both laughed at what a crazy experience going there would be.' Why was she telling him this?

He touched the small of her back and pursed his mouth in a

sympathetic manner. He didn't say a word, but Lili and her sadness felt seen.

Which was why after sifting through bags, after retrieving a gorgeous art deco clock, piles of books and board games and a complete floral crockery set, along with an array of ornaments and old CDs, she couldn't bring herself to say they wouldn't see each other again. She'd have to pick up the crumble dish, anyway.

As she began to drive away, towards the junction at the end of his road, a banging resounded from the boot of her car. She stopped abruptly. Dylan's face appeared at the driver's window and she wound it down.

'I almost forgot,' he panted, out of breath. He brought up his hand and in front of his face held a large, amber-coloured horse chestnut leaf. His eyes were laughing, and she couldn't gaze away; the sight before her was mesmerising – the leaf, of course, the leaf. That was it. He twisted it from side to side, black hair messy, him smelling of bergamot, the joke whirling in his eyes like a leaf in the wind. Gently, he placed it on her lap before running back to his house.

Grinning from ear to ear, she drove home, singing along to 'Jump' by Van Halen. Eventually, her mind drifted to the upcoming week at work. A typical day managing the shop involved supervising the staff, but also mucking in:

Sorting items and bagging up the surplus ones that can be sold, to pass onto other Ware & Care outlets.

Steaming and tagging clothes, putting them on rails.

Rotating stock on the shelves.

Changing the window display.

Taking out time to chat to customers, especially regulars.

Lili loved her job and was fond of everyone who worked with her. She squirmed in the car seat as she thought about her conversation with Dylan about Vegas and how some customers at the shop scrimped to save money. She needed to sort the hotel cancellation and get a refund.

As soon as she got back to the cottage, she placed the horse chestnut leaf on the coffee table, collapsed on the sofa, got out her laptop, and went online for her booking of two adjoining rooms. Lili had expected to lose out financially, 25 per cent of the overall cost perhaps. There was still a month to go, after all. It wasn't as if she was cancelling right at the last minute. But when she clicked on cancel, the penalty seemed much bigger. The travel company's helpline was open until six on a Sunday. She just had time and, coat still on, took out her phone, punched in the number and pressed dial. When you looked closely at the dates, the man explained, and counted the days, which Lili hadn't, the hotel stay was just under thirty days away now. The bigger penalty was correct.

Seventy per cent of the overall cost! She and Em had only been visiting for four days but hadn't stinted, calling the break a last hurrah before really saving hard to build a future. The rooms were deluxe, with silk gold and damask interiors, the hotel incredible with a spa and pool attendants taking bar orders as you chilled on a lounger.

The man told her to look at the small print. She didn't mention Em's death or try to make excuses. He was right. She should have checked the paperwork months ago.

What a waste of money, but how could she go alone, without Em? Somehow, the hotel stay had to be recycled, whether she got back what it had cost or not. Lili spent the evening racking her brains, and then it came to her.

Of course!

Harry! Dylan said his brother had always wanted to go there. He was travelling anyway. She'd lose her money but at least if he could take one of the rooms the booking wouldn't be completely wasted.

She took out her phone and her breath hitched for a second, like it always did, seeing Em's old phone number, once again in her Contacts list, even though it was now listed under Dylan Davis. Fingers moving quickly, Lili texted him.

20

Lili glanced at her phone. It was a quarter to two. She tipped the crumbs and bits of grated cheese left over from her sandwich into her palm and held out her hand. Bobbin flew over. The bird couldn't have looked more festive a minute ago, perched on the branch of a holly bush. The air was crisp and she could almost smell Christmas in the air – mince pies, turkey, mulled wine. It was one month exactly to Christmas Eve. The robin puffed out its chest and pecked at the cheese.

'It's mature cheddar. Your favourite,' she said.

Bobbin stopped pecking and straightened up. Its beak opened. Oh, what notes of pure joy floated into her garden – or rather staccato chirps that quick-stepped. Lili wished she could bottle the song and remove the stopper whenever she needed a lift. Bird recordings on Spotify didn't give the same hit. Lili got up and spotted a beautiful maroon ivy leaf on the patio. Carefully, she slipped it into the back pocket of her jeans, went inside and took off her coat and shoes. She brushed her hair and turned up the heating. She hadn't heard from Dylan since she'd texted about Harry and Vegas, apart from a thumbs up emoji and that he'd ask him. It was now Sunday again, one week later. She'd just lit the incense sticks when the roar of a motorbike sounded out the front. Lili checked the room before hurrying into the hallway as someone knocked. She opened the door.

'Trevor, come on in.'

Trevor was a motorcyclist friend of Tommo. He lived in Portloe. The leather biker jacket had seen better days and had badges sewn across it, some bearing skulls or eagle wings. He came in and took off his boots. Lili hung up the jacket. That was unexpected – underneath he wore a conservative jumper and shirt, both looking as if they'd come from Marks & Spencer. He ran a hand through his chestnut hair that had a Morticia white streak at the front, and he carried a plastic bag into the lounge. Lili pointed to the sofa.

'Would you like a glass of water, Trevor? We've got tea and scones afterwards.'

He gave a nervous cough. 'No thanks. I'm fine. Ta for today. Tommo's reassured me, from the start, that this... this isn't a mickey-take. No offence but it's took me a while to get my head around what you do here. Meeting up with you, for that chat, helped me understand. I reckoned Tommo was joking when he first mentioned it to me – funerals for objects.'

Respect was at the centre of Japanese culture, so it wasn't as big a leap for them to honour this concept. The Brits had wonderful characteristics like politeness, stoicism... and also humour with a generous dollop of sarcasm, which meant that a knee-jerk reaction was often to laugh at the things they didn't understand.

The doorbell rang and Lili left the room again. She opened the door. Rosie stepped in carrying a tote bag with a mental health slogan on it. She was only eighteen with a vital complexion and buoyant bobbed hairstyle – she was the granddaughter of one of the shop's volunteers. The teenager hovered uncertainly.

'Come on in. Pass me your coat, Rosie. Then follow me.'

Sun streamed through the front window as they went into the lounge.

'Rosie, this is Trevor. There are only the two of you today. Would you like a glass of water?'

She shook her head.

'Good answer – hold out for the tea and scones like I am,' said Trevor to her in a kindly tone.

'Who would like to go first?' asked Lili as she sat in the chair.

'You'll both probably think me nuts when I reveal my object. So I may as well get it over with,' muttered Rosie, and she bit a nail.

Rosie stood in front of the window and faced the others and reached into her bag. She took out a soft toy elephant, faded grey and missing its trunk.

'I didn't do that to it, by the way,' she said and gave a wry smile. 'My brother cut it off after an argument, without me knowing, and threw it away. I still loved Jumbo though. Like all the other kids in my class.' She held the toy tightly. 'In primary school the teacher used to give Jumbo to one of the children every Friday. They took him home for the week and had to bring him back and tell a story about what he'd been up to – going to their after school clubs, watching telly, visiting grandparents, that sort of thing. When it was my turn, I was a massive fan of that reality show singing competition *The Voice*, and I made up a story that he'd gone onto the show, trumpeted a song and won hands-down. A record label signed him and Jumbo became a worldwide rockstar.' She gave a sheepish look. 'Not sure what the teacher thought but the other kids clapped for ages afterwards. I was really sad to hand Jumbo in and cried. I'd always wanted to be a singer, right from when I was little, and I felt if Jumbo could make it so could I. In the school choir I was often chosen to sing solo, even at that young age.' She shrugged. 'Then I was in an accident, broke my leg, other stuff, couldn't go into school for a while. The teacher visited one day and gave me Jumbo to keep forever.' Rosie looked at the others. 'Sorry, going on a bit.'

'Not at all,' said Lili.

'Did you keep on with the singing?' asked Trevor.

'You could say that. It became an obsession, fuelled by the fact that everyone thought I was talented. I actually ended up on *The Voice* myself when I was at high school.'

'Wow!' said Lili.

'Hats off to you,' said Trevor.

'I didn't get anywhere, but I got nice comments. That's when everyone else really took notice.' She gave a little sigh. 'Suddenly there was this expectation I'd make it big, not only from me but family, friends, teachers, even local people who'd seen me on television. At the same time I'd begun to realise that singing wasn't for me – I didn't like what being a rockstar like Jumbo would entail.' That wry smile again. 'The focus on how I look, travelling away from home so much, the reaction on socials... Some nasty things were said after my appearance. I didn't go on my social platforms for a month following the show. Part of me feels a... a shame in giving up, as if I've failed – failed the younger me who wanted that career so much. So... I need to let go of Jumbo as a first step. I need to realise that... that I'm good enough just being me; that I don't have to achieve worldwide fame for my life to mean something important.'

Trevor listened intently.

'I've got my A levels and am on a gap year,' she continued. 'The next step will be applying to university.'

'Sounds exciting,' said Lili gently. 'What do you want to study?'

'Psychology,' she said. Rosie looked from Trevor to Lili. 'Um... I say a few words to Jumbo, a goodbye, right?'

'Whatever you want,' said Lili.

Rosie held Jumbo with both hands. 'Thanks, Jumbo. We've had fun, right? Remember when I dropped you in a puddle and Mum put you in the tumble dryer? You looked so happy going around and around and came out super cosy. And all those nights we sat up talking, you were such a good listener, always on my side... such a good friend. And I stashed you in my bag so you could come to *The Voice* with me. You inspired me to do great things. Taking part in that show is an experience I will never forget. But the singing dream isn't for me any more – that was yours, and you did it so well.' She gave Lili and Trevor a self-conscious look, but they simply smiled at her. Rosie ran a hand over Jumbo's ears. 'I know you'll miss me, and doing stuff, but you've had a busy life. Maybe it's time to retire.' Her voice sounded full. 'Thanks for everything, Jumbo. You're the best.' She kissed his head.

Lili got to her feet and held out her hand. Rosie passed the elephant over.

'I'm sure you've got a few already, but would you like one last photo of him?'

'Yes please.' Rosie's voice cracked.

As the gentle instrumental music played in the background, Lili placed Jumbo against the vase of flowers, on the coffee table, took a shot and gave the photo to Rosie, who sat down again. Carefully, Lili placed the toy on the windowsill.

Trevor stared at Jumbo and then got to his feet and went

over by the window. 'I can relate to everything you said, Rosie. Thanks for sharing. I've been so nervous about this but once my friend Tommo explained about the freedom ceremony, I knew I mustn't get scared. I had to do it to move forwards.' He reached into his bag and pulled out a wooden base with a big glass engraved star on top. The end of one of the star's points was missing and the base was scratched.

He held it up. 'This was my dad's. A big award from his job. The only people to get this went onto the board, like he did. It was a big PR agency in London. I hardly saw him when I was growing up.' He tilted the star at different angles. 'Didn't stop him thinking he knew what was best for me. Life was easier if I didn't argue with him, so I did the business degree, got a job in the City. Whenever I visited my parents he'd shake this in the air and say any son worth his salt would eventually gain an award of his own.' Trevor exhaled. 'Rosie's words about not having to scale heights to feel good enough really hit home. He... he only ever told me he was proud once, when I was a kid – when I won a race at sport's day, at high school, beating the son of a neighbour he didn't get on with. Eventually I realised the City wasn't for me. I jacked in the London life, came down here to visit an old uni friend, married her and never went back. I'm a teacher now. Primary school. Love it.'

'Inspiring,' mumbled Rosie and nodded at him to continue.

'Dad died a few years ago. Several days before he passed, he tried to make me promise that one day I'd go back to a corporate life. My dear mum died last year and I kept a few sentimental items. She'd hung on to this, ever so proud of Dad, unable to see the pressure he'd put me under. Yet *she* often told me I made her proud too and she loved my stories about my teaching job.' He lifted the award in the air and stared at it. 'Thanks for... for making my mum and dad so happy. It's not your fault that... negative energy came my way. You are beautiful and served a great purpose, awarding someone for working hard. But I can't hang on to you. I need to be completely free of that voice in my head that pops up now and again saying I'm not good enough.' He looked at Lili, visibly lighter, frown lines softening.

'Would you like a photo?' Lili asked as she took it from him.

Trevor shook his head and sat down.

Their relief almost tangible that the ceremony was over, combined with contentment that they were finally free from those items, displayed itself with a gusto for scones, with laughter, with wiped eyes, with stories about Trevor's dad and Jumbo. As the sun set, Lili passed them their coats.

'Thanks for everything,' said Rosie. 'I really feel like I can make a fresh start now.'

She gave Lili a hug, as did Trevor. He put on his jacket and went to say something to Rosie, but hesitated.

'What?' Rosie asked.

'It's a great idea, giving the kids a toy to take home every week, as part of a storytelling activity. My class would love that. And I think they'd love Jumbo.' He glanced at Lili. 'I know you'll dispose of the items in different ways, so... Rosie – and no problem if it's a no... but—'

Rosie's face lit up. 'You'd like to take him for your class?'

'Yes! How about we bring him out of the shortest retirement ever? My wife's ace at sewing, I'm sure she could fashion a lovely new trunk and spruce him up, make sure he's safe for the children after all this time and perhaps make a little blanket to put on his back.'

'Oh yes, yes please,' said Rosie, eyes shining. 'Jumbo would... I mean... *I'd* like that very much,' she said and gave an embarrassed grin.

'Sounds like the perfect recycling story,' said Lili. She squeezed Rosie's arm. 'I'm sure Jumbo will be very excited.'

Beaming, Rosie left. She'd already said her goodbyes to the elephant. Lili fetched Jumbo from the windowsill in the lounge and Trevor put him in his bag.

She opened the door again, to face someone tall, hand raised ready to knock, with wavy black hair and a charming smile that could get him into any building. He was carrying a bag. What was Dylan doing here? Could he have heard about the ceremony and think he could just turn up? How had he found out?

21

'Dylan? This is a surprise.' Sporty cagoule, chinos, casual but smart and sexy AF.

'I'll be off,' said Trevor, and he squeezed past, lifting his helmet in the air. He looked back. 'Today meant a lot, Lili. I can't thank you enough. I already feel better than I have in a long time.'

'Lovely to see you, Trevor,' said Lili and she smiled, then turned to Dylan. 'Please... come in.' She closed the door behind him.

Over his shoulder, Dylan shot Trevor a curious look and then he went in. 'Thanks, Lili.' He took off his anorak, threw it onto the stairs and lifted up the bag again. In a daze, Lili led him into the kitchen.

'Coffee?' she asked, moving plates smeared with cream and jam onto the worktop next to the sink. Bobbin was on the lawn and looked in. The bird jigged from side to side, a happy dance as if it could tell Lili, despite her questions, was secretly pleased to see the surprise caller.

'Cheers, that'd be great. Sorry to drop by unannounced, it

was a spur of the moment thing. I've been visiting my aunt in Falmouth. I stayed over last night. She's widowed now and hasn't been well, so Dad asked me to call in, seeing as he and Mum are in Italy. Fish and chips in front of *Strictly* – took me back to Saturday nights as a kid. Me and Harry used to partner up and do lifts like the stars and attempt the Rumba.' He swivelled his hips.

Lili covered her eyes. 'How can I unsee that?'

A rich warm laugh filled the kitchen as he took her hand and twirled her around. 'Anyway, my aunt's made me this steak pie.' He opened the bag and took out a dish covered in foil.

Right. Pie. Dylan was as transparent as she'd thought. The opposite of Sean. Lili smiled.

'Truro's on my way home and it's a good size for two. If you hadn't got any other plans tonight... would you like to share it? Food always tastes better with company.'

An evening not to do with business? Perhaps he'd changed his mind and really did want—

'We could discuss my aunt. She's thinking of giving her house a refresh and donating the old stuff to a charity shop.'

Of course. What was Lili thinking? Dylan was into decluttering people's lives; it made sense that he wasn't about to fill up Lili's with romance. And her life was already full, thank you very much. Not that it had always felt that way, this last couple of months, with the anniversary of Em's death. Lili cringed. Had she judged Dad too harshly? The first anniversary of the divorce, he'd got drunk and been arrested after almost picking a fight in a pub. Everyone had a different way of coping.

Maybe Dad's way was simply more honest.

'Sounds good,' said Lili brightly, and she put on the kettle. She shivered. Dylan was wearing a shirt with the sleeves rolled up, so he clearly wasn't cold. Where possible she layered up instead of putting on the heating. Bills were expensive now she alone paid them. Lili made her excuses and hurried upstairs to fetch a cardigan, thoughts about Dylan swirling around her head.

It's for the best to cut all ties. But he gives you all the feels.
You might get hurt. But he's kind and funny.
He's not interested. But he called in.
He's just a friend. He's one hot Roman gladiator.

Hardly focusing, she grabbed the nearest cardigan from her wardrobe. As she went back down the stairs, and almost reached the bottom, her right foot stepped onto the hood of Dylan's anorak that had been left there. The coat slipped against the carpet.

Lili lost her balance.

Went to grab the banister.

But she wasn't quick enough and gave a shriek as she fell forwards, down the remaining few steps. Arms outstretched, she broke her fall, but her head still smacked down onto the hallway floor. Everything was black. Until slowly it wasn't. She felt... warm... comfortable, as if in a deep sleep she didn't want to wake up from. In and out she breathed, her mind empty of doubts and worry and sadness. What a luxury. But gradually, tug, tug, tug, she got pulled away from that melting oasis of contentment. Reluctantly, she opened her eyes. The handsome, tanned face of a man leant over her and Lili's blurry vision focused.

'Hail Caesar...' she muttered.

'Lili? What happened? Lili? Are you okay? You've been out of it for a few seconds.' A touch of panic tinged his voice. What was the problem? She felt quite comfortable.

'We who are about to die salute you...'

'Lili, what are you going on about? Does it hurt anywhere?'

Drip by drip, reality found its way in. She blinked rapidly. Who was he? Was she in a public place? She focused on the wallpaper. Why was this man in her house? She glanced sideways. How come she was lying on the carpet?

'You fell down the stairs,' he said. 'Was it far? Does your neck hurt? Your back?'

She tried to sit up.

'No, just lie flat for a moment,' he said and got up. He paced the room, then dropped back down again.

Gladiators should mind their own business.

She blinked. Reality flooded her brain. Deep lines were etched into the man's face and he took out his phone. Dylan. The pie.

'I'm okay,' she said and pushed herself up. Sitting, Lili leant against the wall. 'Seriously. My left hip's a bit sore but...' She looked up the stairs, pushing down a gag reflex. 'Christ, I was lucky. Stupid too. Should have seen your coat. At least it was near the bottom and not at the top.'

'No, this is on me, chucking it down there, turning up unannounced... Look, let me ring for an ambulance, you need checking over.'

'No way. Those services... are stretched as it is, with... real emergencies,' she said, feeling faint for a second. 'All I need is a glass of water.'

She staggered to her feet and rubbed one of her wrists. Dylan jumped up and led her through to the lounge. How embarrassing. Lili hated a fuss. She'd be fine in half an hour. Dylan gazed at the flowers, the camera and incense before fetching her a drink. Whilst she sipped, he sat down next to her and tapped into his phone furiously.

'Then let me take you,' he said and looked up. 'You blacked out. You were confused when you came around. A rib might be cracked. A&E isn't far. I just googled and the Royal Cornwall Hospital is just down the road.'

'But—'

'No arguments.' He got up and blew out the incense sticks. '*Alea iacta est.*'

22

The two of them sat in the waiting room. A crooked Christmas tree was up in the corner, with threadbare tinsel, chipped baubles and fairy lights. She hadn't put hers up last year. This December she would. She couldn't become like Dad, who'd given up on everything when the divorce had gone through. It'd felt understandable that first year, but after that he only made an effort, with clothes, with going out, with birthdays, with Christmas decorations, if a woman was on the scene and he'd wanted to impress. It made Lili sad that he didn't think he deserved to make an effort just for himself.

She told Dylan to go back to Tavistock, but he insisted on staying. She'd been through triage and had various tests done to check for concussion, to examine her eyesight, her limbs and torso. And bloods had been taken to determine if a CT scan was necessary. The nurse was satisfied enough not to admit Lili, seeing as she'd walked into the hospital unaided, her confusion had cleared and her hip and wrist only twinged a little. The fall hadn't covered much distance.

Feeling more like her old self by the minute, she'd started chatting.

'Tell me about the family business,' she said to Dylan. 'Did you and Harry ever want to do something else?'

'No! We'd been grateful for well-paid jobs whilst friends were struggling to find employment, struggling with bills. And we'd never move away from Devon. Love it here. Love working together – well, speaking for myself, anyway.' He gave a wry smile.

Lili nodded. 'I still miss Manchester but would miss Cornwall too if I moved back up north.'

Their chat moved onto the Vegas trip, the pools at the hotel, the shops and food hall, and Lili explained why she wouldn't go now.

'Not without Em,' she said firmly and then fell into silence. Dylan didn't mention Harry. Perhaps he hadn't contacted him about the trip yet.

A man with a grey beard stained with blood lounged opposite them, his arm in a make-shift sling. A couple sat next to him, the woman with a plastic bowl on her lap, eyes blotchy, her companion with his arm around her. Another man sat on his own, half asleep, stinking of beer and pot. He didn't look much older than Rosie.

'How are you doing?' asked Dylan, his eyes searching her face, concern etched across his features. 'No headache?'

'I'm fine, Dr Davis,' she said. 'Honestly. No need to worry. I'm wasting everyone's time. I definitely didn't faint. I slipped on your anorak.'

'Us doctors have to tick all the boxes and I... I was really worried, Lili.' His voice hitched the tiniest bit.

But why would he care so much? Guilt perhaps. Guilt was a

bastard. That feeling Lili got when she thought about the houseboat party and how she should have insisted on going with Em; how she could have reminded her not to drink loads on top of her painkillers and therefore stopped her from falling into the sea.

Dylan's nose wrinkled as the woman vomited. 'We could do with one of your incense sticks,' he said as if forcing his tone to be brighter. He glanced at Lili. 'Do you mind me asking... Did I interrupt some sort of... religious meeting?'

'What? No! Well, I mean, some might call it that but not me.' He wouldn't understand. Old objects to him were just trash. 'So, did you message Harry?' she asked, keen to change the subject.

Dylan raised an eyebrow. 'Okay, now I'm even more intrigued. You weren't having an orgy, were you? Have to say that guy's biker jacket was a bit of a turn-on, and he seemed pretty chuffed.'

'Stop being a jerk,' she said, wishing her voice didn't sound so tight.

He smiled uneasily. 'Fair enough. Harry... yep, I did. Sorry, I should have said. I managed to get hold of him yesterday.'

Lili nodded, wondering why it had taken so long. Harry had a phone.

'He's really grateful for your offer and gutted he can't take you up on it. He's made friends along the way and they're off to... Vietnam. It's cheap, welcoming and really scenic apparently.'

What was she going to do with the hotel booking? She'd asked for the time off work way in advance, over a year ago – Ware & Care were good like that – and HR had written the request down, saying they couldn't promise but didn't see any obstacles. Lili assumed that the dates off still stood. Even if she could face going and invited Meg along, her colleague had recently moaned about hardly having enough holiday left for Christmas, plus was saving to rent, and Tommo hated flying.

It wasn't long before the consultant saw Lili. Her pulse was taken again, so was her blood pressure. All the test results had come back normal. She examined Lili's hip and wrist and questioned her in detail about how she felt in herself and if she had any pain elsewhere. Lili was allowed to leave on the understanding that if she got a headache or nausea, she was to contact her GP immediately, or return to A&E if it was out of hours.

The drive home was silent. She stole a sideways look at Dylan. Lili had rather abruptly changed the subject when he'd asked about the incense and what she'd been doing. He'd only been curious and she hadn't anything to hide; she wasn't embarrassed about her freedom ceremonies. Lili had simply become tired, over the years, of explaining to people who were taking the piss. Not that Dylan would ever do that. He was thoughtful and caring, having sat with her for hours in hospital. They pulled up outside her cottage.

'Want to come in for a hot drink? There's that lovely pie you brought over,' she said.

'Better not. Work tomorrow. Would you like me to help you inside?'

'No. I'd like you to accept my apology.'

His eyebrows knotted together.

'You asked me what I was doing this afternoon.'

'What? Lili, seriously, I was just being nosy, ignore me. Look...' He sighed. 'If I've been quiet, it was due to talking about Harry. I... I was hoping he'd be home soon, but now I find out he's off to Vietnam. His trip has made me realise how I've depended on him over the years in so many ways – maybe at the expense of making other good friends.'

They looked at each other. She leant forward and gave him a hug, to her surprise with purely platonic motives, wanting to convey her understanding.

'You're amazing, you know?' he said. 'I mean, Em is gone forever but you can still sympathise with me. The last year must have been shit.'

He looked so sad. Genuinely. Dylan understood, or at least he was trying to.

'A freedom ceremony,' she blurted out. 'That's what this afternoon was about. A kind of funeral for inanimate objects.'

Dylan burst out laughing. 'Come on, Lili. You're not still confused, are you? Or am I still your gladiator?'

Shit. She was hoping he'd forgotten that.

'Don't flatter yourself. The fall clearly caused that confusion, due to me loving historical Netflix dramas.' Dylan's laughter wasn't vicious, or sneery like some people, and to be fair, laughing had been her first reaction. 'I got the idea for the ceremony after visiting Japan, and it made sense with the work I do.' She explained about the ceremonies she'd heard of whilst visiting Tokyo and Kyoto, and the customers in Ware & Care who struggled to hand over boxes of donations, occasionally changing their mind. 'And there's also a yearly event in Japan that is attended by seamstresses who honour needles which have been used or broken during that year.'

'But a needle's just a needle. A piece of metal. It can't talk. Can't get a job. It's not living.'

'Objects, humans, they're all made of the same stuff when they turn to dust.' She shrugged. 'But it's not my job to convince anyone. That's the job of your heart. Children are closer to what matters, to the truth. That's why tears come when they have to throw out an old toy that adults consider to be nothing but lumps of plastic or plushie.'

'When an item is old or broken it's nothing but clutter, junk, I reckon, and having worked with cast-offs all my life, I have no qualms about chucking unwanted stuff in the tip. But... I think it's great what you do, helping people like that, giving them the freedom to move on. It's... quite beautiful.'

Lili stared at him and didn't blink.

'In any case, who am I to say my beliefs are any more right than yours? Oh wait... I'm Caesar. What I say goes.'

Lili snapped out of her trance, covered her face as there was that rich, warm laugh of his again.

'Thanks again for today, Dylan.' She went to get out of the car but then reached into the back pocket of her jeans. Yes, the maroon ivy leaf from the garden was still there. As she climbed out, Lili discreetly left it on the passenger seat.

Half an hour later she sat snugly in bed, with a hot water bottle and a mug of tea, cranberry and orange flavour left over from last Christmas. She googled the Latin phrase Dylan had said to her just before they'd left for the hospital. It meant *the die is cast*; that is there was no changing a decision; that a point of no return had been reached.

Lili hugged her knees. Her heart was reaching that point with Dylan, feelings she'd never felt before that were proving hard to dismiss. *Alea Iacta est*, indeed.

A text alert buzzed. It was from him.

> Express House Clearances quietens down in December and I'm well overdue some holiday. How about I take a trip to Vegas instead? I'd be doing it for Harry (that's what I'll tell him, me being utterly unselfish). I'd pay for my room, of course, so your loss wouldn't be so great, and you could laugh at me when I come back to the UK, having gambled away the rest of my money in the gaming machines.

The text ended with a leaf emoji, and her heart skipped a beat.

23

Monday was exactly one month until Christmas Day and the shop was already far busier than normal for the beginning of the week. Festive earnings kept Ware & Care in business, along with its large outlet in St Austell that sold items of furniture. Tommo and Meg had spent the morning transferring donation bags from the outhouse to upstairs. Lili would have helped but her hip was still sore after her fall yesterday.

Slade wished everyone a Merry Christmas as the door jingled open and Glenda walked in. 'Got any new historical romances?' she asked in a tone brighter than the colourful lights that had been switched on around Mevagissey harbour at the weekend. Stories set in the past? The giveaway that all was not right in Glenda's world. Lili took her arm and led her past a mum rocking a crying toddler in a pram. The staff had done a good job, over the last week, bringing down stock to keep shelves full. Lili pointed to a bunch of books that had come from Dylan's warehouse. Foundation couldn't cover the bags under the pensioner's eyes and her mascara was smudged, as if rain was coming down outside instead of the rays of winter sun.

Glenda wore gloves, but not a matching pair. Usually she wore her beret jauntily tipped to one side, but today it was simply perched on her head, like a post-box topper. Lili reached for a Regency novel set during the festive period and handed it to Glenda.

'What are you doing for Christmas this year, Glenda? Visiting your niece again?'

'No. She and her family are off to see the Northern Lights during a week in Iceland. She rang me last night, convinced she'd mentioned their trip before. It's a dream they've always had. And good for them.' She gave an unnaturally wide smile. 'Although I'm personally not sure I'd want pickled herrings for Christmas dinner.'

'What will you do?'

'Oh, I'll be fine. I'm putting money aside so that I can have the heating on all day. The food bank you told me about has been a real boon too. If I'm lucky, it'll be a mince pie in front of the King's speech and then the *Strictly Come Dancing* special.' Her voice sounded as empty as a dish of roast potatoes at the end of Christmas dinner. She looked at the book's snowy, fairy-light-strewn cover and put it back next to the others. 'Actually, I don't think I feel like reading at the moment. See you soon, lovie. Nice to chat.' Before Lili could say anything else, Glenda had left.

Heading back to the till, a shard of indignation rose in Lili's chest. Glenda could barely afford to keep warm after a lifetime of grafting at a cheese factory. That anger grew when Callum came in on his lunchbreak. He had a decent job, worked incredibly hard educating future generations, but still had to watch every single penny. The longer Lili had worked in the shop, the clearer it became that some of what you were taught as a child was a downright lie – that hard work would be rewarded with a nice home, decent life, with independence. It wasn't like that any more, not for everyone, and kids would be better off learning skills on how to pick yourself up if you lost your job, your partner, your house or your health.

'Hi, Lili, it's a long shot,' said Callum. 'I've asked everyone for their Christmas lists early this year, so I can properly budget. I think retirement has brought out a second childhood in Dad.' He smiled. 'He's got a huge collection of old videos, from the 80s, and fancies watching them again – *St Elmo's Fire, The Lost Boys, Ferris Bueller's Day Off...* but his VCR player from back then is broken. He found it in the loft recently and couldn't get it working. Do you ever sell them in here?'

Lili shook her head. 'Ware & Care don't sell electrical goods for safety and legal reasons; they have to be PAT tested. But leave it with me. Some charity shops do. I'll ask around.'

His face broke into a smile as he prepared to leave. 'Thanks, Lili. He'll be looking for ways to play his old *Donkey Kong* and *Tetris* games next.'

Donkey Kong featured in the Mario franchise. Was it not even possible to go one day without thinking about Dylan?

She turned around the Open sign and waved goodbye to the other staff. Tommo and Meg came down last. Meg gave a loud yawn. 'Why did I agree to get up early this morning and go swimming with Gran?'

'The same reason I agreed to walk next door's dog twice a day at the weekend because they're away. We're excellent people,' Tommo said smugly.

'Modest too,' said Lili.

'How was your weekend, Lili?' asked Meg. 'How did Sunday afternoon go?'

'Great. Fine. Apart from falling down the stairs and ending up in A&E.'

Tommo stopped putting on his biker jacket. 'What the hell? How are you, gal?'

'Fine. I slipped on a coat. Just hurt my hip. A whole lot of fuss over nothing if you ask me. But Dylan had popped by, on his way back from his aunt's. He took me to hospital.'

'Glad he was there,' said Meg.

'It's been one thing after another lately. You know that expensive Vegas trip?' Lili told them how she'd left cancelling the hotel until too late. 'Harry can't go, so Dylan said he would, paying his way.'

'Sounds like the perfect solution,' said Tommo. 'You deserve a break and it'll be great for you to have someone to share the experience with.'

Lili frowned and zipped up her jacket. 'No – I mean, he'd go on his own. I... I couldn't face it. That trip was for me and Em.'

'Not even with decent company?' said Meg, and she shrugged. 'A break might do you good. You've not had a holiday all year, apart from those few days in London back in early October.'

'Me go with Dylan?'

'You're right. Stupid idea,' said Tommo, and he put on his helmet. 'Who in their right mind would want to see Vegas at night with its magical lights.' He whistled. 'Imagine biking down the strip.'

'Or the chance to meet celebrities and see amazing clothes,' said Meg dreamily.

On the drive home, Lili couldn't stop thinking about the excitement on Tommo and Meg's faces. She and Em had booked adjoining rooms, as the trip was a luxury treat, so that they each had a double bed. And Em did snore! She'd ruled out the idea of going to Vegas alone but perhaps travelling with someone new might be... okay.

When she pulled on the drive, Lili took out her phone.

So much for cutting ties. But them just being friends was working, right?

> Hi Dylan. Any chance you've got an old video player in your warehouse? It's my day off on Wednesday. Could I come over to look? We can also chat about Vegas!

24

It was always a treat to breakfast in the garden with Bobbin, even if the temperatures hit minus Celsius. With a blanket around her, Lili breathed in her day off, dew heightening the smells of fresh grass and woody soil, whilst the twin boys next door kicked a ball around before school.

She and Bobbin ate breakfast together – cereal and coffee for Lili, the special mix for the robin, along with an upturned dustbin lid on the ground filled with water, for drinking and bathing later.

'Tommo and Meg reckon I should go to Vegas with Dylan,' she said, and the robin, as always, stopped to listen. 'I like him. He makes me laugh. But a holiday together would take our friendship to a whole new level.' She sighed. 'Or am I overthinking? You can never have too many friends, right? Perhaps I should just take the plunge. What do you reckon?'

Bobbin cocked its head. A raisin fell from its beak. The bird turned and swooped towards the ground, but instead of going after the food, it landed in the dustbin lid and dived under the water. After flapping and making a hullaboo, spreading drops of water across the patio, it stopped dead and looked up at Lili.

Her face broke into a smile. 'Okay, my little friend,' she whispered. 'Message received loud and clear. You think I should, indeed, take the plunge.'

After a bath, clean of the house and hour of ironing, Lili drove over to Tavistock and parked up outside Dylan's house. He'd said to drop around over lunch. He'd make them sandwiches. The staff would be out on jobs so it would be quiet. He came out of the warehouse and strode over, wearing worn jeans and a fleecy top. He leant forwards and gave her a hug then bobbed down and scooped her into his arms.

'I'm not risking you falling over on *my* property. The last thing I need is you claiming damages.'

Lili wriggled. 'Dylan! Let me down this instant!' She couldn't help laughing, but not as loudly as he did. Gently, he placed her back on the ground, opened the front door and they went inside. She took off her bomber jacket, gave him a pointed look and in an exaggerated manner, hung it on the end of the banister.

Dylan placed his fleece over her jacket. As he'd taken it off, his shirt rose too, to reveal toned, sun-kissed skin, smattered with black hairs that made her long to run her palm across his chest. If Em was here, the two of them would have giggled like schoolgirls. That was the thing if you stayed close to your best friend from childhood – immature aspects remained. They'd still both race to grab the last biscuit in a packet, and Em still had her one-eyed teddy on her bed, Lili her metre-long plushie snake, Sid. Like the women, those two toys had been the best of friends years ago. The two women would still jump up to dance to 'Single Ladies' by Beyoncé, popping the moves they'd learnt at the age of fourteen. They called it their very own anthem.

Self-reliant Lili Taylor and Em Evans didn't need any man putting a ring on anything.

New intimate habits evolved over time, more suited to a grown-up world. They'd think nothing of borrowing each other's clothes and always bought enough tampons for two. They'd ring each other when out on a date, after an hour, to see if the other needed an escape. Em knew precisely how Lili preferred her tea – not too strong, milk in first – whereas Em's was the colour of tar with two sugars.

More importantly, they knew how to cheer each other up. Lili liked a hot water bottle and a bar of chocolate. Em preferred a hug and a comedy movie. That had been the hardest thing in the months running up to her death – apart from a brief moment when they'd booked the trip to Vegas – day in, day out, Lili hadn't succeeded in lifting Em's mood.

'You stick the kettle on,' Dylan said as they entered the kitchen, 'and I'll make us my famous prosciutto and provolone toasties.'

'Sounds impressive.'

'Not really, good Italian home-cooking, that's all. Ham and cheese to you.'

'What other meals did your mum teach you?'

He opened a cabinet and brought down a wooden recipe box. He passed it to her. Lili flicked through the handwritten cards, some of them stained and curled at the corners. Bean and tortellini soup, pork Milanese, parmesan chicken, pesto lasagna, aubergine Gnocchi...

'My mouth's watering!' she said. 'But no desserts?'

Dylan plugged in the toastie maker. 'No. Mum loves cooking savoury foods and said she could never compete with Dad's favourites – scones, sweet pasties and Cornish saffron cake. You've not eaten proper Italian until you've been to a family dinner. We visit my grandparents when we can. Nonna and Nonno always put on an unbeatable spread, with cheese and fruit, an antipasto platter, biscotti for coffee – all of that's without even eating the main course, washed down with Chianti or Pinot Grigio. Even now, they are approaching eighty, and they take so much pride in feeding us all. I wish I lived nearer to them. But I'll be flying out to Italy this Christmas. There'll be lots of fish, of course, pasta, Nonna's panettone...' He gave a contented sigh. 'And a glass of Limoncello always reminds me of the good times, sitting out in their garden.'

The sandwiches took minutes to make and melted in the mouth.

'Apparently the large buffet experiences in Vegas are amazing,' said Lili.

Dylan took a swig of his tea. 'Have you thought any more about my offer?'

Lili finished the last bite and wiped her lips with a paper napkin. 'How would you feel if... I tagged along? I've not decided 100 per cent. I may not commit fully until the last minute. As the booking was for two adjoining rooms, we'd each have our privacy. We wouldn't have to spend all our time together either and—'

Dylan beamed. 'It sounds great, Lili. Let me know how much I owe you.'

She shook her head.

'I insist!'

'Nuh-uh. The main thing is that the booking gets used.'

'But—'

Lili raised one eyebrow.

'Oh God. It's like my *nonna*'s here in the kitchen,' he said. 'That's the look I get if I steal a slice of salami before dinner.' He looked at his watch and jumped up, put their plates in the sink and drank back his tea. 'This discussion is not over! Either way, Vegas, here I come! Harry won't believe it when I message him later. But for now – sorry to rush you, but let's look through these boxes before my teams get back and I'm needed.'

They made their way over to the warehouse. Dylan pointed to a stack of boxes that were newly in and yet to be sorted. A man in overalls walked past and nodded. Dylan steered Lili away from him.

'Sad story,' said Dylan. 'The owner of all this stuff was only sixty and got killed in a car accident. He'd never settled down with a partner, seeing the world with the Navy for many years. Once back in England, he became estranged from his sister. She passed several years ago. His only living relative was a niece who simply wanted the property cleared, lock, stock and barrel. Even though he'd left everything to her, she didn't want a penny and was giving the proceeds of the sale to charity. She didn't keep any personal items. There are letters and photo albums that will just end up in the bin. Makes you wonder what sort of fallout they had, and it makes you grateful for family that you get on with.' His words petered out and a vacant expression momentarily crossed his face. 'Anyway, me being brutal now, he was the right sort of age to have had a VCR player. I looked in the top of one box and saw a pile of old videos.'

For half an hour they searched. Dylan kept looking at his watch and the road. The man in overalls came back and began to approach but Dylan rushed over and kept him at a distance. Clearly Dylan didn't want staff to stop working. She was about to give up when her fingers ran over a smooth rectangular object at the bottom of one of the boxes. She dragged it out from underneath books, military autobiographies mainly.

'Bingo!' Lili said and examined it. 'Although I feel uneasy

passing it on, as a second-hand electrical appliance should be PAT tested.'

'I've got a mate who reconditions and tests old electrical items before putting them up on eBay. I might be able to twist his arm to take a look at it for you promptly,' he said.

'Oh, thank you. That would be brilliant. How much will it cost?'

Dylan crouched on the floor next to her and swept a lock of hair out of her face, tucking it behind her ear. 'Are you for real, Lili? You're insisting on giving me a fancy hotel room in Vegas and expect me to charge you for a knackered old video player?'

Her throat went dry. His touch took her back to that night.

'But this is business,' she managed to say.

He got to his feet and hauled her up. 'Talking of which, I need to get back to the office.' He looked up and frowned as a lorry trundled down the road and pulled up. It had a bobbing plastic reindeer on the dashboard. The driver jumped out and came over, a lanky man with a dark brown crew cut, in navy overalls. He clapped Dylan on the back. 'I've left the lads at the property. Bigger job than we expected in terms of emptying the loft. Good thing it's just down the road in Whitchurch. I've come to get more boxes.' He looked expectantly at Lili and then at Dylan.

'Lili – this is Jags, our new manager.' Was there a nervous edge to Dylan's voice? No. She must have imagined it.

Jags gave a small bow and held out his hand. 'Nice to meet you. Are you the reason Dylan's been so chipper lately?'

Dylan gave a small smile. 'That's down to all the *mithai* you keep bringing in, Jags.'

Jags rolled his eyes. 'That's Indian sweets to you and me, Lili. Dylan's trying to outdo my Hindi.'

'Jags is something of a sweet maker. And you should try his honey cake.' The phone rang in the office. Dylan didn't move.

'Want me to get that, boss?' asked Jags.

Dylan looked at his watch. 'No, you'd better get those boxes.' Reluctantly, he headed to the office.

Jags beamed at Lili. 'You work in Mevagissey? Great seafood restaurants.'

'Oh. He's mentioned me?'

'You know Dylan, any opportunity to boast about saving someone's life by rushing them to A&E.'

Lili grinned. 'Did he tell you it was his fault I fell down the stairs?'

Jags's expression became serious. 'He did. He was really worried. It's... good to see him have something going on apart from work... Not that, I mean, I know you two aren't...'

'It's okay,' she said warmly.

The office door opened and Dylan appeared.

'It's not been easy for him, having to keep the business on track on his own,' said Jags with genuine concern in his voice.

'I'm off to give a quote on a property,' said Dylan, out of breath, having hurried over.

Lili took this as her cue to leave and the two men waved her off as she walked back to Colonel Mustard. Jags seemed nice. Perhaps being responsible for the business, alone, was more stressful than Lili imagined and Dylan really had found it hard to cope. She turned on the engine and yawned. Lili was about to drive off when her elbow pressed against her jacket and something hard in the pocket. She took out a shiny conker.

25

Thursday, the day after the ham and cheese toasties at Dylan's, was so busy. She was late to work after hold-ups on the road. Then an angry customer came in to return a glass vase that had a crack in it – a flaw that wasn't there before sale, according to Lili's inventory. Clearly the woman must have dropped it. Then a pipe supplying the sink in the staff kitchen leaked across the whole floor. After a series of frantic phone calls, she managed to find a plumber who could come out before water spread into the shop. He worked past closing time. Lili sat in the stockroom drinking coffee, surrounded by once much-loved objects. Em was much loved. Much mourned. Much missed. Lili gazed at the shelves. There were so many different types of loss – after deaths and break-ups, after abandonments. If they were lucky people, and people often were, they found new ways to be cared for, like these objects found new homes.

Was anyone loving Em now? Had her childhood dog and grandparents greeted her at the Pearly Gates? Or had the love she'd experienced on earth kept her here, lurking in the shadows, trying to keep friends and family away from danger?

'You did a shit job when it came to me falling down the stairs, then,' Lili said and stared in front of herself as if her best friend stood there. Lili surprised herself and gave a little laugh.

The plumber called up the stairs that he'd finished. Lili locked up and got into her car and drove away from Mevagissey, humming. She was about to turn onto the main road and begin the trip back to Truro when Callum and Jack caught her attention, in a small front garden, outside a block of flats. They were hanging green and red fairy lights around a leylandii. He'd said Lili had driven past his house before. She pulled over and Callum came over.

'Hi!' he said.

She got out and waved at Jack, who was playing with a cat. 'Hi there. Just letting you know I've found an old video player and am waiting to see if it can be given a clean bill of health. I'll keep you posted. Hopefully it will work out cheaper than buying one from eBay or a shop.'

'Hear that, Jack?' said Callum. 'Lili is helping with my Christmas shopping! So the least we can do is invite her in for one of the Santa biscuits you made at school today.' He turned back to Lili and lowered his voice. 'Best of luck, last week he made fairy cakes and I ended up with a twist tie in my mouth.'

She beamed and went over to chat to Jack, kneeling down to stroke the tabby cat who belonged to a neighbour, apparently. The little boy rushed indoors to fetch his dinosaur collection and whilst Callum disappeared into the kitchen, he set the plastic animals out on the living room carpet and introduced them, one by one, to Lili. Callum carried in a tray and set it on the small dining table near the back window. Jack ran over and picked up one of the biscuits. He took it over to their guest.

Callum shot her a sympathetic look and went over with a small plate. 'Would you like a different one?' he said.

'But that's the best, Dad!' said Jack. 'Santa's got a beard. I forgot to ice it on the others. And I washed my hands, like you told me to, after I played with the cat, so it's okay that I've touched it.'

Lili bit into the gingerbread man. 'Mmm. Lovely! Well done, Jack! Crumbly. Just how I like them.'

Callum jerked his head towards the Christmas tree. 'I know we're not quite in December, but we couldn't resist this from the garden centre.'

Lili ran her eyes over the tree, loaded with a mishmash of different baubles, some homemade, clearly by the little boy, like the card snowman with wonky eyes and reindeer with three legs.

Absorbed in a fight between a T-rex and Brontosaurus, Jack lay on the carpet. Callum looked sheepish and apologised for the bulging black bin bags stashed in the corner.

'Do they hold all the belongings you talked of, that you can't let go of?'

'Yep. An overspill from my bedroom. Nothing I could sell. Nothing worth any money.'

'But they mean a lot to you?'

He nodded and sat next to her on the sofa. 'Going back to my childhood.'

'Relatable. I went through the loft earlier this year. I found a box of all the birthday cards I'd kept since forever – from relatives, school friends even. I decided it was time to let go. I chose one card from each person to keep. And all the ones from special birthdays, like my eighteenth.' And all the ones from Em. She couldn't let go of them.

'Did it help?'

'Yes! They all fit into just one shoebox now. The problem is, the longer we hold on to things, the more emotionally we invest in them, even if it makes no sense. Like... like a coupon I got a couple of months ago for ten pounds off a food shop if I spend forty. I haven't used it. Never will. I don't visit that supermarket. But I've held on to it for two months and because of that it feels wrong to let go of it now.'

'That's exactly how I feel,' said Callum, and he sank into deep thought for a moment. 'Thanks, Lili for... not judging.'

She smiled. 'Always here to chat. I have a... friend who works in house clearance. He's about decluttering, large scale, all in one go. And sometimes that's what's necessary, but for others, a clear-out might be best done in stages. I've learnt that from the many donations I've sifted through over the years.'

Lili put her crockery on the table. 'Right, better be off. See you soon, I hope. Bye, Jack! Thanks for the biscuit.' She could have talked about the freedom ceremonies to Callum, but putting pressure on someone to act might backfire. The tabby cat in Callum's front garden had been very friendly. Normally cats preferred strangers who ignored them. Approaching cats that don't know you made them feel under threat, you had to let them come to you – just like the people who needed to take part in Lili's Sunday afternoons. They had to make the first move, had to find their own way to letting go.

Lili headed to bed after dinner and snuggled under the duvet. She let out a sigh, glad to be safe and warm and cocooned from the challenges in life like traffic hold-ups, angry customers, and leaking pipes – the stuff she'd have normally talked through with Em; the bad stuff that couldn't possibly affect her again, now, until she got up tomorrow. Relaxed and toasty, she closed her eyes and eventually fell asleep...

* * *

Em points to the top of the tree and grins. It is their Christmas sloth. They put it up every year. It wears a Santa hat and hugs a branch. They decided it was their festive spirit animal, as Christmas was a time to veg out. It is the Saturday before Christmas week, when they always cook a festive dinner together and celebrate, as they are never actually together on the twenty-fifth. Yawning, they head into the kitchen for a late breakfast of pancakes with all the trimmings. A traditional turkey roast will be enjoyed late afternoon.

Em wipes away a smudge of maple syrup from her mouth and slides over a long, narrow, wrapped box. 'Happy Christmas, Lili!'

With gusto, Lili opens it. 'Oh, Em...' She lifts up the stained-glass bird suncatcher. 'It's so very beautiful. I can't wait to hang it up.'

Lili hands Em a square gift, tied with a big red and green bow. Em tears open the wrapping.

'You star!' says Em, and she jumps up to fit on the vintage Mexican Day of the Dead jacket. 'I utterly love this. Thank you, thank you.'

Lili gets up too and they embrace. Then Em grabs a strawberry, before heading upstairs to run a bath – a day-off treat. She takes her time. Lili clears up the breakfast dishes and prepares the vegetables for later. The bath water stopped running ages ago. Lili wipes her hands on a tea towel and goes up to the bathroom. She knocks.

'Em? Everything all right? Talk about stringing out this soak to avoid peeling carrots.'

No reply.

Lili's chest tightens as she knocks again before opening the door.

'Em! Em!' She's under the water, hair swirling around her head like Medusa's. Lili heaves her into a sitting position and shakes her friend. 'Wake up! Wake up, Em!'

Lili rings 999. Follows the call handler's instructions. It makes no difference. Em doesn't move, doesn't speak.

Then out of the blue, Em opens her eyes. She looks at Lili with the saddest expression before the light in them dies.

* * *

Heart pounding, Lili wakes up.

26

After work, Lili jumped into Colonel Mustard and drove straight to Tavistock. Last night's terrible dream about Em had left her with a feeling of an unwelcome embrace that tightened throughout the day. Seeing Em in the bath had felt so very real. She'd looked so young, years and years of life stolen from her. Rain pelted down onto the road and took her back to one time when she and Em had been going to the cinema. The sun didn't constantly shine in Cornwall and it had been wetter than Manchester which, despite the rumours, wasn't the rainiest place in the country. A car in front of them had skidded as it stopped at speed, in a huge puddle. Em had slammed on her brakes and narrowly avoided going into the back of it. Shaken, the two of them had turned around. A large lorry had tailgated the Mini for their whole journey and only just steered clear of them as it, too, ground to a halt. They'd skipped the cinema and instead gone for comfort food at Nando's.

'What do you think heaven is like?' Em had asked after a large mouthful of peri-peri chicken.

'Goes without saying that everyone looks like Glen Powell,' Lili had said.

'Idiot.' Em nicked one of her friend's french fries. 'As long as I can see your face, I don't care what the other spirits look like...' She grinned. 'So we have to promise to go together.'

Lili and Em. Together forever. That was also what they'd promised years before, in the playground.

Well, they weren't together now but that didn't mean they couldn't still have fun, or rather Lili could on her friend's behalf to make up, in some way, for everything Em was missing. The nightmare decided it. The Mini gathered speed and the satnav guided her to Dylan's house. Out of breath, she parked up, slammed the driver's door shut and ran up to his front door. She knocked. Her fingers flexed; she was keen to announce her decision before she could take it back. Lili knocked again, her hair getting drenched. Fallen leaves glistened with rain and beads of water hung from nearby bushes, like posh drop earrings worn on nights out.

'Lili!' Dylan's face lit up. 'This is a lovely surprise! But the weather... Come on in.'

'I'm coming to Vegas! I owe it to Em!' she blurted out, not budging an inch. 'So I'll see you there on the thirteenth of December!'

'Wait... really? That's brilliant.' He clapped his hands. 'We'll have to plan our itinerary! We've only got two weeks! Come on, get inside, you need to dry off. I've just pulled a fruit pie out of the freezer.'

She shivered now, the evening chill catching up with her. Rain trickled down her face, and down her shirt, as she hadn't taken the time to do up her coat. 'I didn't plan to visit you today. I had a dream last night, you see.' Her teeth chattered. 'Em would want this. Vegas. If she can't go, I have to, for both of us, and...'

Whilst Lili rambled on, Dylan gave her a curious look. He took her coat, hung it up, and ushered her into the hallway and she sat in the kitchen whilst he fetched a towel and a jumper. He closed a photo album on the table and shoved it into a kitchen drawer. She dried off her hair and put on his top whilst he made coffee and heated the pie. Ten minutes later she was tucking in. She hadn't eaten lunch today, unable to stop thinking about last night, about Em's face, about her friend's life going to waste. However, the dream had filled her with a different, more positive sensation than in the past, one focused on being proactive.

Lili gave herself a shake. 'This is delicious. I love cherries and almonds.'

'Yep, it's Harry's favourite. I was looking for a photo in an old album to snap and send to him from when he made his very first pie. I'd forgotten about it. We'd had an argument. I crept up behind him and pushed his face into the filling before he put the pastry lid on.' Dylan gave a smile at the memory. 'Like Mum, I'm no pastry chef. This pie was ready-made, all I did was heat it up.' They fell into silence whilst they ate, rain easing now against the kitchen window. Dylan pushed his empty dish away and gave a sigh of contentment. 'So, what made you decide to take the trip? You mentioned a dream.'

Without answering, Lili scraped her spoon along the bottom of her bowl.

'Lili? You okay?'

She hadn't told anyone about the recurring nightmares. Not even Meg or Tommo, not Mum and Dad either. She met his open, honest gaze.

'I have recurring dreams sometimes. Em and I are always doing something fun, but then the scene ends with her drowning. I try to save her, but I can't and have to watch her, right until the end when... It's as if I'm actually there, you know?'

Dylan got up and crouched by her side. He slipped an arm around her back and looked into her eyes again. 'That must be so scary. And to keep happening, even one year on...'

She leant her head on his shoulder, didn't know why, didn't care. 'But this time it gave me a clear message: that I should take this break for Em as much as me.'

Dylan sat down opposite her again. He rubbed his hands then scrolled up and down on his laptop. 'Okay. Vegas – aside from the casinos and great food, I remember Harry talking about visiting the Grand Canyon...'

'I wanted to go there too and persuaded Em! And December's a good month to go as the weather is mild. It can reach over forty degrees in the summer.'

'I wonder if we've missed the window for booking a trip.' He started typing. 'I should have looked into all this already but, well... I didn't feel so much of an incentive, going alone. Sappy of me really.'

Dylan was so honest about his feelings, about everything. Like the way he'd invited her to the Bonfire Night evening, saying the few friends he had were married. There was no big ego, pretending to be Mr Popular. There was a sense of sincerity about him that made her trust him.

He shot her a sheepish look. 'And there's me assuming you want to do stuff together. It's fine if you'd rather plan your own activities.'

'No, let's do it! We could take a trip to the Grand Canyon on the Monday, that would be a great start to the break. I remember researching it when we booked the hotel. It's a long day out but should be totally worth it. Quite a drive to get there, but a coach could pick us up from our hotel on the Strip. You can book breakfast at a stop on the way. It should be more peaceful going there at this time of year. It's... nice to have a... a mate to go with,' she said brightly.

A mate. Nothing more. Nothing less. Even if she couldn't take her eyes off him; even if she could have rested her head on his shoulder all evening; even if he did make – okay, heat up – the best cherry pie this side of the Watford Gap. Before she knew it, two hours had passed as they'd researched the best restaurants. The music shows that Dylan said Harry was so keen on were booked up, so they reserved tickets for a burlesque show, instead, at one of the hotels. 'Well, it is Vegas!' she'd said as she'd laughingly persuaded Dylan to go to one with her called Naughty Santa.

'We're only there for four nights,' said Lili. 'The rest of the trip we can fill in spontaneously. I can't wait to see the Christmas decorations and I bet the festive-themed menus are amazing.'

Dylan still looked at the screen. 'One of the hotels has an ice rink. There are shops, restaurants, dance shows, casinos, palm trees... Just walking down the Strip, at Christmas, will be something in itself.'

The kitchen clock caught Lili's attention. 'God, sorry, hope I haven't overstayed my welcome – especially on a Friday night.'

'To be honest, I had a headache coming on, but you turning up seems to have cleared it. You know me though, I always have a full social diary. How lucky you were to find me in.' He gave one of his self-deprecating smiles.

Everything inside her jingled like happy sleigh bells.

He closed the laptop. 'And I'm sorry if I rushed you away last time, when you were talking to Jags in the warehouse. Things just got busy and—'

'No need to apologise.' She went to take off his jumper but he insisted Lili keep it on. She followed him into the hallway and picked up her damp coat before heading for the front door.

'Thanks again for the Vegas ticket. Harry is going to be so jealous.'

'Jags talked about how it hadn't been easy for you to keep the business on track, by yourself. I reckon he thought you'd done a great job.'

An odd look crossed Dylan's face. 'What exactly did he say?'

'That was it. Jags seems like a nice guy.' She touched his arm. 'You can always talk to me, you know.'

'I'm okay. My nomadic brother will be home before I know it and then I'll be complaining about the state he leaves the kitchen in and how he drinks milk straight from the carton.'

'I like this,' she said and waved a finger in the air between them. 'You and me talking honestly about the two most important people in our lives. You meet some people who are afraid of facing their true feelings and it's so difficult to get to know them. Em…' She exhaled. 'Em wasn't in the best place during the last few months before the boat accident. This dickhead guy had let her down big time by cheating. He was the reason she went to that party, to show him what he was missing. She lost her life because of a liar.' Lili's face hardened and she twisted her hands for a second before lifting her head. 'I know I'm in safe hands with Mario. After all, you are the hero of the Mushroom Kingdom.'

Dylan's cheeks flushed the same shade as Mario's cap and his eyes glistened. 'Mario is always here for you, Princess Lili.'

They said goodbye and he shut the front door behind her. Lili bent down and picked up a yellow hazel leaf that had blown across from his neighbour's garden. Carefully, she pushed it through Dylan's letterbox and caught a glimpse of him through the gap, walking back into the kitchen, rubbing his head.

27

After getting back from Dylan's, Lili went for a run. How Em would have howled with laughter, but she was desperate to get rid of the inner tension that had built inside. Her cheeks turned bright red, her chest heaved and she bent over, gasping, when she got back to the cottage. Out of breath, she ran a hot bath. She soaked in it, trying not to think about her nightmare, before ordering pizza. Exercise. Hot bath. Carbs. She should have slept soundly but tossed and turned, fleeting dreams taking her to the Mushroom Kingdom.

In the middle of the night she sat up in the dark and hugged her knees, trying hard not to look at Dylan's jumper hanging on the outside of her wardrobe. She flopped backwards and lay down again, covering her face with a pillow whilst she groaned. Eventually, she pulled it away and, through a crack in the curtains, stared at the half-moon. That was what Dad used to call a croissant, a full-moon breakfast being a circular pain au raisin. Mum would shake her head in an affectionate manner, back in the days when she and Dad got on. Lili's parents hadn't wanted to involve her in the divorce, or encourage her to take sides, but it had been hard not to hear their arguments. Turned out Mum had never been in love with him. She'd got pregnant with Lili and decided staying with the baby's father would be best. He'd loved her passionately, so she'd pretended. And so had Dad – he'd known right from the beginning that she didn't feel the same, but he'd told himself she'd change.

'I adored the bones of you, so it never mattered!' Lili had once heard him shout.

But it did matter because over time, the arguments and resentments kicked in, on both sides. Her parents had lied to each other about what they truly wanted; they'd both lied to themselves about what they could make do with.

The only conclusion a young Lili could make was that commitment was scary unless you met someone who valued honesty as much as you did. One-night stands, casual relationships – they were so much easier due to zero expectations. A person could have goals different to getting married, and life could still be fulfilling – you only had to look at icons like Jane Austen, Coco Chanel and Diane Keaton.

Sean had never intended to be with Em in the long-term and his lies had done untold damage in the way a casual relationship wouldn't have.

Mike, a plumber, who Lili had had a few dates with several months ago, wasn't honest with himself, or Lili. From the start Lili had told him she didn't want anything serious and he'd said that arrangement was fine. However it soon became obvious that he was hoping date after date would change her mind. Other dates too, over the years, hadn't been completely transparent, bigging up their jobs or lying about their age.

But then Lili had met Dylan and, straight away, he'd been transparent, right from that first hour when the man in the Dracula cape insisted she scroll through his messages, proving he hadn't been reading the texts she'd sent Em. He'd laughed at himself over his middle name. He'd been so considerate that night they'd slept together, making sure anything that happened between them was what *Em* wanted.

And now it was time for Lili to come clean.

Confession time.

'I can't deny it any longer... I've fallen for Dylan Davis, hook, line and bloody sinker, deeper and deeper like an anchor that never hits the sea bottom. I don't want us to be nothing but friends. I want *all* of him,' she declared to the half-moon. In the pit of her stomach, a ball of excitement span like a roulette wheel at the prospect of them going on holiday together. Maybe he'd see her in a different light away from Cornwall, away from the charity shop, his house clearance business, away from the one-night stand and their agreement to just be mates.

And maybe, for the very first time in her life, Lydia Taylor felt ready to commit to a relationship.

28

Lili yawned as she drove along the A-road, still not used to Cornwall having no motorways. She'd gone to bed late last night, after a video call with Dylan about their Vegas trip.

'I had a poker game here on Wednesday night,' he'd said, 'and invited some of the lads from work and a neighbour. Got in drinks and snacks. I played Rat Pack music in the background. Really saw myself as some sort of hotshot player.' He'd given a hangdog expression. 'I lost every round and ended up having to bet with Doritos.'

God, he'd made her laugh.

'You need a strong coffee to wake you up, Lili,' said Meg, now. She sat in the passenger seat wearing a classic, bottle-green swing coat and vintage knitted beanie. She'd looked through the old mixtapes and put on a Christmas one. 'Mistletoe and Wine' was currently playing.

'On last night's video call, Dylan and I got sidelined by looking at festive menus on the Strip. Imagine turkey tostadas with cranberry relish, or beef with a bourbon maple syrup, or cinnamon-spiced apple strudel, or chocolate Yule log with peppermint ice cream.'

'Sounds amazing! And talking of food...' Meg pulled a tube of butterscotch sweets out of her pocket and offered one to Lili, unwrapping it after Lili nodded. It was the sort of thing Em would have done.

'Thanks again for asking me along on your shopping trip today,' said Meg. 'Tavistock is a brilliant place for shopping, but the train takes forever from Mevagissey. It was so much easier just getting one to yours.'

'How long has your friend lived there?'

'Six years now. Beth moved when her mum got a new job. You sure you're okay with me heading off to see her at five? You and I could grab an early evening cocktail first.'

'No. I actually have plans of my own,' Lili said airily.

'The fishing boat master?'

'Seeing as I'm over his way, he said to call in. He's doing a winter barbecue. If I'm not in work on Monday, you'll know I've caught pneumonia. Then he wants us to watch the movie *Casino*, to get us in the mood, seeing as it's only one week till our trip.'

'I'm watching a *Twilight* marathon with Beth.'

'We'll both deserve a rest after battling the Christmas crowds. I'm also hoping to tick off everything on my shopping list for Manchester – although Dad just wants a pack of cards from Vegas and Mum a casino-themed fridge magnet. I reckon I'll get Dylan something small from Tavistock. Maybe a bottle of Limoncello if I can find it. He misses Italy and makes the most amazing ham and cheese toasties – using Italian cheese. Now, what was it called...?'

Meg stared at her.

'Lunch is on me today, by the way,' Lili added.

'But you're paying for the petrol.'

'I was coming here anyway. Really, you're not much more than a stowaway.' Lili glanced at her. It was good to see Meg smile. Lili had been so wrapped up in herself this last year but now her focus was widening again.

'I know what you're doing,' Meg said in a soft tone.

'You got me – avoiding one of the busiest weekends in our shop. The great thing about Andrew being such a Grinch about Christmas is he's happy to manage our branch on any Saturday in December.'

'You're trying to cheer me up – and I'm very grateful. It's been a shit week.'

Colonel Mustard was stuck behind a red car with a reindeer aerial topper, on a winding B-road now. Lili gave up on an attempt to overtake. 'I'm sorry that another rental option fell through.'

'I'm beginning to think I'll never find my own place.' Meg reached into the sweet bag again. 'Gran's a star, really is, but the small things grate – she doesn't approve of streaming telly and only likes cosy shows, as she calls them, on the usual channels. But then if I watch on my laptop upstairs, she calls me down, says we should have family time. She sets up a board game, makes me a drink, but sometimes I just want to get home and veg out, doing crap stuff like scrolling whilst eating pizza, or watching some reality show. I don't want to feel guilty that I'm ruining the evening for Gran. The last thing I'd ever want to do is hurt her.'

'Sounds pretty normal to me. There's no way I could go back to living with either of my parents, always having lights out by midnight with Mum, and her tutting if I eat too much chocolate, or having to tell Dad exactly what time I'll be back from a night out and him ringing me if I'm five minutes late.' 'Feliz

Navidad' came on the tape player. 'Your gran was young once, Meg. She won't have forgotten that. Times change, that's all.'

'I think Gran is kidding herself that it won't happen. If only she could see that it's not all bad. I won't be keeping her awake late at night, or making a mess when I cook. And I'm really looking forward to having her over for meals, and if I ever earn enough I'd like to take her on holiday one day. She's always wanted to go to York. She's a bit of a history buff and loves anything to do with the Vikings or mediaeval times.' She sighed. 'Funny isn't it – we're so keen to become independent when we're young, saving every penny to get our own place, to be in a situation where we've got no one else to please. But when you've finally got it, years ahead, mortgage paid, décor exactly how you want it, lots of personal space, you want the exact opposite. Glenda came in yesterday without her usual sparkle. She said I was the first person she'd spoken to in three days as she'd been holed up with a cold. No one had rung, no one had called by.'

The satnav on Lili's phone interrupted them, and directed her off the B-road and onto the final part of their journey heading to the centre of Tavistock and a car park near Bedford Square. The town hall was situated there, with the well-known Pannier Market behind it.

Streets radiated off this central point and once they'd parked up, they walked down one, bustling and noisy. The crisp December air snapped Lili out of her tiredness. They passed an array of independent shops, selling hand-painted cards, Devon-themed gifts, art deco ornaments, stationery, jewellery and clothes. Each shop was either decorated with fake snow in the window or displayed a Christmas tree and provided a different festive music soundtrack – carols from one, jazz from the next and synth pop from another. Lili marvelled at one place specialising in gin, and Meg bought several taster bottles for her gran. Then she took Lili to a shop that sold nothing but flapjacks, tens of different flavours. Lili bought a bagful to take into work next week – and another one to freeze. Both Mum and Dad would love them.

Feet aching, they spotted a table by the window in a coffee shop. They hurried inside and bagged it. Soon they were eating mashed avocado and poached eggs on sourdough.

'Mmm. Don't talk to me for a minute,' said Meg, and she closed her eyes.

'Kristen Stewart just walked in.'

Meg's eyes flipped open.

'Celebrity crush. Works every time,' said Lili.

Meg wiped egg yolk off her chin with a napkin covered in robins and took a welcome mouthful of tea. 'Talking of crushes... Tell me if I'm wrong, but I've got a vibe that something's changed for you, about Dylan. You've come to like him... really like him, right?'

Lili swallowed the wrong way and had a coughing fit, sending an apologetic look to the elderly couple at the next table.

'And there's my answer,' said Meg.

Lili put down her knife and fork on the empty plate. 'Okay. Yes. Yes, I do like him,' she said quietly. 'But he doesn't feel the same. As I told you and Tommo, he's not interested.'

'How do you know for sure?'

'He put a business relationship between us ahead of anything else and hasn't given a hint of regretting that since.'

Meg tilted her head. 'Unrequited love hurts like hell. I can only imagine how bad it is around Dylan, he's so goddam good-looking! And he has a way about him. Even though men are not for me, I completely get why you're into him.'

'At least he's a friend – and, I'm hoping, he might become a good one at that.'

'Fancy sharing your fantasy night with him though.' She laughed out loud at the expression on Lili's face and the elderly couple looked at them again. 'Don't be shy. I'll go first. Me and Kristen Stewart. I go to a fashion show. As usual, her androgynous style is soooo cool. Amongst all the fans and journalists, she spots me and compliments my outfit. I'm wearing suede, pocket micro shorts over tights and a horizontally striped biker-cum-bomber jacket.'

'I can see you've dug down into the detail,' said Lili, grinning.

'She takes me into the VIP area. We only stay for an hour. She's not a fan of the celebrity life. She takes me to a classy hotel nearby, very discreet. We go up to a room. Man, the skyline of Manhattan is amazing. She runs and takes a jump, landing on the biggest bed I've seen in my life. I do the same and land next to her. We can't stop laughing. Not until she reaches for my shorts and—'

'Okay! I think you're done.'

Meg fanned herself with the menu. 'You next.'

This reminded Lili of being with Em. And, she realised, thinking that didn't hurt as much as she might have expected.

'Don't laugh.'

Meg pretended to zip her lips.

'Dylan is dressed as a Roman soldier, in a red tunic, silver armour and sandals. He's holding two swords.'

'Oh God. Don't give me ideas for Kristen.'

'We're both standing in the middle of a battleground. I'm a Celtic Briton – dressed as a man. I won't leave the defending of my community to the opposite sex; our people need all the help they can get. Therefore, I've hidden my long hair, smeared mud on my face, stolen a sword and shield. I've been practising my fighting techniques in the woods, having watched the men train for months.'

Meg leaned forwards. 'I could get into this. Carry on.'

'I hold my own. Wound a couple of soldiers. Help steer the Romans away from our camp. But Dylan spies me. I can tell he's curious. I panic and run away, not wanting my fellow Britons, let alone the Romans, to work out my disguise. But he gives chase and easily catches me up in the woods. I lift my chin defiantly and get ready to lunge. But he's high-ranking in the army, experienced, and before I realise it he's darted to my side and easily pulled off my helmet. My hair tumbles down. His eyes widen and gently he tucks a loose strand behind my ear. Our eyes lock and respect fills his. Before we know it, we're lying on the ground and...'

The grey-haired woman next to them had leant towards their table and jerked back when Lili stopped talking, her chair almost tipping over backwards.

Meg shook her head. 'Dearie me, and I thought it was men who were supposed to be obsessed with the Roman Empire.'

Lili paid the bill and, linking arms, they did a couple more hours' shopping and enjoyed a winter-spice hot chocolate from an outdoor bar. As dusk fell, multi-coloured twinkling Christmas lights zig-zagged across streets, up in the sky. Pockets of light lit up trees and the town hall. The two of them hugged and Meg went off to meet her friend. Lili threw her takeaway cup into a bin before strolling back to the car park, humming 'Waking Up In Vegas' by Katy Perry. As she passed the café where she and Meg ate lunch, a voice shouted out.

'Lili! Hi there!'

Her eyes narrowed. Jags?

He waved and came over carrying handfuls of bags. He set

them on the tarmac and rubbed his shoulder. 'A bit out of area, aren't you?'

'Christmas shopping – and Dylan's asked me over for a barbecue.'

'Nice! He mentioned the other week that winter barbecues used to be Harry's thing. Dylan's brother sounds like quite a character. Wish I'd met him.' Jags consulted his watch. 'Better keep moving. The in-laws are around tonight and I need to hide a few presents before my wife gets home from work. Good to see you again, Lili.' He paused. 'Dylan's a decent bloke and could do with getting out more, with making new friends.' He looked at his watch again and picked up his bags. 'The lads at work say he's hardly left the office these last two years. It's great to see him moving forwards, at last, since Harry died and his world fell apart.' Jags said goodbye and hurried off.

29

Lili didn't know how long she'd sat in Colonel Mustard. The car park was half-empty, her fingers ice cold. She ran a hand over the steering wheel, the nearest she could get to touching hands with Em again, hoping that, somehow, her friend's finger imprints were still there. Sadness had hung over her at first, over Jags's words. Poor Harry. Poor Dylan. But the longer she sat, the more anger brewed like a cup of tea that would eventually be undrinkable.

Lili had been honest about Em, about the person she'd been hoping to meet, that very first time she'd seen Dylan in The Rough Tor. Whereas how easily the lies had spilled out of his mouth. His explanation had sounded perfectly rational – that joker Harry had pranked his brother and was still away travelling. She thought back to how neat and totally unlived in Harry's bedroom had looked. And how Dylan said he couldn't show her the photos of the botanical garden his brother had snapped, saying they'd been put in an Instagram story so they'd disappeared after twenty-four hours. How convenient. Then there was how twitchy he'd been at the warehouse, steering her away from that employee in the overalls – clearly worried, in retrospect, that the truth about his brother might have slipped out.

She turned on the engine. Twenty minutes later, she pulled up outside Dylan's house. Lili knocked loudly. He gave her a hug when she walked in, but she stood as stiff as an ironing board. Having taken off her coat, she accepted his offer of a coffee, before heading upstairs to use the bathroom. However, once on the landing, she went straight into Harry's room and switched on the light. One of the things to learn from Em's death had been to not let a guy's lies ever screw Lili over, and here she was, barely one year on, making the same mistake as her friend. Why? How?

Em's death had to mean something.

Lili sat on the bed. No wonder the room was so tidy. Looking at it now, it was more like a shrine.

She got up and went over to an old-fashioned record player. A Caravan Palace vinyl was on the turntable. She straightened up, studied the poster and gently ran a finger over it. So much life had been stolen away from another young person. Bookmarks stuck out from a couple of the musicians' biographies. A tube of Starburst, half-eaten, lay on the bedside table, the packaging neatly twisted at the end. The alarm clock was set to seven. She opened the wardrobe doors. Clothes hung, neatly, with polished shoes and clean trainers on a shelf underneath, all wrapped up in a slightly musty smell. She closed the doors and went back to the desk. She picked up a photo frame. A shot of Dylan and Harry – she recognised the brother from that Facebook profile Meg had mentioned. By the pile of books was a photo album. That time she'd eaten pie at his, Dylan had been looking through an album when she'd arrived; said he'd wanted to snap a photo in there of Harry's face covered in pie, so that he could send it to his brother – when really Dylan must just have been simply flicking through and reminiscing. Lili picked up a letter rack and went through the post that confirmed what Jags had said.

Almost slipping, Lili sped downstairs. She marched into the kitchen. Dylan went to hand her a cup of coffee, those inky eyes welcoming her in, that shoulder-length hair asking to have her fingers run through it. Christ. Hook, line and sinker. What a joke, falling for the cliché of a tall, dark, handsome stranger – because that was all he was. She didn't know Dylan any more. Was he even half Italian? Was his middle name really Mario? And his physical attributes meant nothing without the charm, the way he'd been, that Lili had believed was genuine.

She placed the letter rack on the kitchen table, next to a plate of raw steak and marinated chicken, the smell of smoke coming through the back door that had been left ajar. Dylan frowned.

'Harry hasn't opened any post for two years,' she said.

'You've been in his room again?' His eyebrows knotted together.

Lili stared at him.

'No, he's not the most organised person,' he continued.

'My God. How quickly the lies slip off your tongue.'

Dylan put down her coffee. He stepped back. Rubbed the back of his neck. 'What... what do you mean?'

'I bumped into Jags this afternoon. He told me that Harry died two years ago. You've lied to me, Dylan. Right from the beginning. And what detail you've gone into, what with the pretend messaging and a video call with your brother, and him turning down Vegas to go to Vietnam and—'

'I—'

'No! You don't get to interrupt me! You don't get to say

anything! Because there's no fucking excuse.' Her voice broke. 'I opened up to you about Em – told you things I've never told anyone before, like about the nightmares. Was it some sort of sick joke coming to meet me in the pub? Did you think it would be an easy way to get a Halloween hook-up? Had you planned it all in advance? How you played coy, like the perfect gent – is that just part of some creepy act? What a fool I've been.'

'Lili, you've got this all wrong—'

'I bet you'd really read those texts I'd been sending Em. Had you deleted them before going to the pub? That would make sense. Did they give you the impression I was vulnerable?' She crossed her arms, heart racing as quickly as she'd driven over here. *Hold it together, Lili, don't let him win*, she told herself. 'Well, you're the one who's got things wrong. It's taken me a while, but I've found you out. And I'm fine.' Her voice sounded hoarse.

He collapsed into one of the kitchen chairs, looking like a criminal who'd finally been proved guilty.

'God, I bet you've had a laugh these last few weeks. After we had sex, you wanted me as a business contact so that you could dump your house clearance stuff out of area – as you said, it would make your life a lot easier. It all worked out pretty well for you, didn't it?'

She wiped her nose with the back of her sleeve and pointed to the letter rack. 'You don't make sense – clinically gutting clients' houses, yet holding on to every part of Harry's life for as long as you can. But then why should I be surprised that you're a hypocrite as well as a liar?'

Dylan got up and walked over to her. 'Lili. I can explain. Just give me five minutes of your time,' he stuttered and placed a hand on her arm.

She shook him off and disappeared into the hallway. She

shoved her feet into her shoes, did them up and pulled on her coat before yanking open the front door.

'It makes sense now why you were so uncomfortable when I visited the warehouse. When Jags arrived... you were worried, weren't you, that he'd inadvertently drop you in it?'

'Look, Lili, I—'

'Go to Vegas! Do it for Harry. Whatever. Or was that a lie too, about him wanting to go there? Did you just fancy a holiday? Either way, I don't give a shit. I won't be going and I don't ever want to see you again. Lies have fucked up the lives of the people I care about most.' She slammed the door shut and ran to Colonel Mustard, tears running down her cheeks.

Somehow she got home, chest still hitching. Lili ignored her phone ringing until she got back. Sitting in the darkness, in the lounge, she felt as if she'd lost something important all over again. Well, she wouldn't let that loser set her back. Tomorrow she had a freedom ceremony to run and helping that person, who'd contacted her out of the blue last week, was more important than her own feelings right now.

Lili's eyes dropped to her phone's screen. Dad had rung. He never did that on a Saturday night, usually down the pub with his football mates. Perhaps there was an emergency. She sniffed, wiped her eyes, and pressed dial.

'Lili, love! Thanks for ringing back. Wasn't sure you'd be in.'

'Hi, Dad.' Normally she'd be pleased. He was happier these days.

'You okay, chick?'

'I'm fine,' she said, almost unable to get the words out.

'Really? You sound funny. Like when you were little and had been crying.'

She bit on her fist. 'No, honestly,' she said, voice higher than usual. 'Maybe I'm... I'm coming down with a cold. Anyway – everything okay?'

'No. Emergency stations. I'm having a panic about what to get you for Christmas. It's only a couple of weeks away. Got any ideas, love?'

Thank God he was okay. Thank God she could end the call quickly. 'I'll have a think and text you, Dad. Gotta go now.'

'Lili, what's going on?'

'Nothing. Love you,' she croaked, and a sob escaped her lips before she could end the call.

30

Lili sat in the garden, wrapped up in a blanket, and breathed in the morning smell of damp soil and foliage. She held out her hand and Bobbin flew over.

'Hello, little friend,' she said and then fell silent.

Even though the bird's favourite mix lay in her palm, with juicy raisins, tasty peanuts and strands of Cheddar, it cocked its head and stared at Lili. Then its beak opened and it gave a joyous rendition of its morning melody. Lili managed a half-smile, nothing more. Still the robin didn't eat. It did a little jig.

'I *don't* want to cheer up. I'm suffering,' she said dramatically.

Bobbin ignored her, did another jig and then started eating. Oh to lead the simple life of a garden bird. Yet they still faced predators. Still lost loved ones. Bobbin flew away and she brushed her hands together.

Scones baked, lounge set up, lunch eaten, make-up applied to hide dark under-eye bags, Lili glanced at the clock. It was almost two. Within the last six hours she'd deleted four texts unread. If Dylan tried to contact her again she would block his number. The doorbell rang and she walked into the hallway, followed by the smell of incense and the sound of soft instrumental music.

'Hello, Elaine, come on in.' Lili held out her hand and the woman put her rucksack on the floor and took off her anorak. She looked sprightly for a woman in her late seventies. Lili had met her once before and had also seen her walking around the harbour. She wore joggers and a sweat top. Elaine took off her trainers. Her short pure-white hair was brushed back.

'Forgive me, I'm not very smart. I've come straight from lunch with the girls. We went swimming this morning.'

'You look great. If you can face more water, can I get you a glass? I've baked scones for afterwards.'

'Daff, one of my swimming pals, told me that's what happened. You... you didn't tell Meg I was coming, did you?'

'I'm a woman of my word,' said Lili.

Meg's gran followed Lili into the lounge and sat on the sofa. She put her empty glass on the floor. 'I don't like keeping things from my granddaughter but I think, in this case, it's best. Right.' She exhaled. 'I'm ready to get on with it.'

'Would you like to stand up?'

Elaine nodded and went over to the window, rucksack on her shoulder. Lili hadn't been able to meet her in person first to discuss the process, as this was late notice. But they'd had a video call on her day off, when Meg was in work. Lili had pushed a little, checking Elaine was really ready to let go of her object.

'Thanks for fitting me in. It's felt pressing, what I have to do. Meg has been so down this last week. Have you noticed?'

'I can't discuss Meg with you,' Lili said gently.

A sheepish look appeared on Elaine's face. 'Of course, I

understand. That's why you are such a good friend to her. Loyal. Supportive. She's lucky to have you as her boss as well.'

'Thank you. And anyone can see how much she loves you.'

Elaine stood by the window. 'I love her with all my heart. That's why I had to come today.' She let the rucksack slide to the floor, opened it and took out a doll. It was made from plastic and dressed in a faded yellow smock dress, with black shoes, a little scratched, and shiny blonde hair tied into bunches, threadbare in places.

'My daughter loved this. We got it for her third birthday. I passed it on to Meg. She loved it as much as her mum had.' Elaine ran a hand over one of the pigtails. 'My daughter named her Tinker Bell and would pretend she could fly through the air. She always was chasing the impossible. Whereas Meg simply called her Annie and would beg me to make more clothes for her. I used to cut up items I was going to give to the charity shop.'

Lili gave Meg's gran an encouraging nod.

Elaine cradled the doll in her arms and looked directly at the pale face. 'You hold so many happy memories. Of my Lucy, before the drugs got her – she was the sweetest thing at primary school and used to make me and her granddad breakfast in bed. We loved our Lucy so much we'd happily drink down the fizzy cola and eat the thick Bovril on bread, at six in the morning. Then you…' she nodded at the doll '…you belonged to Meg. She'd read you books and make up stories about animals that wore clothes.' Elaine took a moment. A tear trickled down her cheek. 'But those two girls are grown up now. One I never see and the other I see all the time. Both of those things cut deep into my emotions and you represent those feelings.' Elaine hugged the doll to her chest and cried quietly for a moment. Lili passed her the box of tissues. Elaine pulled one out and dabbed her eyes.

'This is no good,' she said and stood up straighter. 'I've a job to do here and scones are waiting.' Elaine stared at the doll again. 'You bring me treasured memories from the best times of my life, but I have to let go now. By saying goodbye to you, I'm freeing myself of two things. Firstly, the hope that Lucy will ever come back. I've known for a long time she won't but the prospect of Meg moving out has made me realise that even healthy, loving family members leave eventually. And secondly... I need to free myself from the selfish hope Meg will change her mind and always live with me.' A tear ran down her cheek again and she wiped it away.

'You're doing brilliantly,' said Lili quietly. 'Do you want to sit down for a minute?'

Elaine shook her head. 'No. I need to get this done. For my sake. For Meg's too. You see, what's brought me here today,' she said, talking to Lili now, 'is Meg's upset this last week, after that latest renting opportunity fell through. She tried to hide it but her eyes were blotchy for several days. It's time for me to put my own feelings aside and help her look for her own place, to help her financially if she'll let me. Meg has her own life to lead, just like I have done. I left home at eighteen and got married the next year. I know Mum missed me but she never once complained.' Elaine turned back to the doll. 'Thank you, thank you, Tinker Bell, Annie. You've been a wonderful addition to my family and meant so much to our two little girls. I hope you understand why you can't live with me any more. I... I love you too. Beautiful, smiling, you were always there for Lucy and Meg. Often I'd go in to wake them up in the morning and you'd be in their arms.' Elaine kissed the doll on one cheek.

'Would you like a photo?' asked Lili.

Elaine nodded. Lili sat the doll on the coffee table, next to the incense, and took a shot, passing the photo to Elaine. Then Lili sat the doll on the windowsill.

Elaine stayed for another hour. They ate scones, talked about swimming and chatted about the charity shop, laughing about how Meg should credit her gran for any career to do with clothes, due to Elaine making clothes for the doll all those years ago.

'Thanks, Lili. Daff was right. I feel so much better. And I... I'm sorry about your friend, Em. It sounds like you've coped brilliantly. Loss affects us all in different ways. One of my friends used to swear she'd seen her husband often walking in the village for the first year after his death, and admits she still thinks that occasionally now. Yet take my Lucy, even though she's alive I've finally accepted that I'll never see her again.'

The women hugged and Lili saw her out before tidying up in the lounge and putting the doll in the cupboard under the stairs. Another text arrived from Dylan and she was about to block his number when the doorbell rang.

Elaine must have forgotten something. Lili hurried into the hallway and pulled open the door.

Tired face. A huge bunch of flowers and a box of chocolates in his hands.

'Dad?' said Lili, taken aback, winded, happy, and unable to stop herself from falling into his arms crying.

31

'Next time, jam first, Dad,' Lili said. They sat at the kitchen table. 'You're in Cornwall, not Devon. Did you know that the cream tea originated in Tavistock? In 997 AD the Benedictine abbey there was damaged by the Vikings. The monks gave the workers, who were repairing it, slices of bread with clotted cream and jam. So the tradition started in Devon, and—'

'Enough of the diversion tactics. What's going on, chick? What's happened?' He swatted crumbs away from his woolly green jumper, as if they were flies and not bits of scrumptious dough. 'I love scones, love cream even more, but I haven't travelled four hundred bloody miles to talk about them.' He smiled. 'Not complaining about eating them though.'

Silence fell.

'Look... I'm fine, Dad. Honestly. I was simply... pleased to see you. And I'm home in just over two weeks for Christmas. But thanks for the Quality Street chocolates. December wouldn't be the same without them. The flowers are so pretty too, with that gold-sprayed holly added in.' Lili got up and pulled down the window blind. 'How long did the journey take?

I wished you'd spoken to me first, I could have put your mind at ease.' Feeling tearful once more, she sat down again.

'Seven hours – but I'd travel seventy, if it meant checking you were okay. And your mum agreed.'

Lili's eyebrows shot up into her hairline. 'You bothered telling her you were coming?'

'No. I rang up to *discuss* it.'

'But you two... you keep contact to a minimum.'

'She wanted to come too but had a shift at work. She said, "Go down straight away, Johnny, and keep me posted. Give Lili my love and tell her I'll ring her this week."'

Johnny? Since the divorce, for Mum, it had been strictly 'John'.

John wiped his mouth, scrunched up the paper napkin and clenched his fist. 'Em's death... it really affected us too. Maybe you didn't know that, but it did. We'd watched that girl grow up, growing ever cheekier by the year.' He gave an affectionate but sad smile. 'Em drowning made us realise what was important – that life was too short to be unkind, to hold on to grudges. God knows we've both said a million hurtful things to each other over the years. But we're trying to stop.'

An uncomfortable sensation spiked in Lili's chest. She'd never considered how difficult Em's death must have been for her parents. 'Guess I would have noticed the change in you and Mum if I'd visited more this year.' Her cheeks reddened. 'Sorry about that. I... I haven't felt like seeing many people. But that's changing now, so you've no need to worry.'

He dropped the napkin and placed his hand over hers. 'No, *I'm* sorry. So is your mum. We should have both come down this year and supported you more. I've only visited a few times since you and Em moved in.' He picked up the napkin again. 'I've been thinking a lot lately. The divorce wasn't only about me and your mum. And I... I wasn't there for you properly. I was so self-absorbed, could only see what had happened to *me*. I should have put you first.'

'Dad, it's okay, I—'

'That's the main reason I charged down today. I'm here for you now, love. Always will be. Why are you so upset? I'm here to listen. Here to help if you need it.'

She opened her mouth.

'No more of that "there's nothing wrong" nonsense. I may be a bit grey around the edges, but I'm not doolally.'

'You always did know when I was keeping something from you. Like the time I got a detention and pretended I'd joined the school choir.'

'Yes, no offence, love, but your singing voice has always sounded like the train brakes squealing at Deansgate station.'

Lili put her elbows on the table and rested her chin on her hands. 'I... met someone I liked. Really liked.'

'Oh. A guy?'

She rolled her eyes. 'Yes, Dad, I haven't been keeping my sexuality from you.'

'It's just... you haven't really ever been... serious about anyone before.'

He asked it as a question. Lili replied with a nod.

'Your mum and I wondered but never liked to ask. I came across a term on the internet – aromantic – and I get it if—'

'Oh my God, Dad! Stop being so embarrassing! I'm straight, okay? And I have had brief romantic relationships, but I prefer to keep things fun and casual and—'

'Whoa! Who's being embarrassing now?'

They looked at each other and laughed.

'I don't get involved because... I don't want to get hurt. Not like, well... People in long-term relationships often suffer badly when there's a break-up.' She broke eye contact.

'It's okay. I realise, now, how much our divorce affected you. And I'm sorry. So sorry. If there's any way we could have avoided—'

'It's not only that, Dad. Em fell for this guy last year. She got serious. He really let her down.' Lili shrugged. 'It's safer to keep yourself to yourself.'

'But that's life, love. You can't avoid putting your feelings out there.'

'I have. All these years I've not committed to any relationship and life's been great.'

John looked puzzled. 'What about Em?'

'That was a friendship! Please, Dad. I. Am. Straight!'

Now he rolled his eyes. 'All I'm saying is, more like friendship, that's what some marriages turn out to be, once the honeymoon period is over. How long did you know Em? Since primary school, since you were five? That's almost a quarter of a century you were together. You've already had one of the longest relationships ever.'

'But that's different.'

'I don't think so. And yes, you got hurt in the end. Terribly. But if you had your time again, would you still choose to become friends with her?'

'Of course!'

'Right, and that's how I feel about your mum. Despite how things ended, I wouldn't change a thing. We had lots of good times. I loved her passionately – some people never know what that feels like. And we had you... Think of the many great times you had with Em – the nights out, the nights in, the travel, the laughter. You could have those with a romantic partner. Sure, getting close, it's a risk. But I reckon people on their deathbed don't regret the things they did do, they regret the things they didn't.'

Lili looked at his third finger, where his wedding ring had been.

Was he right?

She didn't regret one second of her time with Em, even though the loss, this last year, had seared her heart.

John helped himself to another scone. 'This guy... has he got a name?'

'Dylan.'

John slathered jam, then cream, onto another scone and bit into it, waiting for Lili to explain. So she told him about the texts mix-up, about their growing friendship, even agreeing to go on the Vegas trip together. Then about bumping into Jags and him revealing Dylan's brother Harry was dead, not travelling.

'He's been lying to me for over a month, ever since we first met on Halloween.' The tips of her ears turned pink. 'That may not seem long to really get to like someone, to be so upset when you find out they aren't who you thought, but...'

'When you know, you know,' her dad said. 'The first time I set eyes on your mother, I knew I was going to do everything I could to be with her. We were in a pub, one of the busiest in Stockport, but when she caught my eye and smiled, it was as if we were the only two in the whole of the world, let alone that room.'

It had felt like that when Dylan came over to the shop to return the sock.

John rubbed his stomach in a satisfied manner. 'Weird though... if he had some sort of agenda, wouldn't it have been more clever, to have been honest about Harry? There'd have been more common ground, both of you having lost someone close. Maybe Dylan was having a bad day, and that evening pretending his brother was simply away was his way of dealing with the tragedy.'

'But I opened up to him! Told him things about Em that I've not told anyone else.'

'But, love, that was your choice. I'm not approving of this Dylan lying to you, but it could have been his coping mechanism.'

Maybe.

'Does he seem a decent lad?'

'Yes. But none of that matters. He lied, like the dicko Em dated.'

'Language!'

They smiled at each other.

'She went to that houseboat party because the guy was due to be there, and she wanted to show him she was fine, even though he'd been cheating whilst they were together.'

'Unexpected, horrible things happen, love,' he said firmly. 'That young man's lies didn't cause her drowning.'

Later they sat on the sofa, listening to John's favourite radio station, Smooth. He had one arm around her shoulders as they both sipped hot chocolate and she snuggled up.

'Thanks for coming, Dad,' she said. 'This is nice.'

'Any time, chick. Let's see more of each other from now on. And no more trying to fool your old dad on the phone.'

'Promise. But enough about me. How's *your* dating going?'

'I've met someone as well, although it's only been a couple of months. She's called Sal,' he said. 'But she lied to me too at first, you know; said she was a supervisor at the supermarket. Turns out she stocks shelves, a job she didn't feel was impressive enough for a dating profile. God knows why, any job that pays the bills is great, and she's an amazing woman, but we've talked it through.' He took another sip and looked sideways at Lili. 'Sal's lies weren't about her actual feelings. She wasn't cheating. What you need to ask yourself is what this Dylan's lies were *really* about. And Christ, I've made mistakes in my life, but most people deserve a second chance now and again – apart from the dickos.' He chuckled then gave her a sharp look. 'Not a third chance though. Us Taylors aren't mugs, right? But if he means as much to you as I think he does, perhaps you should at least hear this Dylan out.'

John put his drink on the coffee table, removed his arm and fully faced her. 'Also, speaking Taylor to Taylor, you've a ticket for Vegas. Why on earth would you miss out on a trip like that? Em wouldn't approve. Go for it, girl!'

He had a point. Em would be mightily pissed off if Lili avoided going on their dream trip because of a bloke.

'You go to America. See the sights. And remember to get me that pack of cards.'

32

Leaving the body scanners and passport checks behind, Lili stood in Harry Reid International Airport next to her case, glad to stretch her legs after the eleven-hour flight. She admired a nearby glittering Christmas tree before winding her way between bustling travellers, cleaners, a row of stewards, and a pilot. The mish-mashed aroma of duty-free booze, sweat and coffee welcomed her to Sin City, as Glenda had called it yesterday, along with intercom announcements, squeaking luggage trolleys and babbling tourists.

Lili had made it through the tense wait in the departure lounge back in Heathrow last night. Saturday 13 December, an unlucky number for some – but her luck must have been in, because there had been no sign of Dylan, and she hadn't seen him on the plane either. They'd booked separately so he might have chosen a different flight. She hadn't been able to relax until her delayed aeroplane finally took off in the early hours of Sunday. He hadn't contacted her at all last week. She'd checked her phone numerous times. Of course, it was a great relief. It was.

Maybe she should have heard him out, like Dad had said, but Dylan had dropped contact now, so he couldn't have valued their friendship that much. A shard of emptiness cut through her chest. Damn Dylan Davis for tapping into the space inside her that had emptied out since Em died. She'd allowed him to fill it with all the good things again, like hope and excitement, like laughter, but then his lies had pierced through and all the newfound warmth and comfort had trickled away.

Stupid Lili had forgotten how important it was to rely on no one but yourself.

Meg had waved her off from work yesterday with strict instructions to photograph any celebrities, and Tommo wanted snaps of any cool American motorbikes – or classic cars. A mate of his was into them. Lili had landed in Nevada early afternoon. She passed through crowds, to the taxi rank outside, and took a moment, in the fresh, mild air, enjoying the quiet away from the bustling travellers.

Myrtle Evans, I wish you were here.

She didn't feel like making small talk during the taxi ride, so she put in her ear pods and prepared for a snooze. However, she soon started paying attention as they drove along a solitary road through the flat desert. The surreal scene was like something out of a spaghetti western, passing the occasional box-shaped café, house or shop. The taxi driver got chatting about Nevada's mountain ranges, the mafia introducing casinos in the 1930s for workers who built the Hoover Dam, and how the words Las Vegas actually meant *the meadows*, hardly a glitzy name.

What a contrast the desert drive was to the Strip. As they arrived, Lili sat back, overwhelmed. Her eyes adjusted to a kaleidoscope of buildings and signs advertising restaurants and shops, the architecture so tall and bold. Discreet wasn't a Vegas thing, with its flashy cocktail lounges and sports bars. Dusk was approaching and the buildings were already lit up, along with extravagant Christmas decorations in windows and street fairy lights. At this time of year, the palm trees looked out of place. The taxi driver offered to drive her up and down the Strip – but said it was busy and the tour might take a while. Still, she was only there for four days. *Blow the expense*, said Em's voice in her head.

Wow. What a dopamine hit for the eyes. The drive created a medley of incredible sights, like Caesar's Palace, with its awe-inspiring Greco-Roman design that made her think of the Trafford Centre back in Manchester. The Fountains of Bellagio as well! And there was the Eiffel Tower, about half the size of the original Paris one! Mentally, she ticked off the iconic sights that she and Em had seen online. The Luxor hotel was pyramid-shaped and the Excalibur had a medieval castle theme, with impressive turrets. Las Vegas was so extra, as Meg would say. One surprise was how ordinary everyone looked, but then most passersby were tourists. Also there were homeless people, sporadically camped along the roads. She and Em had imagined that every person in Vegas would be decked out in designer suits, sunglasses and shiny medallions. Yet they'd read the bad reviews as well – the stinky drains, the super-high prices – but it hadn't put them off. A holiday destination was like a book, they reckoned. One person's desert was another person's oasis.

The taxi driver chatted again, giving her tips on the seasonal sights, such as how The Cosmopolitan hotel's outdoor Boulevard Pool had been turned into an ice rink, and that there was an attraction called Winter PARQ where snow fell every half an hour. Eventually, he pulled up at the Pleasure Star hotel. Lili paid and got out. She squinted up at the building, with its thousand rooms. Not as many as the MGM Grand further down the

Strip that had more than five times that. The word 'scraper' in skyscraper came from the Old Norse 'skrapa', meaning to erase, but not even the colossal stainless steel and glass structures in Vegas would have been able to erase the sky that earlier had been as blue and clear as the Greek island waters she and Em had swum in, one summer. Lili smiled at the doorman and entered the hotel, excitement running through her veins.

Em would have grinned at Lili as they walked in, a grin that would have said so much: *Look at us! We don't belong here! But who gives a shit, we're here to paint the town green!* That was a joke from their teenage years, before they'd understood their tolerance of alcohol and after a night out often ended up being sick.

Lili inhaled. *How lucky are you to be here, living in such luxury, a place built for nothing but pleasure? How lucky to simply be living*, she told herself. *Vegas is for partying, not pity-partying.*

Whistling, Lili passed a Christmas tree, decked out in silver and gold baubles. She got her room key, then stood and digested her surroundings, as if they were a rich, decadent meal that couldn't be hurried. There were a few shops ahead, a pizza kiosk as well, and a kiosk that sold pastries, both with queues. There was no Sunday downturn here. Far behind that was a selection of restaurants. Further back from there were the outdoor pools; she'd seen them online. To her left, at the front of the hotel, was a bar and casino area, with croupiers patiently teaching tourists the rules of Blackjack, and a sign pointing to a poker room. Because any member of the public could walk in to use these facilities, when she went up the stairs, to use the lifts that took residents to their rooms, a member of staff checked that she had a key card. Wearing the burgundy uniform with gold trim, he was seriously cute, and by the look in his eyes, he thought the same about her. She imagined him taking Lili to her room and insisting on a personal tour. He'd open a bottle of bubbly from the minibar. They'd chat and laugh and he'd turn down the sheets, raising an eyebrow to see if she wanted anything more than housekeeping service and...

Meg would have been impressed with the fantasy had the mental picture not fizzled away without so much as a quicker heartbeat. Damn Dylan Davis. He'd extinguished her desire to think about other guys, even here, at the world's epicentre of hedonism.

The lift hummed its way upwards. How many floors did this place have? There was one for the spa and indoor pool, another for the food hall. Finally she found her room, realising how very tired she was. It was five in the afternoon here, but already Monday in Cornwall. Lili felt as if she'd been travelling forever.

'Holy... Look at this, Em,' she said out loud and gasped. The bed was long, wide, deep and a chocolate nutcracker doll lay on each of the pillows. It shouted luxury with its gold sheets and damask headboard. The voluminous curtains matched those colours. She picked up a nearby iPad. When they'd booked their rooms here, this had been a feature mentioned. It controlled the lights and heating and you ordered room service via it. When Lili turned on the screen, a dancing reindeer was the first thing to appear. She quickly worked out how to use it and opened the blinds. What a sight! She gazed at the skyline, a disorderly, fun, bright, flashing patchwork of neon signs, of moving lights, of hooting cars and blaring music that even reached the floor where she was staying.

'Remember what we promised to do as soon as we arrived?' Lili asked, tilting her head upwards. She got out her phone and went onto Spotify, found 'Waking Up In Vegas' by Katy Perry and put it on full blast. Lili threw her phone on the bed and began singing as loudly as she could, jumping up and down in the air, closing her eyes and shaking her head at the chorus. When the song ended, Lili grinned.

'Woo hoo! Luv ya, Em!'

She sat up. But what was that? Another knock rapped on the connecting door and a familiar voice came through.

Dylan? So he had travelled here?

An urge overwhelmed her to run into his arms and lean her head against his chest, to lose herself in the familiar in such unfamiliar surroundings. But then she relived the sense of humiliation, feeling like a fool for believing his travelling stories about Harry.

With a frown, Lili unlocked and opened the door. The one opposite opened too.

She almost gasped, and angry sentiments were replaced by an uncomfortable sensation. He looked exhausted, as if he hadn't slept for days, his shoulders were hunched, his hair a mess. No doubt it was jet lag; yes, that had to be it. However, Lili could swear she smelt the whiff of alcohol coming from his direction, and the lines in his face dug deep, making him look years older.

'I didn't see you at Heathrow, in the departure lounge,' she said with a blunt manner.

'I decided to come at the last minute,' he muttered. 'The people at the airline's desk were very kind and agreed to hold up the plane for a couple of minutes. I just made it.'

Of course. The flight had been delayed. 'But I didn't see you on board and we must have walked off together at Harry Reid.'

Harry. There was that name again.

'I looked for you,' he said and shrugged. 'I didn't want me being here to come as a shock but the airport was so busy and I just wanted to get away from all the noise.'

The connecting space still stood between them, filled with so many unanswered questions.

'I wasn't sure whether to come. But I'm doing it for Harry. Although I think it's going to be harder than I thought. He... he should be here. I... can't pretend any more that... that he's in Vietnam.'

'I'm doing it for Em,' Lili replied stiffly.

He put his hands in the air. 'I'll keep out of your way if you want. You call the shots.'

'Fine with me.'

He coloured up. 'My brother died, Lili. My brother, my buddy, the most infuriating person in my life, the fucking funniest. He *died*.'

Her fists curled. No. She wouldn't be moved by the agony in his voice.

'You're the one person who knows how it feels to lose someone you'd put your own life on the line for.' His voice sounded jagged. 'He was so young.' His eyes flashed. '*So* young. He didn't deserve it. He deserves to be here wasting money on machines and plastic mementos and living the carefree spontaneous life that I always secretly admired. I wish I'd told him how much I looked up to him.' The words caught in his throat. 'But now it's too late.' Lili's eyes prickled. 'I know I did wrong and I'm so, so sorry, Lili, about lying, to you of all people who... who's been where I am, but—'

'There's no *but* that can make this better, and no excuse for your behaviour,' she said sadly and pushed the door shut.

33

After ordering a sandwich from room service, Lili scrolled on her phone, without taking much in. Eventually she showered, went to bed and slept for ten hours straight. Lili got up at eight and dressed. She picked up the iPad and found the room service page for breakfast, and was about to order when a knock came on the connecting door.

Dylan again, in a linen shirt and trousers. The clothes hung off him. 'I'm going to the food hall. I can't come to America and not have pancakes.' He gave a tentative smile that didn't reach his tired eyes. 'Hungry?'

Lili thought back to her chat with Dad and how he'd been so wrapped up in his divorce he'd not considered how deeply it must have affected his daughter. And how she'd been so wrapped up in losing Em that Lili hadn't thought about how it must have affected her parents. Grief could make you selfish and thoughtless.

But that was no excuse. Lili hadn't lied to anyone about Em.

Yet she had to eat. The food hall would be easy. They didn't need to sit together.

'I'll probably be going down in about ten minutes,' she said in a flat voice.

The food hall was down on the second floor, a more casual – and slightly cheaper – option to eating in the restaurants. The two of them didn't talk in the lift. They walked out and into a circular dining area with various food booths all around. The seating space, in the middle, was decked out with an eclectic mix of furniture. Some tables were low with upholstered armchairs, others were metal with practical seats, and running around the edge was a narrow, long, semi-circular dining bench with high stools.

They took a lap. Breakfast could be pancakes, yes, but also fry-ups, fruit bowls, or turkey and avocado paninis, as well as waffles. One outlet even served French toast with a selection of festive cocktails and another nothing but donuts, including a bourbon apple flavour, cranberry and orange or decadent eggnog. Lili's stomach rumbled as she breathed in the smell of fried dough and sizzling meat.

'Wish I'd brought elasticated trousers,' she muttered.

Dylan caught her eye.

'That comment was for Em, not you,' she said abruptly.

Shoulders sagging, he went off to order pancakes. Lili stood and watched him. He'd lost weight. As he got to the front of the queue, Lili tapped his shoulder and he turned around.

'If you get the food, I'll get the coffees. Just order me the same as what you're having.'

They chose one of the tables with practical seats. Lili raised an eyebrow at her plate. 'Bacon with syrup? And the pancakes have got bananas in them?'

'It sounds so bad that it's got to be good, right?'

Secretly she agreed, and she cleared her plate. Dylan played around with his fork, ate one rasher and half a pancake and then pushed his plate away.

'I ordered that meal because Harry loved bananas. And bacon,' he said.

'I took a chance on this dish because Em would have. Whenever we travelled, she'd be the first to try unusual foods – even fermented soybeans that looked as if they were served in dog dribble.'

Dylan wiped his mouth and put his hands, clenched together, on the table.

'I meant it last night, I am really sorry, Lili, for lying about Harry. It's unforgiveable. If I could take it back I would. You were right, last night, there is absolutely no excuse.'

'You just did it so easily. There was zero hesitation. It was as if you'd planned it.'

'I promise I hadn't.'

'That time I drove over, to tell you I was going to Vegas, and we ate your crumble... I told you how much I hated liars, that Em died trying to prove herself to one; I said how great it was that we were being honest with each other about the people we were missing. Yet still you didn't fess up.'

'I... I know. After you went, I was wracked with guilt.'

Oh. Lili thought back to that day. She'd peered through the letterbox just after saying goodbye, when the front door was shut, to push through a leaf, and she'd seen him, walking back to the kitchen. Had he been rubbing his head because he was upset?

She leant forwards. 'But what were you thinking? You must have known I wasn't Harry when you got those texts.'

'Did you truly believe the texts sent to you were from Em though?' he said, staring at his mug.

She'd wanted to. Oh, so much. But deep down perhaps...

perhaps she'd known the truth, yet still she'd hung on to the fantasy. Lili tilted her head and took in Dylan's crushed demeanour. Crushed by reality.

'What happened to him?' she asked, tone a little softer.

'He went missing on a backpacking trip two and a half years ago. He'd been gone six months, keeping in touch with us, and then suddenly all contact was lost. Eventually remains were found but...' Dylan talked about how his dad went on antidepressants and his mum had lost over two stone. He looked up. 'I never got to see his body, so now and then I would tell myself they'd made a mistake.'

That could have been Lili talking about Em.

'Mum and Dad took it so badly – as you'd expect. It's why they spend so much time in Italy now. I tried to manage the business for a year, but it all felt much harder after he died. I threw myself into work, putting on a brave face. But sometimes it felt impossible to get out of bed, as if my whole body weighed a hundred tons, as if I was lost in a dense fog or... or a maze where each corner just led to another jumble of paths. You... you must have felt the same, Lili, and I feel for you. Em sounds like a really great person.'

A lump formed in Lili's throat.

'I became burnt out and hired Jags. He's one cool dude.' Dylan exhaled, body shuddering. 'The worst thing is... I've never told anyone this... Harry and I had a massive argument the day before we lost contact. He was always so spontaneous and said a friend of his was going to meet up with him and it would mean extending his trip for a while. He was supposed to be coming home soon but that plan changed. I told him that it was selfish, leaving me in charge for longer. Harry said just because I was a boring sod, didn't mean he had to be and that if the situation were the other way around, he'd cover for me in a flash.' He swallowed. 'It was just one of those silly arguments between brothers. Previously, Harry had offered to help me recruit someone to help out, in his absence, but I'd insisted that I'd be fine. He said his twenties were the age to see the world and he didn't want to look back when he was older and regret not having done it. We're different like that. I haven't ever had the travelling bug.' His shoulders bobbed up and down. 'I think that's why I've struggled so much. If only my last words to him had been kind; had meant something.'

'Like mine to Em?' said Lili and cleared her throat. '"Knock him dead, bitch, and don't bother coming home if your tongue ends up down his throat."'

They stared at each other and a rumble of laughter rose up her throat. Dylan's eyes lit up and the two of them started giggling, but before long, tears appeared in her eyes.

'I haven't told anyone this,' she said, 'but the worst thing for me... I knew Em had been drinking alcohol whilst taking her painkillers. I worried it was dangerous, should have said more to her. Then, perhaps, that night on the boat, she wouldn't have drunk, she wouldn't have fallen off and would still be here...'

'I think guilt goes hand in hand with grief,' he whispered. 'Doesn't mean it's justified. Guess it's a way of processing the shock; we like to think there might have been a way of preventing what happened.'

She sniffed and nodded. 'Yes. But like my dad says, sometimes unexpected, horrible things just happen.'

Their coffees had gone cold and Lili fetched two fresh ones.

'Even though you aren't much of a traveller, you must be looking forward to seeing your family next week?' she said, opposite him again, sipping her hot drink, the tension easing in her neck. 'Where do you fly to?'

'Naples. It's not far from the Amalfi coast. Yes, I can't wait.

Italy's my second home. Even though...' A shadow crossed his features. 'I don't know how we got through the last couple of Christmases, without Harry. Oh, we go through the motions, opening presents, eating too much, getting a little drunk. But it's not the same. Still. I keep waiting for it to get easier, but Harry loved Christmas. The pain of losing him runs deep, for all of us. I'd never want to relive the weeks in between knowing he was missing and the authorities finding his remains.' He stared Lili in the face. 'But then you know what it feels like, getting through the festive season without someone you loved so much.'

'Yes, it was hard going up to Manchester last Christmas and visiting shops and pubs that had been our favourites. I couldn't wait to leave. Perhaps this year will be better for both you and me.'

'I hope so.'

'Is it your parents who want Harry's bedroom left like that – to remember him by?' Lili asked.

He ran a finger around the top of his mug. 'No. They told me to empty it but... I can't. It says everything that was important about my brother – his love of music and reading, his clothes that were far trendier than mine. And family meant so much to him. One of his drawers is full of physical photo albums he's made over the years, whereas the rest of us just leave snaps on our phones, promising ourselves that one day we'll do something with them.' He put a hand to his chest. 'At the same time, it hurts like hell going into that room, and I wish it was bare. It brings back memories and reminds me that's all I have now. But I can't bring myself to strip it. And then your texts arrived and just for a moment, I wondered what it would be like if Harry was still travelling. God, it felt good to think that, so I pretended to myself it was true, even getting myself a Dracula costume for the evening. And the world seemed a better place again. I shouldn't have carried on the pretence.'

Lili paused, then reached across the table and took his hand.

'I am sorry,' he said.

'I know. It's okay. I... I get it. You're right. I think I knew Em wasn't texting me but, God, the unadulterated joy at dreaming I was wrong, it became addictive, as if I'd found a drug that would finally lift my spirits and make me feel whole again...'

He squeezed her fingers.

'It should have been me,' Dylan croaked. 'I'm the eldest. It's against all laws of nature that my kid brother died first.'

'Em was older than me. Never let me forget it. More mature, she pompously reckoned, a glint in her eye. I was looking forward to the day when grey hairs appeared and me being younger was finally an advantage.' She smiled. 'Come on, let's get out of here,' she said and took her hand away. 'We've got the Grand Canyon tomorrow, the burlesque show Wednesday and then home Thursday. That leaves minimal time to do any Christmas shopping or gambling.'

'I'd say we've both gambled enough the last couple of months, wishing for things that are unlikely to happen.'

That didn't stop them calling into the Paris Las Vegas Hotel to try the slot machines though – once they'd stopped staring in awe at the décor, beautifully representing a Parisian avenue. Each slot machine – there were almost two thousand – had a comfy chair in front of it. Before they knew it, they'd spent two hours spinning wheels.

Lili walked outside and squinted in the winter sun. A group of carollers sang nearby. 'So we doubled our money. Then lost it. Racked up a debt. Then got into profit again and just broke even. Nerve-wracking times.'

'I know. Almost losing twenty quid, just imagine…' He let out a long whistle, and she pushed him playfully.

'Could we be any more boring?' Lili complained. 'I can't believe that guy in the next row won twenty thousand dollars.'

'Harry would have loved that place! The risk-taking, the noise, the colours, the music. He was always seeking the next thrill.'

'Em would have called everyone a bunch of losers, but then given a sheepish grin and settled down at a machine for the whole afternoon.'

They sat down at an outside table of a coffee house, on a patio surrounded by green bushes twinkling with fairy lights, even though it was still daytime. It opened out onto the Strip so that customers could watch the Vegas brouhaha pass by. In an attempt to be less boring, they both ordered a Winter Wonderland Blue Sapphire Latte that actually had crushed gems in! And a hot sandwich that sounded as if it belonged in a posh Subway shop, with beef, Swiss cheese, cheddar, lettuce and mustard along with a seasoned tomato sauce.

'When Harry and a mate of his were both fourteen, they got into parkour,' said Dylan as they waited for their food. Dylan had been studying the skyline opposite.

Her eyebrows knotted together.

'It's where people jump from building to building, navigating objects instead of walking around them.'

'I've seen videos of that – looks scary.'

'Not a lot scared Harry. He tried jumping from a garage roof to a garden wall, missed and broke his ankle. Mum and Dad couldn't believe he'd be so stupid. I could and told him as much. Although I secretly admired him for it. He rang me first. I helped him plan how to tell our parents. Not that it helped; he still got grounded.'

'I admired Em too. She was more fearless than me in so many ways. Wild, carefree – although deadly serious about selling crystals. But I think that's why our relationship worked. Any differences complemented each other. She told me once that I was her mooring post, always there, loyal, reliable, and much needed in what can be a turbulent world. It sounded funny but she didn't laugh, and the comment meant a lot to me. Perhaps that's how it was with you and Harry.'

Dylan's face brightened.

Their food arrived and they ate in silence.

'This sandwich is amazing,' he said and smiled away his tired eyes, his haunted face. 'What would you do with twenty thousand dollars?' he asked.

An answer came into her head straight away. Instinctively, she gave a little shake of her head.

'What?' he asked.

Lili wiped her mouth. 'I don't ever think about having loads of money, so I've not asked myself that question before. Weirdly, the first thing that came to mind was to sell Em's car and get a newer, more modern, comfortable one with aircon and satnav, with heated seats and a bigger engine.'

Dylan drank from a glass of water. 'It must hold a lot of memories.'

'Yes, exactly, so why would I want to get rid of it? Like Em teaching me to drive. I accidentally went right over a mini roundabout once. She got really cross and threatened to stop my lessons. Then there was the time we broke down, in the summer, on a country road. Em's phone was out of charge and I couldn't get a signal, so I suggested climbing over a fence and spending the night asleep amongst a pile of haystacks, even though the field stank of cow dung. Colonel Mustard was way too small and cramped. When we woke up, a bull was staring straight at us. We'd never run so fast in our lives.' She lost herself in the memory for a moment. 'What about you?'

'It is very boring, you've been warned. I'd just like to give the house a refresh. Modernise the décor, perhaps add a conservatory. The rooms are so dark it can get depressing, especially in the winter.'

She could almost hear him say the words 'especially without my brother'.

'I tell you what won't be depressing,' said Lili, and she finished the last mouthful of sandwich. 'A swim back at the hotel. Have you seen the photos? The indoor one is a kidney bean of blue. Cushioned loungers are everywhere, glossy plants too, and these incredible swim-up bars.'

Dylan gave a thumbs-up. 'You had me at kidney bean. As long as the water isn't too *chilli* con carne.'

Lili rolled her eyes but couldn't help smiling at his joke.

34

In Riviera-turquoise swim shorts, Dylan strolled towards her, softly toned, a guy who didn't try to look like a model strutting down a catwalk. A group of young women in the pool checked him out as he passed. Oblivious to the admiring glances, he sat down on the lounger next to Lili. He put in his ear pods, closed his eyes, put his hands behind his head and lay back, one leg bent.

Understated. Unassuming. And sexy as hell.

A woman lay on a lilo at the far end of the pool, bobbing up and down. She held a fancy drink with a sparkly cocktail stick in it. Behind the loungers, on the far side, the wall had been designed like a rocky cliff, with a waterfall flowing down that people used as a shower. Palm trees and laughter complemented the background dance music. An oasis of summer in the middle of winter. The air as well as the water was heated. For a second Lili wished she could stay here forever. It was just over a week till Christmas Day and when she got back it would be hectic in the shop, with busy evenings doing last-minute shopping and packing for Manchester.

Dylan stood up, stretched and walked to the pool's deep end. Easily, he dived in and surfaced at the edge, near Lili's feet. His torso appeared, water trickling down his pecs, his black hair drenched and curling more now it was wet. Dylan was hot. No doubt about it. Heat smouldered between her legs at just the memory of the night they'd had together.

* * *

He clambered out of the pool, did a small run-up and went to dive in again. He couldn't have seen that the tiled floor was wet.

He slipped, at speed.

Falling backwards, Dylan managed to straighten up but then another slip threw him forwards. As he skidded to the edge of the pool his ankle twisted and both legs gave way. He toppled headlong and fast, into the water.

It felt like minutes, but seconds later he surfaced and pulled himself to the side, spluttering. To save him any embarrassment Lili looked away, focusing on a magazine that had been left on her lounger.

But there was shouting. Wait... What was going on? She looked up. Where was Dylan? Lili rubbed her head as the lifeguard jumped in and disappeared beneath the water's surface. She couldn't see Dylan.

Shit! No. No, no, no. Lili got to her feet.

He must have gone under again, must have suffered some sort of... of... heart attack? But he couldn't have; he was only young. The lifeguard soon resurfaced, with Dylan in his arms. She ran over to help, risking slipping herself, but another guard appeared and the two of them got him onto the side.

The kiss of life? That meant...

Was that water running down her face or tears? She wiped

her eyes, kneeling by Dylan's legs as the lifeguards continued to work on him. This was like a scene from a tragic movie.

The prospect of Dylan not being around any more left her heart shattered in pieces...

* * *

Heart pulsating, Lili shook herself and sat up on the lounger. When Em first died, when the shock was still raw, Lili would play out traumatic scenes like this, in her head, about other loved ones, and they felt so real, had been so vivid. Dad in a car accident. Mum getting cancer. She'd torture herself with these imaginings, afraid of losing someone else. It only happened with people she felt really deeply about and hadn't happened for months now.

Not until now. Not until Dylan.

As he got out of the pool and came over, Lili could deny it no longer – here was a man she wanted to have a grounded, long-term... *loving* relationship with. No more pretence. Not about Em. Not about Harry. And not about her true feelings for this man who'd entered her life and shaken it upside down as if making a cocktail full of fizz, full of flavour, full of zest for the next chapter. Lili could see now that she'd had a committed, platonic relationship with Em – and that had been fucking brilliant. So this could work with Dylan, right? If he felt the same? If he saw her as more than a friend, than a business contact?

Dylan picked up his towel and bent over her, shaking his head so that water drops fell onto Lili's dry skin. The two of them laughed.

Heart spinning like a roulette wheel, her decision was made.

Before they left Las Vegas, she'd share her true feelings with him.

35

A 6 a.m. start wasn't what you normally expected from a holiday, especially when you were still a bit jet-lagged, but it was several hours to get to the Grand Canyon. They'd leave Nevada and enter Arizona. Lili and Dylan were given bottles of water as they clambered onto the coach that picked them up outside their hotel, in the dark. On the journey, the guide handed out a breakfast menu. The trip included a stop-off at a canteen. Dawn arrived as they sped through the desert, along the dusty route, punctuated by the occasional small settlement. Dylan fell asleep, his head resting against her shoulder. She didn't move an inch, not wanting to disturb him, glad to see him catch up on sleep – he looked so tired, so strained, and obviously hadn't slept much since their fallout. And then they'd stayed up late last night, after dinner, talking in one of the hotel's bars about work, family, Christmas, Cornwall, Devon… Effortless chat over a couple of margaritas. Despite the pull of pancakes again, when they took a break from the journey, they both chose eggs sunny side up and hash browns, with black coffee – the full American experience. Egg yolk dribbled down

Dylan's chin and Lili leant forward to wipe it with her napkin. Her fingers brushed against his stubble and they tingled. Did he feel it too?

Rays of sunshine greeted them as they emerged from the canteen, reenergised. They climbed back on board the coach, fully awake now. This leg of their trip passed much more quickly, and they arrived at an official entrance point. After parking up, they queued for a shuttle bus that ran on loop and took visitors to Eagle Point first, ten minutes away, where the Skywalk was located to allow people to discover the Grand Canyon West Rim. The Skywalk was a large, glass, horseshoe-shaped cantilever bridge that stuck out over the canyon, which was one mile deep. Lili was glad she'd layered up, as the air had a crisp bite. The bridge even had a glass bottom and was owned by the Hualapai Indian tribe. They sold gifts nearby and performed traditional dances.

However, it was the next stop, Guano Point, that really took their breath away, 0.8 miles, to be exact, above the canyon floor. The ridges and layers of rock went on forever, carved out over millions of years by the Colorado River. But then the canyon *was* recognised as one of the seven wonders of the natural world.

'Talk about a panoramic view,' said Lili as they stood near the edge of one viewing point, struck by how few railings there were around. Her eyes scoured the ridges of black, brown and red rock, rising up from the canyon's gorge, with the occasional patch of green plants. Their guide pointed out the muddy river way down below. The canyon's vastness overwhelmed her, but in such a different way to the Strip, which was bustling and noisy. The majestic canyon, solid, timeless, could withstand any act of nature, unlike the trail of glitzy hotels that looked transitory in comparison. Lili tilted her head to the sky, as blue as ever, and then walked off on her own, joining the beginning of a trail, whilst Dylan took photos and spoke to another passenger.

Eventually, Lili found a quieter spot, higher up, following the instructions of signs to keep five feet away from the edge. She stood for several minutes, breathless, not because of the exertion, but because of the surrounding magnificence. The chat of tourists faded into the background, and she watched a bird of prey soar overhead before swooping down into the valley. Lili had read a leaflet on the coach and it said that the Hopi Tribe believed that the Grand Canyon was the gateway to the afterlife. For some reason, away from their cottage, away from Crystoffees and Colonel Mustard, Lili felt closer to Em here than she had since she died.

Standing here, in the face of such staggering beauty and simplicity, and a sense of being shown what really mattered, inside Lili an unfamiliar sense of peace grew at the thought that Em was now at one with nature.

A sense of... release.

'I love you, Em,' she whispered. 'Always will. But... I've got to move on. That doesn't mean I'll ever – *ever* – forget you, but I'm ready to commit to another person. If I lose them too, it's a risk I have to take. The prospect of opening up to Dylan about how much I like him, about becoming invested in his life, about sharing hopes, dreams, worries, makes me feel like I did stepping onto that glass-bottomed Skywalk, waiting for the ground to give way and me to fall, fall, fall. But I can't let that fear control my life. Even if I were to fall, like I did after losing you, Dad's right – you being such a big part of my life was still totally worth it. Thank you, Myrtle Turtle, for the gift of your friendship.'

Tears ran down her cheeks. Dylan came over and started talking but stopped when he saw her face. She looked at him.

'Em,' she choked. 'I wish she could have stayed in my life for just another day. I'd have told her how much I loved her; how much I was going to miss her. That...' Her voice faltered. 'I was sorry I didn't insist on joining her at that party. And I'd have made sure Em knew how special she was. She lit up people's lives without even realising it, always ready with her affectionate banter.'

'Oh, Lili...' Dylan's eyes filled. 'I understand. I'd do anything to have another day with Harry. I'd have told him he did the right thing by extending his trip. That life is for living and for him that meant travelling. I'd have made sure he knew how much his big brother admired and respected him, even though he hadn't shown it, not at the end.'

Lili looked out, across the canyon. 'Do you think they know?' she croaked. 'Do you think they are here with us?'

Dylan wiped his face. 'They're probably rolling their eyes over the sentimentality.'

She caught his eye and the two of them smiled through tears before Dylan took Lili in his arms.

36

Thursday morning arrived too quickly. It was less than one week away till Christmas Day. She'd be leaving the busyness of the Strip for hectic festive preparations. Yesterday they'd gone to the Grand Canal Shoppes at a hotel called the Venetian, having overheard a couple at the table next to them, at breakfast, rave about the canal down the middle of it. Shoppers could take gondola rides, which Lili and Dylan did, sailing past restaurants and luxury shops. Late afternoon they'd gone to the burlesque show called *Naughty Santa*. With its skimpy outfits, tinsel boas, sexy music and topless dancers, and Santa, in very tight trousers, Dylan had pretended to cover his eyes, widening his fingers just enough to get a good view and looking at Lili through it.

They'd laughed. A lot.

Being with him was effortless.

So why hadn't she been able to open up about her feelings for him? Since the visit to the Grand Canyon, it was as if the pure blue sky, strewn with sunbeams, had penetrated her skin and infused her with a joie de vivre. But what if he said no and the world became a darker place again?

Lili looked firmly at her reflection in the bathroom mirror.

Then so be it. You'll find the light once more. You know that now.

They'd be leaving for the airport mid-morning. When they entered the food hall, both went for waffles. Lili offered to get them whilst he fetched two coffees. She'd sent photos of their food all week to Meg, having failed to spot celebrities, and found a biker bar on the Strip with a Harley Davidson parked outside, and an amazing neon-yellow sports bike that looked like a Transformer. Tommo loved the snaps and replied to Lili's message with wow face emojis.

But she wouldn't be sending Meg a photo of Dylan's waffles today. Lili carried their plates over to the table where he was waiting. She put down hers first and then, stomach in knots, placed his plate in front of him.

Dylan rubbed his hands and picked up his cutlery, shadows under his eyes not so dark as a few days ago, his hair shiny and tidier. 'So ready for this,' he said and looked down. His eyebrows knotted together as he glanced at Lili's plate. 'Is mine a special order?'

His stack of waffles was covered in cream, and bright red hearts of coulis were dotted around, along with cranberries. Whereas Lili's coulis was in a puddle on the side, next to a mini jug of cream and slapdash pile of berries.

Lili clenched her hands under the table. 'I asked the server to do that. Because, well, I like you, Dylan. A lot. I've known for a while but didn't feel I could cope with anything... deeper than that one-off night at the pub. Not after losing Em. But that's changed.' Awkwardly, she took a sip of coffee.

He studied the plate once more, then lifted his head.

'God, Dylan, put me out of my misery, say something!'

'I've got nothing to say.'

The knots in her stomach tightened and insecurities filled his silence. In her black one-piece she hadn't been half as glamorous as the other women at the pool, in their eye-catching metallic bikinis, as if Dylan—

He shot her one of his disarming smiles. 'Actions speak louder than words.' He swapped their plates over and turned the hearts to face Lili. 'I feel the same. Have done since we first met.'

The sun in Lili began to shine even more brightly.

'Not just about liking you, but also about getting close to someone again,' he continued. 'When we first met, my emotions were still so focused on the loss of Harry. But it's become harder and harder not to see you and me, us together, as a chance for happiness that I'd be a fool to let go of. Vegas proves that getting that lucky break often involves taking a gamble.' He leant forwards, took her hand and kissed her palm, his lips remaining there as he gazed into her face.

Lili cut a big piece of waffle, stuffed it into her mouth and bit into the sweet gooiness, slowly digesting his words.

'I wonder if your bed is as comfortable as mine?' he whispered, feeding her a cranberry.

Her eyes crinkled. 'Only one way to find out. And I think we've got time.'

They practically ran to the lift and once in Lili's room, they undressed faster than the spin of a roulette wheel.

An hour later, she lay in his arms, utterly content, having hit the jackpot after the sweetest breakfast a person could want.

37

'And then what happened?' asked Meg, and she bit into an egg sandwich, chewing avidly as her eyes widened.

Lili had got back from Las Vegas yesterday, and today was the last Saturday before Christmas. Tommo was holding the fort with other volunteers whilst Lili and Meg grabbed a much-needed break in the staffroom.

'We finished our waffles, talked a bit, agreed we'd… give our relationship a go. Then we checked out of the hotel and headed to the airport.'

Meg's face fell. 'That's it? After your romantic declaration of love with that berry coulis, the two of you stayed in the food hall and chatted?'

Lili's face pinked up.

Meg put down her cup of tea. 'Lili Taylor! You absolute liar!'

Lili grinned. 'Okay. I might have invited him back to my room. Let's just say we were a few minutes late checking out.'

'So you're dating?'

'Do we have to label it?'

'Label what?' Tommo stuck his head around the door.

'Because I don't think we can cope with much more pricing up and tagging today. We still need to get those elf-themed egg cups on display.' He screwed up his face. 'Ah, yes, the reason I came in. Callum's here and would like a minute with you, Lili, if possible. He and I have had a good natter about the football but he looks like he's leaving in a minute.'

'I forgot to mention – Callum came in twice whilst you were away,' Meg added as Tommo disappeared. She got up and put their plates in the sink. 'I'm really pleased for you and Dylan.'

'How about your news? Any luck on the rental front?' Lili chuckled. 'God, it's only been four days, but going that far it's felt like a month. Did I tell you about the burlesque show? That was one *bad* Santa. Wearing a thong, in the cold snow on stage, didn't reduce the size of his prospects, if you know what I mean.'

Meg burst out laughing and spluttered tea down her jumper. 'Jeez, Lili, you sound like my gran. Prospects? If you simply mean he had a large—'

'Boa,' cut in Lili, eyes twinkling. 'They wore tinsel boas. It really was a great performance – hot for all the right reasons.' She shivered. 'Speaking of which, we couldn't believe the drop in temperature when we got back to Heathrow. That frost this morning! And now it's sleeting.'

'I hope it doesn't snow for your trip up north. It's due to get even colder.'

'Fingers crossed. Anyway, back to you and renting... Seen any new places?'

'No. It's a quiet time of year on the selling and letting front apparently. Everyone's busy with Christmas. But...' Her voice skippity-jumped. 'This last couple of weeks, something's changed with Gran. She's always been supportive but wants to help me out financially. I've said no, but she's been persistent.

She wants to help me with a deposit for a new place, and to even go shopping with me, when the time comes, to buy any furnishings or kitchen equipment I need. She's also done research into the vintage clothes business, and has offered to have a brainstorming session with me.' Her voice became thick. 'No one's ever done that. Her research threw up that it's best to focus on a specific area, to stand out. That hadn't crossed my mind. Might be one reason I've not moved forwards much. One of her swimming friends used to run her own business. Gran spoke to her and she's offered to look at my business plan. I... I feel so much better about moving out, with her so interested in my future.'

Lili felt toasty inside, as if back by the pool in Las Vegas. It was so good to hear that Elaine letting go of that doll had made such a difference.

Tommo stuck his head around the door again and adjusted his glasses. 'Callum's really leaving now.'

'God, sorry, coming straight away,' said Lili. She gave Meg a quick hug. 'I'm so pleased for you. I'm no expert but, if you like, I'll cast an eye over that plan before your gran's friend takes a look.' She made her way into the shop, full of children now that schools had broken up. Callum was turning up his coat collar and heading for the door. Sleet pelted against the window as she hurried over and touched his arm.

'Callum? Hi. How are you? You've been looking for me?'

They moved over to the side of the door, by the Christmas tree that Tommo had decorated a few weeks ago. They stood awkwardly for a few seconds. Festive music played in the background. 'Santa Tell Me' by Ariana Grande came on, and Lili couldn't help smiling. Callum shot her a quizzical look.

'This song,' she said. 'It reminded me of something funny I saw in Vegas.'

'I heard you'd gone there. Sounds amazing. But I might wait until Jack's over eighteen before I take him, if I can ever afford it.'

'Advisable,' she said and shot him a humorous look.

'About the VCR player,' she said. 'A friend of mine is bringing it over to the shop tonight. It'll be here waiting for you Monday, all sorted.'

'Lili! I owe you one. That's ace.'

'I know you've been dropping in. Apologies for not texting, but I didn't know until I was back from Vegas that the machine had been given the all-clear.' She jerked her head towards the bag. 'Father Christmas been shopping again?'

'Kind of. Marge next door is looking after Jack.' Callum hesitated. 'But that's not the reason I've been in. You see, I got talking to Marge a few days ago. She saw you leave the other week. What she said, about your Sunday afternoon events, sounded odd at first, but the more we talked... I know it's late notice, and you're probably busy, but I've been wanting to ask... are you holding one of your ceremonies tomorrow?'

No. She had a million things to do. Wrapping up presents for Manchester, baking the chocolate log she promised to take – Mum's favourite.

'As a matter of fact, yes. Two o'clock, it starts.'

'Really? Is there any way I could come?'

'It's to do with the bin bags in your lounge?'

He nodded.

'Of course.'

'Really? That would be great!'

'Normally I like a chat in person first, but without much time... can we have a phone call later tonight so that I can talk you through everything? I haven't time now. In fact, I'd better get a shift on.'

He left just as Glenda came in, her coat wet from melting sleet. She hurried straight over to the book section. Lili wanted to chat but had to take over the till. Over half an hour later, and Glenda was still in the shop. This was unusual. She'd stopped looking around now. In fact, she was just standing, looking shattered. Lili went over.

'Anything I can help you with?' she asked gently.

'Oh no, don't mind me! Just got lost in my thoughts for a moment. I'll be on my way!'

Lili frowned as Glenda's smile dropped and she navigated the clothes rails and passed shelves of ornaments, stopping by the front door to pull down the unstylish but thick bobble hat Lili had never seen her wear before.

Oh Glenda. Of course. She was here to keep warm with the drop in temperature. The library was closed on a Saturday afternoon and she'd been trying to save her heating for Christmas Day. Lili hurried over.

'Glenda, will you do me a favour?' Lili's mind raced. Yes. That would do it. 'Fancy making a deal?'

'Gosh. Sin City really got to you, didn't it?' said Glenda. 'Was it everything I imagine it to be?'

'More than, and...' She shot Glenda an apologetic look. 'I'm rushed off my feet at the moment, but I'll tell you about it another time. I'm hoping you could help. We've been given a bundle of Christmas jigsaws at the last minute. They always sell quickly in the run up to the big day. I'd like to put them out on Monday. If you haven't got anything on this afternoon, is there any way you'd consider checking each one for me? All you need to do is count the number of pieces, to make sure none are missing. You could do it in the staffroom, over a coffee. And Tommo brought in a Christmas cake he's baked.'

Glenda's eyes narrowed. 'Are you sure this needs doing?'

Lili held eye contact. 'Absolutely. It would take some pressure off me. I'd be very grateful. But no problem if you're busy.'

Glenda paused and then stood a little taller and beamed. 'Okay, dear. Happy to do my bit. I can see you're all busy. You fetch those jigsaws and I'll fill the kettle.'

* * *

'You really are just an old softie, aren't you?' said Tommo as he put on his leather coat and put his bike helmet under his arm. She thought about his Christmas secret. Poor Tommo. She wished he would be more open about his festive plans.

It was almost six. He and Meg had stayed longer to help Lili tidy up from one of the busiest days of the year, reorganising items on the shelves and pricing up the jigsaws Glenda had checked, to make the start of the day on Monday easier.

'*Me* old, says the man who raved about a Liberace vinyl that came in today? I'd never even heard of him!'

'Don't swerve the compliment,' he said airily as Meg appeared with her anorak on.

'I won't. But back atcha. I saw you slip Glenda an extra slice of cake to take home.'

Tommo muttered goodbye gruffly and was about to leave Lili and Meg grinning when a face appeared outside, gorgeous, stubbly, and giving off fishing-boat-master vibes.

Tommo unlocked the door before Lili could speak.

'Get yourself in here, man, it's freezing today.'

Scarf thrown around his neck, black hair curling from the sleet, Dylan came in carrying a big parcel in his arms. Must have been the VCR player. Lili indicated to him to put it on the counter by the till.

Tommo slipped an arm around Meg's shoulders as Dylan

came back over. 'Come on, gal. Let's give Lili and her boyfriend some space.'

'He's not my boyfriend,' Lili protested.

Tommo's arm dropped back to his side and he rolled his eyes. 'Don't tell me – there's a whole load of rules about dating these days?'

'Of course,' said Meg. 'First you go out. Then you go out on an exclusive basis. Next—'

'Pah!' Tommo shook his head. 'You like each other, right? Have you been out for a meal together?'

'Yes,' said Lili and gave Tommo a pointed look to stop talking.

'Several times?'

'More than once,' said Dylan, eyes crinkling.

'Kissed?'

'Tommo!' said Lili, and she turned to Dylan. 'I do apologise.'

'Might have,' said Dylan.

'You're as bad as Tommo!' said Lili. She folded her arms as Meg bent over laughing.

'You've been out on dates, you've kissed and you're obviously going to continue seeing each other,' Tommo said. 'In my book that makes you boyfriend and girlfriend.'

Dylan looked at Lili. 'Fine with me.'

Under the gaze of three pairs of eyes, Lili forced an exasperated sigh and, doing her very best and failing to look anything but happy, threw her hands in the air.

38

Lili yawned and opened her eyes. Solid arms with fine black hairs had wrapped around her during the night. She'd lain awake, relishing the sound of Dylan's breathing. Lili turned over and kissed him on the lips.

'I'm not Snow White, you know,' he said and his eyes flicked open. Mercilessly, he tickled her. Shrieking with laughter, she shouted at him to stop...

When they got up an hour later, both of them showered and Lili went downstairs to make breakfast. First, however, she went outside and called for Bobbin. She hadn't seen the bird since she got back from Las Vegas. She poured some seed mix onto the garden table and went back into the kitchen. Lili flicked on the radio as Dylan walked in. He stopped dead as she bopped in time to the music.

'That's Caravan Palace. One of Harry's favourite tunes,' he said.

'It sounded familiar. I remember there was this week where Em wouldn't stop playing this track, after she got back from a music festival.' A squawking caught Lili's attention. She gazed out of the kitchen window. Two pigeons were scoffing Bobbin's food. The robin, who always visited in the morning, hadn't appeared yet again. 'I can't promise my pancakes will meet Vegas standards, but do you fancy a stack with golden syrup?'

She turned around to hear the front door close and went into the hallway. A scribbled note lay on the stairs, on the back of a tissue. It reminded Lili of their first night together.

Sorry, Lili, no time to explain, but I've got to fetch something. I'll be back in a couple of hours. Dylan x

Whilst the message baffled Lili, she couldn't stop staring at the kiss. Humming, she took the tissue into the kitchen, not having the heart to throw it in the bin.

One o'clock arrived and Dylan still hadn't returned. Just as well; Lili had been busy baking scones, along with wrapping presents for Manchester. She was still reeling from the phone call on Friday, when she'd rung her parents about her trip. Yes, she had got Mum's Vegas fridge magnet, to add to her collection of seventy. Yes, she'd got Dad a pack of cards; the hotel sold a special line on reception. But no! She was *not* expecting to hear that the two of them had gone out to the pub together whilst she'd been away, in the spirit of trying not to hold grudges. Dad's new friend Sal had joined them, along with Geoff, who'd been dating Mum for almost two years and now lived with her. The four of them had a Christmas dinner and stayed drinking until last orders!

Lili grabbed a sandwich and set up the lounge for the freedom ceremony, having had a long chat with Callum last night She had just lit the incense sticks and put on the music when there was a knock at the door.

'Sorry about that. I needed to fetch something.' Dylan

carried a plastic bag. He came in and slipped off his coat and shoes, then picked up the bag again, clutching it tightly. 'I completely understand if the answer is no, because I'm throwing this on you, and I know there's a process, but... could I take part in the freedom ceremony? I have given this a lot of thought and our trip consolidated, in my head, what I need to do.'

'Oh. Right. I don't know... I mean... didn't you think funerals for objects are a bit of a joke?' she said, a mischievous look on her face. Was this his sense of humour, like the pranks Harry would play on him? 'This is a serious business, Dylan Davis.'

His cheeks reddened. 'I know. The concept initially took me by surprise but I get it now. Please, Lili. Honestly. I need this. It's the right thing to do.'

Oh. He seemed genuine.

'And we've talked about stuff already. I've opened up to you about things I've never told anyone.'

The argument with his brother? She studied his earnest face. She didn't often make an exception but Dylan's need felt thought through. The doorbell rang. She glanced at it then back at Dylan and nodded. Callum came in carrying two full black bin bags and Lili introduced the two men to each other. Callum disappeared outside again and came back in, dragging three more bags. He looked at Lili sheepishly but she gave him the thumbs-up. Lili and Dylan helped him drag them into the lounge. Callum and Dylan sat on the sofa, Lili in the armchair after fetching glasses of water.

'Would you be okay going first, Callum?' she asked. At least that way Dylan would see, first hand, how the ceremony worked.

Callum smiled nervously. 'Suits me.' He tugged the bags over to the window and stood in front of it, breathing heavily.

'Talking to you, Lili, about when you cleared out that stash of birthday cards in your loft, really helped.' He gave Dylan an embarrassed look. 'I'm a high school teacher and, well, as Lili now knows, I have found it impossible, over the years, to throw away any of my own school work from when I was a child. I mean, *any* of it. I've kept all the folders and exercise books for every subject, going back to primary school. One bag contains nothing but artwork from those early years. In fact there's even some from preschool – a whole pile of stickmen drawings.'

'Wow! That's amazing,' said Dylan.

'I used to think so, and it was okay when I lived with my parents – they had a huge loft – and when I was alone, but the bags became a real sore point with my ex as they took up so much room in our old place. We didn't have a loft and I haven't in my new flat. Now I need the space for Jack's stuff.' He glanced at Dylan. 'He's my young son.' Callum reached into the nearest bag and pulled out a pile of exercise books. 'Guess I'm lucky. I had such a good time back then – lots of mates and we all moved up into the same high school. Loved my teachers too.' He ran a hand over one of the book's covers. It was covered in doodles, signatures, love hearts and comments ending with exclamation marks. 'At the beginning, university was hard. I'd never had to work at making friends before. Looking through these bags when I went home for the weekend reminded me of better times. The longer I held on to all the notes, all the books and drawings, the more I felt as if I'd regret giving them up.' He put the exercise books back. 'But it's time now. I'm back at school in a different way, and happy – and I have a son at school, making memories of his own.'

'Have you kept a selection of what you're going to give up, like I did with the birthday cards?' asked Lili.

'Yes. That was a great idea. I chose a huge ladybird painting that I did in Year 6; it won me a small trophy. Also a test sheet where I got a poor mark in Year 9, but the teacher had written encouraging comments all over it. Mr Jackson was my favourite and keeping that sheet reminds me of what sort of teacher I want to be. Then there's the exercise book from Year 10 that a girl who I fancied to bits signed. I was so excited! And another one filled with messages between me and my mates. We'd secretly passed it around during one very boring maths lesson. The banter makes me laugh to this day.' He exhaled. 'In so many ways, what with my divorce, I need to focus on moving forwards.' Callum cleared his throat, crouched down and lay his hands on top of the bags. 'Thank you for reminding me of the wonderful schooldays I had. Thank you for getting me through that tough first year at university, when I developed anxiety and almost left. You kept me going and made me realise that I *would* make friends and that studying was my life.' His fingers clutched the black plastic. 'It's because of the memories you hold that I became a teacher, a job I love. Thank you. Thank you.'

Callum's eyes shone as he stood up and he stared at the floor. Dylan strode over and gave him a side hug. Lili took a photo and gave it to him, before the three of them dragged the bags nearer to the windowsill. Dylan fetched his bag and then went back to the window. He took out... the Caravan Palace poster that had been up on Harry's wall.

'Thanks for sharing in such an honest way, Callum,' he mumbled. 'My object is to do with my younger brother. He died a couple of years ago. I've thought about him a lot lately, and about grief. For me it's been about not wanting to move on, but thinking I should... but then when a happy moment comes my way I feel guilty that Harry isn't enjoying it too.' He studied the poster. 'It's been about anger as well. Not because he left the business for me to run, not because of the argument we had, but...' His voice trembled. 'Angry that he left *me*. We were supposed to be there for each other, always.'

Lili didn't blink, thinking about Em.

Dylan gazed upwards, towards the ceiling. 'Harry, we were going to be each other's best man at our weddings; uncles to any nephews or nieces. Now that's all gone, along with the small stuff that mattered so much – the disagreements that would become outrageous, like when you cheated watching a Netflix series we were supposed to go through together, so I changed the password and wouldn't give the new one to you. Or the wrestling matches we had whenever you called me an old man.' Dylan gave a trembling smile. 'But I... I can't keep your bedroom like it is any more, because it's frozen in time, at the moment of your death, of your body being found. I relive getting the news every morning when I go in to pull the curtains open. It hurts too much.

'Taking down this poster is a first step in dismantling that room and redecorating it. I'll sort through your stuff like I should have months ago, keeping personal items to look through, every now and again. Like that green, white and red teddy bear that Nonna crocheted for your fourth birthday.' Dylan looked at the poster again. 'But as much as anything else, you loved this band. They gave you so much joy.' He ran a finger over it. 'Thank you for making my brother so happy.' Dylan didn't need a photo, and Liliput the poster gently on the windowsill.

However, she didn't sit down again.

'You've both done brilliantly,' she said. 'In fact... you've both inspired me to take part too. It's something that's been on my mind ever since I first met Dylan, and our trip to Vegas also consolidated my feelings over something. Especially when I went off on my own at the Grand Canyon and... Em...'

Dylan nodded with understanding.

This wasn't normal procedure but neither had it been with Callum or Dylan. But the aim, the sentiments, were the same as in the other ceremonies. Standing in front of the window, Lili hesitated and then reached into her pocket.

39

Lili dangled a set of keys in the air. She took a deep breath and removed her house key, putting that one back in her pocket. The keyring was still Em's, a Mickey Mouse one from Disney World in Florida. When travelling in their twenties, the trips had been about visiting authentic places, and they hadn't expected to enjoy the manmade pleasure centre as much as they had.

'Colonel Mustard?' chorused Dylan and Callum at the same time.

Lili was still staring at the car keys. 'Yes.'

'But that's a great little car,' said Dylan.

'Jack loves it,' added Callum.

What with the last-minute organisation, she'd forgotten to tell the other two that they must never question another person's decision at her ceremonies. Yet, she understood. Colonel Mustard was special.

'I know,' she said quietly. 'Colonel Mustard is one of a kind, that's for sure, for so many reasons – and that's exactly why I need to free myself from it. All I can think of – on every journey

I make – is Em and the places she drove us to, and the good times in the car, eating snacks and singing along to her 80s mixtape.' She raised her head. 'Em, I need to make memories of my own now, and I can't do that in the Mini. Every drive, I picture us together in the front seats. I hear your voice pointing out something silly or asking me to clarify directions. Remember how many times I'd send you the wrong way? You were most unforgiving!' Lili would speedily remedy the situation by passing Em half a KitKat or the correct directions to the nearest Starbucks.

'I need to sell Colonel Mustard.' There. She'd said it out loud. Tommo had a mate who knew about classic cars. It was likely to sell at a decent price and she'd do her best to convince Colin and Shirl to take the money. Lili lifted the keys in the air. 'I don't do this lightly, Colonel Mustard. You've been brilliant, given me such great memories, and for your age you've been incredibly reliable. I know you'll go into good, caring hands. Cars like you are always well looked after.' Her voice caught. 'You gave Em so much pleasure, and her aunt before her. And me – even if your engine is noisier than a Formula 1 car, or so it seems. How fine you've looked, how full of personality. Thanks for everything. I'm so grateful.'

A lump in her throat, Lili placed the keys on the windowsill next to the poster. She didn't need a photo. Perhaps she'd have one taken of her next to the Mini, before Tommo's friend helped her sell it. Lili glanced out of the window at the yellow car that was so small compared to modern beasts, with their airbags and big wheels and crash structures. However, Colonel Mustard was huge when it came to character and she'd miss the Mini sitting on her drive – although she definitely wouldn't miss the backache after a long journey. One thing she'd keep, or rather continue to borrow, if Shirl didn't mind, was the 80s mixtapes. Lili would have to buy an old tape recorder to play them on. Music had been so important to Em.

Whilst eating scones in the kitchen, the three of them got talking about Christmas. Dylan would leave for Naples on Christmas Eve morning. Lili would drive to Manchester Christmas Eve afternoon, after closing the shop at lunchtime. Callum was going to his ex's for Christmas Day; they got on okay and Jack would love it.

Callum spread on more clotted cream. 'Another reason I kept all my school stuff was that I honestly believed, if I ever had kids, my old books and notes would help their studies!' He shook his head. 'Education has changed so much.' Callum wiped his mouth. 'Today is about more than saying goodbye to a load of books and drawings,' he said. 'It's hard to explain, but I already feel different inside, as if... a balloon full of tension, in my chest, has been popped and is now deflating. I have felt stressed about the clutter.' He put down his knife. 'And I've got plenty of memories of my school friends down at the harbour – and on Facebook. There's even a reunion coming up.'

'Yes, I've got memories of Em along the routes we used to take, whatever car I am in,' said Lili.

'That's a perfect explanation, Callum, because I feel the same.' A sheepish look crossed Dylan's face and he looked at Lili. 'Apologies for when I laughed at the idea of these funerals for objects.'

'I laughed too when I first heard,' said Lili. 'But everything on earth, breathing or not, is made from the same building blocks – blocks that become invested with emotions, good or bad.'

'Yeah, boy did I cry when I lost my comfort blanket as a child,' said Callum. 'I drove my parents mad, always taking it in the car and to family gatherings. I was a shy boy and it made me feel everything would be okay. I reckon they threw it out in the end but still won't admit it!'

Dylan nodded. 'My dad threw out my plushie collection when I started school. He didn't want me getting teased when mates came around. I was gutted. Stupid really, but it upset me for ages that I never got to say goodbye to them.'

'Not stupid at all,' said Lili. 'Harry kept his little teddy your *nonna* made all these years, didn't he? I've still got an ornament I bought from an Oxfam shop whilst in sixth form and volunteering there. It's a squat rainforest frog with big eyes and an angry face – always makes me laugh. It reminds me of how much I loved working there – and how that time shaped my career.'

The three of them reminisced about other objects that had been important to them. Today's ceremony had been about much-loved items. The same couldn't be said of everything that temporarily ended up in the cupboard under her stairs. But part of the ceremony was about recognising that any bad feelings attached to objects weren't the objects' fault; it was about saying goodbye in a respectful, kind manner.

Toasters, people, car keys, plants, bird feeders, turtles, posters, bacteria... Every single thing in life started off the same way, regardless of whether it ended up running for president or percolating coffee.

40

Lili blew out the incense sticks she'd left burning in the lounge, having found the smell comforting as it had wafted through the cottage, after she'd taken the first step of her monumental decision to say goodbye to Colonel Mustard. She and Dylan waved Callum off. The crisp breeze at the front door said a refreshing hello.

'Fancy a drive out?' she asked Dylan. 'I know it's dark and biting weather, but there's a walk I haven't done for a while. It takes an hour if we go from Mevagissey, but I feel like I need it today. It always clears my head. We'll need to wrap up. I've got a scarf you could borrow. Or have you got to get back to Tavistock tonight and be in the office tomorrow?'

'Nah. We're closed now until the first week of January. A walk sounds great!'

An hour later they had parked up in the fishing village and were lucky enough to buy takeout coffees just before the last café open lowered its shutters. Lili led the way towards the coastal path until Dylan took her hand and, grinning like two high school sweethearts, they walked side by side, away from the closed gift shops and the boats moored for the night yet dancing a jig on ocean ripples. The village looked even prettier than usual with the Christmas lights. She built up the pace and, sipping coffee, they passed Portmellon and eventually reached Gorran Haven beach.

'Never been here,' said Dylan, squinting in the darkness as they made their way down onto the pebbly sand, rocks jagged and shiny either side of the little bay. Choppy black waves did taekwondo across the ocean, and Lili led him to the rock where she always sat. Frost glinted, sparkling and subtle, on the stone, as magical as the twinkling fairy lights back in Mevagissey, in shop fronts and across streets. She breathed in the sulphur smell of a nearby patch of seaweed, glistening and writhing in the wind.

The two of them sat down. Lili turned to Dylan and kissed him. He put his arm around her shoulders. How easily they fitted together. Lili never thought it would be possible to feel so at ease with a guy you fancied even more than Glen Powell. She gazed out far, across the water, hoping to see her friend, realising it was unlikely the seal would be bathing at night. Far, far away in the distance, the lights of a ship passed by on the horizon. The sky was as clear as black diamond, stars and satellites easily visible. Her eyes dropped back to the water.

'Em had a tattoo of a dolphin, you know,' she said. 'Except, of course, it was no ordinary dolphin. This one cheekily had its tongue stuck out and was diving over a rainbow. She got it done at a music festival where Rick Astley was a guest performer, much to her mum's envy. There was a pop-up tent and she didn't think twice about going in and getting one done with zero planning.'

'Ever seen dolphins here?' he asked.

'No, but they've been spotted a few miles out to sea.' She

pointed. 'And see that sea stack, about fifty metres out? Whenever I usually come, a large grey head pops up to say hello. I prefer to think it's the same seal every time and have called it Neptune.'

'Not got a tattoo of it, then?' he asked. 'Can't say I've noticed one. I might need to examine you again later.'

She laughed and leaned in for another kiss, longer this time, despite the coldness of their lips and noses. She could have sworn the breeze whistled *wit woo*.

'No. Tattoos were Em's thing, not mine, along with her music festivals. She used to go with a group of friends when we were younger – they'd set silly dares like high-fiving twenty people in less than a minute, or peeing in the most unusual container, as the loos were often filthy or had thirty-minute queues. One of her friends filled a Coke tin without spilling a drop. That takes skills.'

Dylan had been looking out to sea. He faced Lili. 'Harry was the same, although he'd head off with a big backpack filled with home comforts, like a blanket, food and drink.' Dylan went to say something but then changed his mind. He gazed out to the sea again. He rubbed his forehead and turned to Lili. 'Can you describe Em's tattoo again?'

'A dolphin sticking out its tongue, diving over a rainbow. Why?'

'This is going to sound crazy, but did she get that done at...' He screwed up his face. 'It was a festival in the summer of 2021, in South Wales.'

Lili's brain scrolled back through the years. 'How on earth did you guess that? Are you a fan of Rick Astley? I remember her talking about that one incessantly afterwards. Wildtown festival, that was it. Post-Covid, some music events still weren't going ahead. This one did. She said everyone went a little crazy, getting drunk, getting tattoos... Can't say I blame them, after the lockdowns.' Lili's eyes narrowed. 'Em wouldn't shut up about this guy she'd hung out with. He was apparently a bit of a joker and reckoned rickrolling was hilarious. You won't believe what he got tattooed – they went into the tent together.'

'Try me,' said Dylan, an odd look on his face.

She grinned. 'I'd completely forgotten. This guy got a QR code linking to a YouTube video of Astley's "Never Gonna Give You Up" on his arm, so he could rickroll everyone who asked him what it stood for. Em thought it was iconic and was gutted when she lost him in the crowd on the second day and never got his contact details.'

Dylan put down his coffee cup. 'Lili. I know about that tattoo already. Because... it was my brother's.'

'You mean he had one like that?'

'No. I mean, that man at the festival was Harry.'

Lili sat very still.

'He came home raving about this girl he'd met. Said she had awesome purple hair and grew up in Manchester. She'd shared her crisps and fruit with him and these amazing cinnamon buns from the café where she worked. In return he bought them burgers and chips.'

'Em and Harry... they knew each other?'

Slowly, Dylan nodded. 'Yep, I reckon so... She was into astrology and when the concert was over, she took him to a nearby field where the lights were less glary and pointed out different star constellations. He tried to track her down on social media, but he only had her first name to go by, and the fact that she lived in Truro. They'd got separated on the second day during a crush when a really popular band came on.' Dylan picked up a handful of sand and let it run through his fingers.

'He said this girl had so much energy, the best banter and she actually laughed at his jokes.'

Lili's jaw dropped. 'This is mad.'

'I'd never seen him so buzzed about a girl before. I remember him telling me about her wearing some sort of sleeveless, floor-length silk coat that was totally impractical for roughing it outside.'

Lili exhaled. That coat – it was the one of Em's that Meg always talked about and said showed true style. Her mind scrolled back again. 'Yes, I remember now, she said the tattoo guy was from Tavistock, and he'd pretended he'd got her a vegan burger. He insisted on calling her his little potato all weekend. He told her to google the Italian for it when she got home. She did and... Oh, of course... now it makes sense.'

'It's an Italian term of endearment – *patatina*.'

'Yes. Because well-cooked potatoes are soft and tasty. We laughed about it. We laughed even harder when she talked about his tattoo – but in an affectionate way on her part. Em tried to find him afterwards as well but she gave up eventually, because he'd said how he was going backpacking and... Oh, Dylan.'

He nodded. 'That music festival was shortly before his trip.'

She linked arms with him and the two of them gazed out at sea, chatting about Em and Harry and how well-matched they would have been.

'Look!' said Dylan, and he pointed towards the sea stack.

Lili stood up and grinned. A head bobbed up and down under the moonlight. Neptune had come to say hello. Dylan stood up and put his arm around Lili. They turned to face each other.

'I can't help thinking Em and Harry somehow orchestrated our meeting,' she said.

'It would be just like Harry. He was always trying to get me on dating apps.'

'And Em would have seen you as the perfect antidote to me moping around after her death, as she'd have seen it.'

'It would be a shame for their hard work to go to waste,' said Dylan, his jet-black eyes twinkling along with the stars.

A lump rose in her throat. 'It does feel as if fate had to get involved, because Mario and Bacteria don't sound like a match made in heaven,' she whispered.

'Why don't we ship our names together? Bario? In Italian, that's the word for barium, a chemical element. Your ceremonies are about going back to the basics of life. That's us, building our relationship from the ground up.'

'You are so romantic,' she said and pulled a face.

When they stopped laughing, he held her tight. Lili leaned into him and closed her eyes. Despite the cutting wind, the crashing waves, the December frost, everything felt absolutely right.

41

After leaving a yellow hazel tree leaf on her bed for Lili to find later, Dylan left the cottage on Monday morning at the same time as Lili headed to work, both of them navigating roads covered in black ice. He had packing to do before going to Italy and last-minute shopping, joking about buying a new full-length raincoat. The weather on the Amalfi coast was getting worse after heavy rainfall last week.

Feel-good Christmas music had been the order of the day and by the time she got home, Lili couldn't get Bing Crosby out of her head. Callum had picked up the VCR player and Jack was full of how they were going to a nativity play later on. Glenda had dropped in to sort through more jigsaws. They weren't for Christmas, so there was no urgency. But she didn't need to know that and Lili simply said it would be a huge help to have them ready for the January sale period.

'Are you seeing Dylan again before he heads to Naples tomorrow?' asked Tommo. He wore a Santa hat and a scarf of tinsel around his neck, like the dancers in Vegas. It was Tuesday now and his last shift volunteering before the visit to his sister's for Christmas, in Norfolk, that he'd told everyone about. Lili passed him the biscuits. Despite counting every penny, Glenda had dropped off a tin of cranberry and orange shortbread, a thank you for the staff's good service and friendliness over the last year. The tin was ornate, bright green with holly around the edges and a beautiful robin in the middle.

'He's coming over tonight. I'd go to his, but he said I've got enough driving ahead of me, up to Manchester.'

'A real gent. I like that. Not that you gals need special treatment,' he added hastily as Meg came in.

Meg gave him a bemused look and took a biscuit.

'After the festive hoo-ha, my mate who's into classic cars will look at Colonel Mustard,' said Tommo. 'He's very excited. Any idea what you're going to replace it with?'

'Something quiet. Smooth-running. A car I can stretch my legs in.'

'And how's everything with you, Missy?' he asked Meg.

She sat down. 'Still not dating Kristen Stewart and the rental market is as dead as a dodo at this time of year. But my business plan is taking shape nicely – your suggestions really helped, Lili.' She clasped her hands together. 'And Gran's massively got into researching the vintage clothes market. We've spent hours brainstorming together, listing stuff I need to set up, even if it's only online at first – working out costs. I feel like I've got more direction now, a real goal. As a result, I've decided…' She mimicked doing a drum roll. 'I'm going to focus on 1940s World War Two fashion for women. That era has always fascinated me – the tea dresses, wool suits, white gloves, turbans, the angle hats, wraparound coats, the reefer and box ones too. Polka dots and stripes galore! Those are the styles I often wear myself and… Sorry, going on a bit.' She took a glug of the tea Tommo had passed her. 'The clothes were so elegant and simple back then. Hollywood had a real influence. I love the contrast of that glamour against the backdrop of the ordinary person having to manage during the war.'

'You should target advertising at those festivals that relive the 40s,' said Tommo. 'If you like I could ask my mate who's buying Colonel Mustard. He goes to all sorts of classic car events and some of them aren't just about the motors.'

'Cool, thanks, that sounds brill. I'm giving Gran's loft a good tidy out over Christmas. She said her mum had some wonderful pieces from when she was younger, and they could still be up there. But enough about me.' She beamed. 'You'll never guess who just came into the shop. I'm sure it was the lead actor from that detective TV show episode filmed down at the harbour during the summer, and...'

Lili was staring at the tin.

'Lili, he's even offered me a part in the next season – if I sleep with him.'

'Oh, great...'

'Lili Taylor! You aren't listening!'

Ears red, Lili looked up. 'Sorry. What were you saying?'

Meg pointed to the tin. 'Why is the picture on that biscuit tin more interesting than my prospective fame?'

'What? Oh, nothing... it's just... the robin...'

Tommo picked up their empty mugs and took them to the sink. He turned around. 'Cheeky little chaps, aren't they? Not that I've seen one this autumn, it's mostly sparrows and pigeons in my garden. But robins are definitely more tame.'

'Yes. I... I trained one over the summer. Got it feeding out of my hand. It's visited me every day for months now.'

'Wowww! You've never told us that before! It's so cute. You should have filmed it. You'd be a TikTok sensation!'

'Because nothing's real unless it's online, right, Meg?' said Tommo.

Meg affectionately flipped him the finger.

Standards really had slipped. Lili would have to have a word with her staff in the New Year about inappropriate behaviour. She couldn't help smiling.

'I called it – her, to be specific – Bobbin. And it sounds silly but... I swear the bird understood everything I said. She really listened, you know? Especially if I was feeling down. She used to make me laugh as well.'

'Used to? So she doesn't visit any more?' asked Meg.

'No. Not since I got back from Las Vegas. It's only been a few days but the bird never missed a single morning. Not even if I'd been away for a break, like my trip to London. Bobbin the robin's always been waiting when I get home. I'm trying not to think about it, but the tin reminded me.'

'You've not seen her since you got together with Dylan?' said Tommo.

Lili frowned. 'I haven't neglected her. I've still been going outside with food in my hand.'

'No, gal, I mean... you've not seen this bird since you've decided to sell Colonel Mustard and move forwards with your life either?' He pointed to the tin. 'Lots of people believe robins are the symbol of, or a messenger from, a loved one who's passed.'

They did?

'I don't profess to understand everything in this universe,' he continued. 'But perhaps this is a sign from Em that... it's time – time to accept what happened last year; time to make your peace with it. Maybe this Bobbin disappearing means Em believes you're strong enough now, to live your life without her, without her memory being such a big focus. Or I could just be a silly fool,' he added gruffly, and he shot Meg a warning look not to agree.

Lili studied the tin again. Bobbin would cock her head whilst Lili offloaded, and sometimes do a silly dance on her little legs, wings flapping. Em always did love Cheddar cheese. And peanuts. Raisins too.

Blinking away tears, Lili went to the sink and ran the tap. She and Em had always dreamt of flying when they were little girls. How lovely to think Em might have finally got her wish.

42

Dylan was a little late, which suited Lili as she'd just made a call to the property owner over an idea she'd had for her cottage, and it had overran. Hearing the doorbell, she rushed into the hallway, then slowed at the last minute and gathered herself. But as soon as she saw her gladiator, all notions of playing it cool vanished out of the door and into the sleet. She dived in for a kiss before he'd even got into the hall. Lili pulled off his beanie, took his coat and stood on tiptoe as Dylan leant down for another one.

'You aren't the only one who can cook Italian,' she said when they'd settled in the lounge on the sofa, with glasses of red wine. 'Although when I say cook, I use the word loosely... What I actually mean is I've ordered in pizza. Hope that's okay.'

'More than okay,' he said, voice a little flat. He took a large sip of his drink. Two large cardboard boxes lay on the floor. He jerked his head towards them. 'You aren't actually moving to Manchester, are you?'

'No. How do you feel about helping me put up the Christmas tree tonight? I've brought it and the decorations down from the loft. I wasn't going to bother but' – she thought back to what Tommo had said about Bobbin – 'now the time feels right.'

'Sure,' he said.

She leant sideways and dug him gently in the ribs. 'You okay?'

'Sorry, Lili. Just waiting for a text. It's why I was late.' His phone buzzed and he put his drink on the coffee table. Lili undid one of the boxes whilst he tapped into his phone, gave a big sigh and slipped the phone back into his pocket.

Lili scooched over and sat at his feet, her chin resting on his knees. 'What's up?'

'Flights are being cancelled from everywhere going into Naples airport, including mine. But worse than that, Vietri sul Mare, my grandparents' village, is cut off by flooding. A storm had been building in recent days and was due to miss their area, but it changed course late yesterday and things got much worse overnight.' He ran a hand through his hair. 'As soon as I heard the word storm, I should have changed my flight and gone over earlier in case they needed me. It's no excuse but what with Vegas and... other distractions.' He shot her a wry smile. 'I wasn't thinking of my family over the weekend as much as I could have been. The water has got into Nonna and Nonno's garage. They've got sandbags around the house. The weather's due to get even worse in the next twenty-four hours. The upshot is, I'll be spending my Christmas in Tavistock.'

'Oh no! Dylan, I'm so sorry.'

He read his phone again. 'It sucks, big time. I'm not bothered for myself, much as I was looking forward to it... I'm worried about my grandparents. They're getting on now.'

'Maybe you can get over there once the storm has passed.

Go for New Year's instead. Help them clear up if they do get hit?'

His face brightened. 'Why didn't I think of that! I'll text Mum and Dad and then get onto the airline and see if it's possible.'

She got up and sat next to him. 'Don't spend Christmas on your own. Come to Manchester with me. My parents would love to meet you and I can't believe, in all these years, you've never visited the north.'

'I couldn't come, Lili. I wouldn't want to intrude.'

'Then do it for me,' she said and grinned. 'Just so that I can see Auntie Sheila's face. Every Christmas she wants to know why I haven't settled down yet. And seeing you, in the flesh, will prove to Dad that I'm not aromantic.'

'What?'

'Don't ask!'

He hesitated, a spark in his eye now. 'Well, okay, being purely selfless here though.'

She grinned back.

'But ring your parents first. Honestly, if you get a vibe that they just wanted a family Christmas, that's fine. Right, I'd better call the airline company.'

An hour later, Lili was setting out plates in the kitchen. She had baked beans on the hob to go with the pizza, a throwback to her childhood. She stood looking at the garden as Dylan came in. A pair of arms wrapped around her from behind and she smiled ahead at his reflection in the window, despite the frown across her forehead. Sleet still tapped against the glass.

'All done,' he announced. 'Mum and Dad and my grandparents sounded relieved that I'd be going over there at some point. The weather's due to ease off at the end of this week. I've even managed to change my flight. It was easier online, in the end.

I'm just waiting for a confirmation email.' He took a moment. 'This way, I'll have some time off work at home, and I can set about emptying Harry's bedroom.'

She squeezed his arm.

'Did you ring your parents?' he asked. 'Whose house are you staying at for Christmas?'

'Dad's was the plan as he's got the most room, but heading to Mum's for a late turkey dinner – the first Christmas Day all together since I was at school.'

'Wow. That's special. And were they okay with me coming?'

She turned around to face him. 'No. Really sorry, Dylan, but—'

He held up his hand. 'I get it. Completely. This is quite a monumental year for your family. And Jags texted me over a work issue he'd forgotten to raise. We got chatting and he said I'm welcome at his. What time are you leaving tomorrow?'

'I'm not. That's the thing. When I called, turns out Dad was about to ring me. He sounded terrible. He's got Covid. So has Mum. They both tested positive today and reckon they caught it last week, on their trip out to the pub. Apparently Mum's ringing me in the morning. She's already gone to bed. He's really upset but says there's no point me driving all that way as I'd not be able to go near them.'

'Oh, Lili. Talk about bad luck.'

'Dad's asthmatic so I hope the cough doesn't worsen. But get this... Mum's insisted he goes around to hers anyway. Geoff's ill too, so they may as well all convalesce together and try to make the most of it. I never thought I'd see the day...'

'What are the odds of both of our Christmases being ruined?' he said. They gave each other exasperated looks.

'Wait... Is it too much of a stretch of the imagination to think this is Em and your brother up to no good, still manipulating our love life? Determined that we spend Christmas together?'

Dylan gave a chuckle. 'Wouldn't put it past Harry. So, is that what we're doing? I mean, I have got another invitation,' he said airily, 'or maybe I was looking forward to Netflix and chilling.'

'You do know that phrase has a double meaning?'

With a wicked glint in his eye, he nodded as the doorbell went.

'Plans might change, people turn you down, but one thing you can always rely on in this life,' said Lili with certainty as she walked into the hallway, 'is a margherita stuffed-crust pizza, with garlic bread and cheesy fries on the side. And baked beans.'

It didn't take long for them to devour the pizza. 'Nonna and Nonno wouldn't understand why anyone would get any sides. Italians consider pizza to be the whole meal.'

'I order chicken wings too sometimes. Or mozzarella balls. Talking of food.' Lili pulled a face. 'What are we going to eat on Christmas Day? I bet all the turkeys are gone.'

Dylan spotted a notepad and pen on the windowsill. He fetched it and sat back down again. 'I'll go home tonight and pack the stuff I'll need for the next few days. Then first thing tomorrow I'll get to the supermarket. What are you thinking? Chicken? Beef?'

Lili popped a bit of garlic bread in her mouth. 'I'm thinking of getting a whole lot actually. Because we might have to cook for more than two people, if you're up for it?'

'You're that hungry?'

Lili threw her napkin at him, laughing. Then she told him about her idea. Dylan gave an enthusiastic punch into the air. He scribbled on the notepad, insisting he'd start the food preparation tomorrow afternoon, whilst Lil made some very important Christmas Eve visits.

43

Christmas Eve, and what a morning. Ware & Care had never been busier, filled with the people forced to do last-minute shopping due to work and other responsibilities, such as small children or elderly relatives. She had no time today, but a stroll along the harbour after work often grounded Lili and took her away from the twenty-first century buzz, letting her focus on the simple things – the red and white buoys riding waves, or seagulls strutting around puddles as if offended by the very element that provided them with so much food.

Instead, she hurried to the library, three streets away. It closed at two. She had only fifteen minutes, having stayed a bit longer at work to tidy so that they wouldn't be greeted by a mess when they reopened after the festive break. The slate clouds looked bulbous and full, as if holding on to snowflakes for as long as they could, trying to time their release for Christmas Day. As Lili arrived, Glenda came outside. She tugged on her gloves and readjusted her thick bobble hat so that it covered her ears.

'Glenda! Hold up!' Lili hurried over, turning the air white with her heavy breaths.

'Hello, love,' she replied in a listless tone. 'What are you doing here? The library is about to close.'

'No matter, it's you I've come to see. I hoped you'd be here.'

'Shouldn't you be heading off to Manchester?' Her voice sounded flat.

Lili filled her in about her parents' illness and told her about the flooding in Italy. 'It'll be a quiet one for both of us now, so we came up with an idea. Wouldn't it be wonderful to invite friends over?'

'Go for it, love. I hope you both have fun with your crowd. But why did you want to see me?'

Lili raised an eyebrow. 'Glenda – I hope you consider me a friend, as I do you.'

'Of course.'

'Good. Because you're part of my "crowd" and I'd be chuffed to bits if you came over tomorrow afternoon. I can't promise it'll be a traditional dinner. Dylan went shopping this morning. The turkeys had sold out, but he did get a large chicken and a joint of beef and—'

'You want *me* to come?'

'I'm counting on you, Glenda, to bring a bit of glamour to the occasion.' Lili smiled, but to her dismay, Glenda started crying. Lili pulled a clean tissue out of packet in her handbag and handed it over. 'I didn't mean to upset you. I... I'm sorry, don't feel obliged to—'

Glenda gave a big sniff. 'You're a good girl. I'd love to.'

She dried her eyes. They exchanged phone numbers and after a hug, Lili paid her next visit, a fifteen-minute drive away on the outskirts of Mevagissey, on the same estate as Callum. She stood outside the small terraced house, took a deep breath and rapped on the door. A light went off in the lounge. She waited for a couple of minutes and then knocked again. Still no reply. She bent down and opened the letterbox.

'It's me, Lili!' she called through.

The light in the lounge flicked on again. The door creaked open.

'What are you doing here, gal?'

Tommo's eyes had dark circles underneath, his hair hadn't been brushed and he was still wearing his pyjamas.

He glanced down at himself. 'I... I've had to delay my trip to my sister. I've got a train booked first thing tomorrow and will get there just in time for Christmas dinner. I haven't been well. Must have caught a bug.'

'You sound fine to me,' Lili said and folded her arms.

A sparkle of humour, ever so small, but definitely there, shone in his eyes.

'You'd better come in,' he grumbled. 'That air is bloody freezing.' He led her into the lounge on the right, and it smelt of cigarette smoke. A comfortable room with big cushions and thick carpet, its centre point was a striking painting of a motorbike on the wall.

'How can I help?' he asked and pointed at the sofa for her to sit down.

'Come to mine tomorrow afternoon. The fishing boat master will be there – floods mean he can't go to Italy. My parents have got Covid. Glenda's family is off to Iceland, so she's coming too. I'm going to ring Meg and ask if she and her Gran want to drop by. There won't be turkey, it's all a bit last-minute, but—'

'Hold your horses, gal! Thank you for the invite, but I'm off to my sister's, I told you.'

Her cheeks flushed. His secret. 'I know, Tommo,' she said quietly.

Tommo interlocked his fingers. 'What do you mean?'

'You don't have a sister. Let's face it, you only ever mention her at Christmas. Last year I spotted you in Mevagissey on my last day at work, before I travelled up north, when you should have been in Norfolk. You wore dark glasses and a scarf around your mouth, but it was definitely your hair.'

His hands clenched together. 'I don't know what you're talking about.'

'I get it,' she said gently. 'Last year I didn't want to celebrate the festive season. I know you miss Joe, that you probably can't imagine enjoying Christmas without him, but... remember what you said to me yesterday – about maybe it being time now for Em's memory not to be such a big focus for me?'

Tommo grunted.

'Maybe it's time for you to take a step forward now too – by making real plans for Christmas; by not spending it alone.'

'What would you know?' he muttered.

'I know what it's like to only want to attend parties that are pity parties.' Her voice became more firm. 'But that, Mister, isn't going to get you anywhere. You don't strike me as someone who's simply all talk. So listen to your own common sense. What would Joe say?'

He looked up. 'That's a low blow.'

'Is it? Because I know what Em would think to the way I've been wallowing. She'd tell me to pull my head out of my arse and get on with life, grateful that I can because hers has ended.'

Tommo's mouth dropped open and then his eyes crinkled. He laughed. 'Jesus. Okay, okay. I'll bike over. Anything for a bit of peace.' Tommo sprang up. 'Fancy a cuppa?'

'A quick one would be lovely,' she replied, eyes twinkling.

'I'll put the kettle on whilst you get changed and then we can talk about the best party games to play on Christmas Day…'

* * *

'And I'm so sorry that quick one turned into two cups,' said Lili as she sat down in the kitchen at home, coat still on. She looked up at Dylan. 'I feel really guilty. Not only have you done the shop, you've also started the food prep for tomorrow.'

Dylan sat down next to her and took her hands. 'I love everything to do with cooking and, for the record, what you did this afternoon for Glenda and Tommo is far more important.'

'More important than a magnificent roast? Don't get carried away.' She leant forwards and they kissed. 'I did find time to pick up a tin of chocolates, a box of Christmas crackers and plenty of nibbles. Also some Santa paper napkins. And I just drove past an off-licence. I'll nip out and stock up. Might get a bottle of Bailey's – not a huge fan of it myself, but I bet Glenda is. I also called Meg – she and her gran will definitely drop by but will only want a mini dinner as they've bought in everything to eat at lunchtime with a neighbour who's on their own. Oh, and Meg messaged Tommo and the three of them are going to share a taxi over, and pick Glenda up on the way. I've given them her number.'

'Whoa, slow down!' Dylan said and grinned. 'Sounds like hot chocolates are in order for an energy kick before I tackle making dessert and you do the booze run.'

'Dessert? Didn't they have Christmas puddings?'

'Yes. I got a large one. Two boxes of mince pies too. And, of course, a Panettone. But Christmas isn't Christmas without a Tiramisu. Whilst you're out I'll ring Mum and Dad again. Naples airport is still only running a limited service but, fingers crossed, where they are, the rain's slowly abating. The water hasn't reached their sandbags yet. It's a huge relief.'

'Thank God,' she said. 'And Mum rang me at work. She's well enough to blame Dad for the Covid as he chose the pub they went to.' She grinned. 'It was good to hear. A bit of realism in their new relationship – it was starting to sound a little too perfect. He's still invited around to hers but better prepare himself for a guilt trip.' She took off her coat and Dylan made the hot chocolates. They took them through to the lounge, turned on the Christmas tree lights. They sat on the sofa and he put an arm around her shoulders.

'It's weird. Us. It doesn't seem new. It's as if we've been together for ages. Or is that just me?' she said shyly.

'No,' he replied softly. A smile crept across his mouth. 'Does that mean I can leave the toilet seat up and my dirty laundry on the floor?'

His smile widened as she pretended to glare and said, 'Bario won't last long if that ever happens.'

44

Lili stood back in the dining room and admired the table, set with six places, each with a cracker, Santa napkin and wine glass. She'd put out the condiments, and a box of mints to have after dessert with coffee. A clementine and clove candle was lit on the sideboard and Christmas jazz played in the background. Darkness was falling as she went to the French patio doors and bit on her fist. Silly really, but she felt excited, joyous, grateful... This cottage hadn't known much positivity in the last twelve months and it was almost too much. A teacher at high school had taken Lili aside once. She'd spotted that Lili had been crying in the toilets about her parents' divorce.

'Difficult things happen in life, Lydia,' she'd said gently. 'My boyfriend broke up with me the day before our engagement party. Not only that, but shortly after – only five years ago – I got diagnosed with cancer.'

Young Lili's eyes had widened.

'I'm telling you this because the way I coped was to follow a piece of advice my granddad gave me when I was little, which I'm passing on to you now. He said that however bad things get, imagine yourself one year ahead, looking back on that difficult time. It won't seem as bad. I did that and it got me through. And as fate would have it, that boyfriend turned out to be fiddling the tax office and went to prison – and my cancer was caught early. I'm completely cured now.' She'd patted Lili's shoulder. 'Time might not make you forget, but it will teach you how to get through and you'll be stronger as a result.'

The front door rang and Lili shook herself out of the past. She hoped Miss Brown was doing well now. She hurried into the hallway, secretly pleased Dylan loved cooking so much and was happy for her just to help with the washing-up and arrange the table. She smoothed down her Christmas jumper that had a reindeer with a lit-up nose on the front, a present from Dad last year. She'd worn it on a video call with her parents, a couple of hours ago. Not that either noticed; they were too busy looking at Dylan and quizzing him about his job, Italy, cooking... He already had an invite up to Manchester in the New Year.

Lili opened the door. Tommo saluted and did a jig over the doorstep. She took his biker jacket. Glenda came in next and slipped out of her anorak immediately to reveal a red blazer with gold buttons and green velvet trousers. A necklace made of flashing fairy lights completed the festive combo. She was talking to Meg's gran, Elaine, about Meg's vintage clothes business. Elaine was saying that Glenda clearly had an eye for fashion and suggested the three of them got together to brainstorm further about Meg focusing on 1940s fashion. Once inside, Elaine passed Lili a bottle of bubbly and a box of truffles.

'They are from all of us,' said Meg. 'A big thank you.'

'Thank *you* for coming over to Truro,' said Lili.

Glasses of champagne accompanied chicken, beef, Yorkshire puddings, sprouts, parsnips, and roast potatoes. And groans of contentment went around the table after the main.

Meg and Elaine had been served mini plates but had both gone back for seconds. Gasps then sounded as everyone dug into the Tiramisu, creamy and decadent with a rum kick. They toasted the chef with Bailey's and mints, chatting about 2025, now it was coming to an end, the world events, personal ones. Glenda went to fetch a glass of water, but the others could hear her starting to tidy up. The guests went to get to their feet and help, but Lili gestured for them to sit down again and called Glenda in. Lili topped up their Bailey's glasses and raised hers in the air.

'Here's to the absent friends,' she said.

'My Alf. I miss him so much,' said Elaine.

Meg raised her glass. 'My parents. Especially at Christmas. I miss what could have been.'

Glenda nodded. 'I've been thinking a lot about my parents lately too. They always put out a glass of sherry and a carrot on Christmas Eve.'

Tommo lifted his drink. 'Joe, my sweetheart, Happy Christmas, hope you've found your favourite trifle where you are now. You always were the fruit to my custard.'

'To Harry, the best brother a man could ever want. I should have said that more often.'

Lili gazed at the ceiling. 'Em, I'll always miss my sister from another mister.' Her throat caught. 'Love you.'

Tommo and Dylan cleared the table whilst Elaine and Meg volunteered to help Glenda with the dishes. However, Lili tapped Meg's shoulder and said to follow her upstairs. She led her to Em's room, barren and cold, the radiator switched off, the wardrobe and drawers empty, the bed stripped back to the mattress.

'Em filled every room she walked into with so much colour,' said Lili.

'And jokes. Or a friendly punch if she thought you were

being an idiot.' Meg gave a sad smile. 'What do you want to do with this room? Do you need a hand? I know you like recycling objects. You could move out the bed and...'

'It's yours if you want it.'

'What?' Meg stepped back.

'I've spoken to the property owner. She's happy for you to live here as long as your references are good and the rent gets paid.'

'But I couldn't afford—'

'We can travel into work together, and you're learning to drive – until you pass you'll have to catch the train on the days I'm off. But that should be doable, right?'

'Lili, it would be a dream come true, thank you. But there's no way I could afford the rent for a cottage like this. It's in such a nice street.'

'What are you looking to pay for a flat? Come on. Cards on the table.'

Meg stuttered a figure.

Lili shrugged. 'Then that's how much your rent is here. It feels like money down the drain, me continuing to pay the lot. You're helping me out. I can't promise how long I'll be here though. I am hoping to buy in the next couple of years but—'

'God, I'd love to, Lili. You are so very kind, but...' She sighed. 'I can't take charity.'

'Quite right too,' said Elaine crisply, and she walked into the room.

'Gran! Were you eavesdropping?'

Elaine flushed pink. 'I was going to use the bathroom but heard voices, and when I realised what Lili was suggesting...' She folded her arms. 'I'll pay the difference so that Meg is responsible for half. I can afford it. This is your future, Meg – a first rung on the renting ladder; a bit of independence. I should have supported you long ago, and I'm sorry about that.'

'You've done more than enough over the years,' Meg said, voice thick. She looked at the two women. 'You're both amazing, but it's too much.'

'Nonsense,' said Lili. 'If nothing else, trial it for six months. You can always keep looking for somewhere cheaper. I've nothing to lose. In fact...' Her voice wavered. 'I've everything to gain. I've always had Em, you see. I've never lived on my own until this last year, so we're both in the same position, really.'

Meg paused before stepping forwards and pulling them both into a group hug.

Lili went back downstairs, leaving Meg excitedly talking to her gran about the plans she had for the bedroom. Glenda and Tommo were having a friendly argument in the lounge, over the pros and cons of watching the *Call the Midwife* festive special. Dylan appeared at the kitchen doorway holding a tea towel, and she went over.

'Everything okay?' he asked.

She told him about Meg moving in.

'No more Netflix and chilling at your place then,' he said and pulled an injured face before grinning. 'That's a great idea. I bet she's thrilled.' He brushed a strand of hair behind Lili's ear. 'And I'm thrilled too, spending today with the first person, in a long time, to remind me about the good things in life. In fact, to make me think about what it means to be alive. That poster of Harry's didn't have a pulse, couldn't replicate or breathe, but it held memories and emotions and happiness – the most important aspects of living.'

Lili reached up and ran a thumb across his cheek. 'It has been a fab Christmas Day,' she whispered. 'And I can't wait to see what next year brings. I've spent the last twelve months looking backwards to the past, as if I'm flicking through photo albums, revisiting my teens, my childhood, all the times with Em... but now it's as if I'm looking forwards again, with empty photo albums waiting to be filled with new memories.' Lili stood on tiptoe and kissed him on the lips, heart pounding, heat rising, a vortex of lights in her head. Shyly, she stepped back and took his hand. 'I... I can't promise anything about the future... I'm scared of getting close, really close, to someone like I did with Em, in case I lose them as well. But how about we take it one day at a time? Will you stay another day, Dylan? With me? In my life?'

Dylan took her other hand. 'Nothing would make me happier, Lydia Taylor, than if you'd stay another day with me as well.'

And in that moment it felt as if there was no one else in the house apart from them. Nor in the street. Nor in Truro.

Apart from at the kitchen window where a robin peered in, against a backdrop of falling snow that the humans hadn't noticed yet. The small bird tilted its head and watched the couple, before it did a happy dance and flew away, a flash of red across the patio lights that disappeared into snow clouds for good.

45

Once their guests had gone, Lili and Dylan finished tidying up and then went to bed, looking forward to eating the leftovers on Boxing Day. After kisses, caresses, gasps, laughs, and the promise of an early morning bracing walk they both knew they wouldn't keep, eventually the pair of them fell asleep...

***

Lili and Em sit down on a large rock, up on a cliff edge. They'd both bought new walking boots on moving to Cornwall and have spent many a weekend exploring coastal paths. It's August and the middle of a heatwave. Lili takes out a flask and they both chug back squash before scoffing apple and custard pasties from Crystoffees. They pack up and head downwards and into nearby woodland.

Em gasps as in a clearing ahead, basking in the sunlight, a beautiful oasis of water sparkles. She runs ahead and Lili follows but trips and falls. One of her laces has come undone. By the time she arrives, Em is nowhere to be seen. Oh no! Had she fallen in?

'Em!' Lili hollers.

Whoosh! Suddenly, Lili rises up, above the woods, into the sky, higher and higher until she's surrounded by pure blue air.

Now she's on a white fluffy cloud with two swings. She finds herself sitting on one and looks sideways. From the other, Em gazes back with her characteristic jaunty grin and colourful hair.

'We had fun, didn't we?' says Lili, and she gestures down to Earth.

'Sure did. The travelling. Nights out with friends. Bingeing box sets. Pursuing career dreams. Chasing hot guys.' Em gives an impish grin. 'Even arguing with family. We lived life to the full. Not bad for Myrtle Turtle and Lydia Bacteria.'

Lili stretches out her hand. 'And we loved each other.'

Em's face softens. She interlocks her fingers with Lili's and nods.

'Then that's all that matters,' declares Lili. 'The rest is just ego and followers and likes.'

'If you say so.'

The two friends look at each other, laugh, and hold the swing ropes again. They move their legs forwards and backwards, the swings going higher and higher, until the two friends' whoops of joy brighten up the whole sky.

* * *

Lili wakes up, Dylan's arms around her. A sense of peace envelopes her as well. She looks through the crack in the curtains, up at the starry night sky. A smile crosses her face.

* * *

MORE FROM SAMANTHA TONGE

Another book from Samantha Tonge, *If You Could See Me Now*, is available to order now here:
https://mybook.to/IfYouCouldBackAd

ACKNOWLEDGEMENTS

I'd very much like to thank...

Boldwood Books – for continually striving to make my books the best they can be, and not remaining static with the way they market and sell them. A special mention to Jenna Houston, Claire Fenby, Isabelle Flynn, Candida Bradford, and the rest of the team.

Isobel Akenhead – my eagle-eyed, hardworking editor who always makes me feel as if my stories are worthy of her talented attention! Who points out flaws yet cheerleads with gusto.

Clare Wallace – my wonderfully supportive agent from Darley Anderson Agency & Associates who carries out her job with an open mind and open heart.

My author friends, published by Boldwood and elsewhere – you keep me sane, hopeful and smiling.

The bloggers and reviewers who support my books – having you in my corner means more than I can ever say, and it's not often I am lost for words!

Lovely Debra Brown on X who inspired the character of Bobbin with her story of encouraging robins to feed out of her hand.

The Friendly Book Community on Facebook. Thanks for feeling like a staffroom I can pop into for a laugh, when I need a break and a brioche!

To those readers who've joined me on my twelve-year

publishing journey, and those who've hopped on board recently – thank you, thank you, thank you.

Martin, Immy and Jay, for always being there during the highs and lows. I love you to Neptune and back (the furthest planet from Earth and the name of a rather special character in this story).

I'm one lucky lady.

Sam x

ABOUT THE AUTHOR

Samantha Tonge is the bestselling and award-winning author of over fifteen romantic fiction titles. Her books for Boldwood mark a broadening of her writing into multi-generational woman's fiction. She lives in Manchester with her family.

Sign up to Samantha Tonge's mailing list for news, competitions and updates on future books.

Visit Samantha's website: www.samanthatonge.co.uk

Follow Samantha on social media here:

facebook.com/SamanthaTongeAuthor
x.com/SamTongeWriter
instagram.com/samanthatongeauthor

ALSO BY SAMANTHA TONGE

Under One Roof

Lost Luggage

The Memory of You

When We Were Friends

A Single Act of Kindness

The Promise of Tomorrow

If You Could See Me Now

Will You Stay Another Day?

BECOME A MEMBER OF THE SHELF CARE CLUB

The home of Boldwood's book club reads.

Find uplifting reads, sunny escapes, cosy romances, family dramas and more!

Sign up to the newsletter
https://bit.ly/theshelfcareclub

Boldwood

Boldwood Books is an award-winning fiction publishing company seeking out the best stories from around the world.

Find out more at www.boldwoodbooks.com

Join our reader community for brilliant books, competitions and offers!

Follow us
@BoldwoodBooks
@TheBoldBookClub

Sign up to our weekly deals newsletter

https://bit.ly/BoldwoodBNewsletter